RECKONING AND RETRIBUTION

The Collector #4

MATHIAS G. B. COLWELL

ISBN: 978-1-68046-921-9

Melange Books, LLC
White Bear Lake, MN 55110
www.melange-books.com

Cover Design by Ashley Redbird Designs

"For Michelle, I love you. Here's to all the days to come."

CHAPTER ONE

Philip felt the bite a split second before he awoke, sharp teeth sunk deeply into his forearm. An instinctual reaction led him to yank his arm away as he opened his eyes. Dark eyes glittered above him, reflecting the flickering light of a midnight fire. A pale, regal face outlined by silken-black hair atop a lean frame, hovered above him. Mischief and malice mingled in equal parts in the vampire's face.

With a roar of anger and pain Philip thrust himself upwards to his feet and eyed his attacker. They circled each other warily with cautious eyes. The night-dweller darted in for a few lightning fast feints, but Philip was too experienced a fighter to fall for them. The vampire was quick enough to land a few blows, however, and Philip felt his eye swell, and the slash of what had to be nearly claw-like fingernails on one of his arms. Philip closed the distance and landed a few blows himself. His knuckles were calloused like only a long-term fighter's could be and he could hear the pain in the vampire's grunts as he connected, even if the creature danced back out of range with an eager glint in its eye.

Philip had had enough of this. He was a direct individual and he fought like it. He tackled the night stalker. A moment of surprise flecked the vampire's eyes followed quickly by its own deep-seated rage before the two bodies collided. Philip bore the vampire to the ground in a brawler's tactic and tried to force him down with his own body weight, landing a quick, forceful blow or two as they scuffled. The vampire was

1

not weak, however, and turned the tables on Philip, forcing his own body beneath the weight of the attacker.

The vampire soon lost all sense and appearance of regality as it clawed, kicked, and bit into Philip's shoulder and neck, with a vicious desperation—a desperation likely born from Philip's change of tactics, a switch from landing awkward blows to a steadily-tightening constrictor's grasp.

Philip ignored the pain bites and squeezed even harder, forcing air out of the vampire's lungs until it stopped biting and began struggling just to catch its breath. Its angry scrabbling turned anxious in a bid to escape. Blood welled up from tens of bites across Philip's shoulder and arm, but he ignored the wounds. He healed even faster than he used to these days. They were of little concern.

One last jerk of my arms. That's all it will take. The thought came and he eagerly sought to pursue it. He had the vampire where the creature was least effective, on the ground, in a vice-grip, where its speed and agility could do it no good. One titanic tightening of his powerful arms would be enough to break its back. Troll blood infused into Philip's body as a child would enable him to accomplish such an act. As well many other feats.

He coiled to make it so, to end the fight, when a voice cut through the night. "Stop! Philip, stop!"

Alayna's melodic voice rang out singsong into the dark, even if it was filled with concern. She spoke again.

"I said stop. Both of you. Philip, Azir, you're being childish. Stop the fighting at once!" she finished with an imperious toss of her strawberry-blonde hair. Only the slight crease of her forehead betrayed the depth of her worry.

Philip weighed her request only for a short moment before expelling his breath in a huge sigh and letting go. He released his grip and rolled away quickly into a prepared fighter's crouch, mimicking what the vampire Azir had done. They eyed each other warily, coals from the fire illuminating their faces. Philip saw hate there, an emotion he was sure the vampire could see reflected in his own eyes. However, the vampire was noticeably the worse for wear compared to Philip. Azir was trying to catch his breath and slightly twisting and stretching his back as he watched Philip, no doubt attempting to undo the damage Philip had begun to inflict during their conflict.

"Stop, doesn't just mean *quit fighting*. You've both got to relax around each other. And stop preparing to fight as well. You're so on guard that the slightest thing sets you off." Alayna's exasperation did little to make Philip feel guilty. He maintained a wary gaze on the vampire.

Azir transformed at her words. He straightened and smoothed the anger out of his face. "Of course, Alayna. Of course." He nodded courteously to her. "I was merely defending myself from attack." His thick eastern accent was mitigated by the way he pronounced every single syllable that he spoke completely and clearly.

Philip rolled his eyes. "He bit me. He took a chunk out of my arm." Philip wiggled his forearm up in the air for all to see. He hated the plaintive note he heard creeping into his voice. Hated the way he felt around Alayna and Azir.

"That is only because you pulled away so violently."

"I pulled away because you bit me. You were drinking my blood. You were eating me!" Philip's outrage grew.

"I suppose I was. But only a little," the vampire smirked.

Philip shook his head and was about to reengage the fight, Alayna's wishes be damned. He saw Azir's muscles tense and eyes narrow as he saw the flickers of danger in Philip. But before he could attack Alayna intervened again.

"I said enough! You're being childish. Both of you." Her frustration cut him.

Philip couldn't hide the hurt on his face. How could she take Azir's side in this? He might have technically started the fight, but he never would have been pushed to do so were it not for the actions of the vampire. However, a subtle, angry glance at the vampire showed that Azir's face reflected almost what he would have guessed his own did; annoyance at being lumped in by Alayna with the other.

Everything had been strange in the week that had passed since they left the Manor. Philip had gone from believing Alayna was dead—killed by Collectors—to going half-mad with grief, then removing the trace with the help of The Alchemist, to wanting revenge on the Guild, before finally discovering Alayna was actually alive. It had been a whirlwind of emotions spanning a short period of time, and he was still recovering from it. It hadn't helped that upon discovery of Alayna, he had also encountered Azir with her, a character he had whole-heartedly hoped he would never see again upon leaving the shores of England. And yet here the vampire was, healthy, whole, and somehow having managed to worm his way deeper into Alayna's affections than Philip would have ever thought possible. Philip didn't know where he and Alayna stood. Their hurry to put distance between themselves and the carnage left behind at the manor and the menagerie had left little time for discussion. It had certainly been a confusing week.

The fourth member of their party stepped in between Philip and Azir to create a physical barrier between them. Beathan, the half-fairy, half-human put a hand on Philip's chest and pushed him away from the vampire.

"Walk it off, mate," he murmured with his Irish lilt. "But don't stray too far, the Transylvanian woods are no place t' be alone for long."

Philip shrugged his hand off but acquiesced to the advice. Blood still dripping from cuts, he stomped away from the coals.

"Philip, let me tend those bites," Alayna's voice took on its first sound of care since she'd broken up the fight. For some reason it annoyed him, and he ignored her to walk deeper into the forest. He'd probably regret it later. They had to talk eventually—things couldn't go on as they were—but for now, ignoring her felt like the easiest option. Or the most satisfying at least. He walked into the darkness of the night and pulled the chill air around him like an imaginary frozen cloak. The snow on the tops of tree branches and the soft blanket of snow on the ground calmed him and he soothed his anger and pain with the cool balm of late-winter, and reminded himself of home, of the north.

CHAPTER TWO

"They shouldn't be fighting like that! He'll hurt him." Beathan heard the furious whisper as Alayna half spoke to him and half spoke to herself.

"What's that, eh? Who'll get hurt?" Beathan asked, cocking his head to hear her better.

Alayna turned red as if she hadn't really expected an answer. She opened her mouth and then closed it again without speaking, shaking her head in answer to his question. Almost as if she wasn't even sure what she meant, wasn't sure who *he* was.

Beathan put a hand on her shoulder as Azir stared moodily into the darkness from across the campfire. The vampire had resumed his watch, but with Philip out wandering, clearing his head and the rest of them wide awake it didn't look like anyone would be getting much more sleep tonight.

"Let it go, love, nothin' like a fight t' warm a body's blood in wintertime. Didn't mean nothin'." His calming words and quirky smile didn't seem to have his desired effect. Alayna returned the smile, but it seemed half-hearted. She squeezed his arm in thanks for the words, and then despite what Beathan had just been thinking, went back to her bedroll and wrapped herself up in her cloak. Whether she would actually sleep was another story.

He shook his head slightly as he looked at her. Red-gold hair cascaded

5

around her elegant and slightly exotic features, features that were only partially visible beneath an upturned hood. She was lean and lithe, beautiful by almost any man's standards. The kind of female he'd pursue if she didn't happen to be one of his closest friends. *No need mixin' up in that*, he thought with a laugh to himself, *Azir's doin' a job o' that himself already. Don't need no more trouble*. Besides, even if she wasn't a good friend, he'd never betray Philip.

Her breathing slowed as he watched, but he didn't believe she was sleeping, just avoiding the present for a while. Beathan sighed and slipped his way over silently to stand next to the vampire who was seated against a tree.

"Unrequited love isn't really a good look for ya', mate," Beathan lilted mockingly at the hybrid vampire—half vampire, half Elfas like Alayna was.

Azir snorted slightly, a condescending look in his eye. "You are right, it is not." Each word he spoke was precise despite his accent. "But unrequited means that there is no hope," he paused slyly, "and I definitely have hope." The vampire winked and flashed his teeth, gleaming in the faint moonlight. "Besides, life is dangerous, especially around you three. All I really have to do is outlast him," Azir finished with a nod out into the brooding darkness that had swallowed Philip when he left.

Beathan went cold at that admission. "Ya'd better not betray him in a moment o' need." The half-fairy's eyes were flat as he stared at the vampire. "Ya'd not long survive, I promise ya' that. A Fairy's vengeance is swift an' brutal."

Azir waved him off, unconcernedly. "Please, as much as I might enjoy hurting him, she'd never forgive me. No, Fairy, I can bide my time."

"Besides, Ya'd be hard pressed t' get the best o' him, judging by this latest tussle." It was Beathan's turn to wink at the vampire. Azir's face darkened considerably.

"Begone, half-breed. I tire of speaking with you."

"Who ya' callin' half-breed, hybrid?" Beathan retorted good-naturedly. Azir grimaced in annoyance. The sight was pleasant to see. Beathan was a Fairy—well, half of one at least. He even had some Leprechaun in him way back down the line. But he was also half human, and had the roving, wandering in his blood from both sides. He was also prone to mischief and months in the wilderness—mostly prior to the attack on the menagerie—had him practically itching for some prey. He could hardly pick his friends' pockets, but Azir was not off limits. In this case, needling the vampire's bloated ego would have to suffice.

Beathan left the vampire and wandered the few feet back toward the fire, thinking of following Alayna's lead by trying to catch a few more winks himself, when a rustling could suddenly be heard from the woods. A muffled shout followed, and everyone—even the supposedly sleeping Alayna—was on their feet and ready for combat in a heartbeat. Crashing noises grew louder as something approached, making no effort to hide its progress.

As it got closer and closer, the three around the fire clutched weapons tightly in hands, ready for whatever was coming. Determined lines creased hard faces. None of them were easy prey for whatever was headed their way. It was a letdown of sorts then, when instead of some angry beast of legend, Philip emerged from the bushes. Beathan was about to spout a jibe for being so loud when he saw the person Philip was dragging behind him. No wonder he'd alerted everything in the forest within a half mile of their camp. The man was clawing at Philip's hand, which was clutching his collar. He was scrabbling and making spluttering noises as the angle of his collar choked him. Philip tossed the man into the light of the fire.

A Collector.

Beathan grimaced sourly. He hated his friend's former employers, and not just because they'd imprisoned him in their hideous prison in England. It had taken Philip and Alayna to break him—and by default Azir—out of St Thomas. No, Beathan hated the Collectors Guild and their people simply because they thought they were better than everyone who was not human. They took it upon themselves to monitor and judge the world on behalf of humanity, despite the fact that humanity was, as a whole, one of this world's youngest creations.

"Kill him already and be done with it," Azir's angry voice growled.

Philip turned to the vampire and shot him a disdainful look. "You aren't that stupid, are you, Azir? He was skulking around our camp. We need to ask him a few questions. Then maybe we will." His voice hardened at the end, ice in his eyes. Beathan swallowed involuntarily. He knew first hand just how terrifying Philip could really be. He'd experienced that terror in the aftermath of Alayna's supposed death when Philip had gone mad with grief and chased Beathan across the countryside intent on making him a meal, more troll than man.

Azir grumbled something under his breath but seemed to recognize the folly of his statement. Beathan turned to Alayna, half expecting her to counsel peace to Philip in light of how he ended his last statement, but surprisingly—or perhaps not, considering what she'd endured at the hands of the Collectors Guild in the menagerie—she appeared to have the most blood-thirsty look of them all. Pain and torture could do that to a person, hardening them in ways they didn't even realize.

Philip squatted down near the man in the dirt next to the fire. The captured Collector was doing his best to put on a good face and show some courage, but he wasn't fooling anybody. In fact, the closer Philip got to the Collector's face, the more he seemed to cower.

"What are you doing here? Why are you following us?" Philip asked.

The man stuttered something incomprehensible. Philip smacked him lightly, arrogantly across the face. It seemed to embarrass the man enough to shake him out of his fear.

"I said, why are you here? Did someone send you? Helmsted?"

"No, nobody sent me. I just took it upon myself," the Collector said hurriedly.

"Why?" Alayna interjected harshly.

"Why does anyone follow? To gain information. You killed all my brothers. I wanted to bring valuable information back to the Guild. I thought I could glean something by spying."

"They deserved it!" Alayna practically shouted.

The man cocked his head at her, confused.

"Your brothers," she clarified. "They deserved it, and I'll not hear a word in argument."

Philip motioned her to silence, which seemed to annoy her. "So you just followed us here from Helmsted's menagerie. You were one of her men?"

The man nodded. Azir growled angrily. Beathan knew that he'd been subjected to as much pain as Alayna had been during their time in the menagerie. Torture, fighting pits, and who knew what else.

Philip, Alayna, and Azir continued to question the man, but Beathan gradually lost interest. The man was bold to have followed them, but somehow had become terrified upon being caught. He wet himself and babbled incoherently at times. He must've been a new recruit. He looked fairly young. In general, there was not much to be gleaned from his mind. Precious few details of import did he possess. The only thing of note was that he believed himself to be the sole Guild member in the area. It was good to know there weren't others lurking, waiting in the night as well.

When Philip had grown tired of questions, he stood and hauled the man to his feet. "Kill him," urged Azir, and again, Beathan was surprised not to hear Alayna discouraging him. He should stop being surprised.

"Why are you even here? Seriously, why?" Philip turned his head and shot the question at the vampire, clearly annoyed at the vampire presuming to tell him what to do. Azir shook the question off with his own annoyed look and did not answer, just maintained a snarl as he stared at the frightened Collector.

Philip stared long and hard into the man's eyes before taking his hands from his collar, by which he'd hauled him to his feet. "Go," Philip said firmly, quietly.

"What?" Alayna exclaimed.

"We can't just let him go!" Azir agreed.

Even Beathan was unsure. "Mate, we've been movin' quick t' avoid notice ever since leavin' the menagerie. Whole point was t' avoid unwanted eyes an' now ya' want t' just let a self-confessed spy go?"

"I've changed my mind," Philip said suddenly, "we aren't hiding anymore." He looked the man in the eyes one last time. "Go. Go on back to your masters, to the Guild. Go to Helmsted and the Council for all I care. Tell them where we are. It doesn't matter. Because," he paused dramatically as he pushed the stumbling man into the dark of the forest, "I want you to deliver a message. Tell Helmsted—tell them all—I'm coming for them. I'm coming for them all!"

CHAPTER THREE

A solemn hush fell over the group. The sound of twigs breaking and branches snapping grew quieter as the Collector disappeared into the brush of the dense woods.

"Was that wise? Sending him back with a message. It'll mean war." Alayna sent a questioning look Philip's way. She couldn't help but feel a bit worried at such a bold declaration. They'd been running and hiding from the Guild for so long now it felt strange to imply the opposite.

"It was always going to come to a head eventually, I'm just speeding things along." Philip clenched his fists, as if in anticipation of what he knew was to come. "I meant what I said when we left the menagerie; the Guild has gone rotten, and I aim to make them pay!"

Azir spoke, "Well, there are hardly enough of us to do significant damage to such a wide-reaching organization."

Alayna saw Philip's face tighten in disagreement as it always did whenever the vampire spoke. Azir could claim the sky was blue and snow was white, and Philip would want to dispute it, and vice versa. She would have to do something about that.

Beathan was nodding along to Azir's statement, even as Philip rejected it. "We just laid waste to a Guild complex with only four of us. We can hurt them the same way. I know of many safe houses and facilities all across the continent and even the Americas. There's no limit to what we could do."

The fairy shook his head. "Azir's got a point, mate. We did some damage t' the menagerie, no doubt, but at what cost? Injured half t' death and lickin' our wounds. We won't survive endless encounters of that kind."

"We have to strategize," Alayna agreed.

Philip got a stubborn look in his eyes, but Alayna raised her eyebrows and stared at him, silently questioning his logic. Finally, he gave in. "Fine, you're right, Beathan," Philip's grumbling agreement was directed at the fairy even though it was Azir's initial comment with which he was actually agreeing. Alayna knew that Philip would never admit to agreeing with the vampire.

"So what do we do?" Alayna prompted.

"We need an army. The fairy is correct, any assault on the Guild with even a hope of success needs to have manpower and plenty of it. There will be casualties. As much as I hate to admit it, the Collectors are not weak, even if they are human." Azir pursed his lips as he thought out loud.

"We'll never muster an army," Philip eagerly jumped down the vampire's throat.

"Not so fast, don't give up on an idea before we entertain it," Beathan said. "There's plenty o' folk out there who hate the Guild somethin' fierce."

"I doubt my kind would commit to full scale war," Alayna commented dubiously, "we aren't naturally as warlike as other species."

Beathan nodded along thoughtfully. Alayna could practically see the thoughts turning in his head. Azir and Philip were glaring at one another across the fire, not contributing as much as would have been helpful. An idea began forming in Alayna's head. It was dangerous, and probably a bad idea, but they'd been down that type of road before and emerged alive. It could work. Maybe.

"I have an idea," she put forth, almost hesitantly. Involuntarily her eyes found Azir's. She stared for a moment before continuing. The vampire's features seemed to narrow as he guessed her thought. He tilted his head in silent reproach, a shake of the head partnering the motion.

Alayna continued anyway. "What group of creatures is organized enough, plentiful enough, and dangerous enough to take on the Guild? We need allies and there's only one group of beings that can even come close to meeting that criteria." She left the statement hanging in the night air.

Silence filled the crispness of the winter night, even around the campfire, as recognition filled all their eyes one by one. Philip and Azir were already shaking their heads but stopped when they realized they were mirrors of one another. Beathan, however, seemed to be entertaining the idea.

"Interestin'. Very, very interestin'."

Philip cut him off harshly. "No. Not a chance."

"It is a terrible idea, my dear," Azir agreed with Philip, although it seemed as if his words were bitter in his mouth.

Beathan narrowed his eyes as he thought. Alayna needed an ally in the argument. Truth be told, she wasn't sure herself that it wasn't a terrible idea, but she had no others.

The fairy spoke. "Let's not dismiss the idea out o' hand, without entertainin' it at least. It has certain merits."

Philip finally said out loud what they all understood to be talking about. "I will not work with the vampires." He said every word firmly, clearly, brokering no response.

"She's right, mate. They have the most extensive network on the continent. No other beings have even close t' the kind o' culture they have. At least not so widespread."

Philip shook his head again, even as Azir reluctantly joined him. "The One Who Rules would not likely condone working with even a former Guild member like him," jerking his head toward Philip. "Besides, it would be too dangerous. The One Who Rules—The Shade King—he always exacts a hidden price. Something extra. You would not enjoy the accord."

"Shade King?" Alayna questioned.

"The leader of the vampires," Philip responded, "they have many names for him: 'The One Who Rules', 'The Shade King', or one you might have already heard, 'Dracula'."

A nervous chill fell over the group as Philip named him, especially Azir, of all people. The vampire seemed the most unsettled of all of them.

"No, no, no. A bad idea entirely, my dearest Alayna," Azir counseled.

"I agree." Philip's voice was hoarse from disgust at agreeing. They eyed each other sideways.

Beathan however, was still considering. "There's really no other way. We'll need the extra muscle t' accomplish the assault ya' have in mind—unless ya' want t' risk Alayna and our lives at every turn?"

That perked Philip up, and a guilty look crossed his face.

Determination, warred with worry, and Alayna's heart went out to see the concern in his eyes each time he looked at her. The love there was real. Confused perhaps, but not tarnished.

Beathan was still speaking. "Besides, it's like me ma' always said: 'A deal with the Devil's just a trade, and traders can be tricked'." He winked as he finished. "Probably her Leprechaun blood speakin' through—there's a wee bit o' it way back on me ma's side. Ireland an' all." He shrugged with a wry smile as if that explained the statement.

Philip bit the side of his lip as he began to truly consider the idea. Alayna could practically read his mind. A deal with the leader of the vampires would indeed be akin to a deal with the devil, something Philip would not undertake lightly. But then again, Philip was capable of nearly anything that he considered necessary to keep her safe.

"Even if I decide to do this—and I haven't yet—what would it entail? How would we even get an audience with this Shade King?" Philip ran a hand idly through his shoulder length brown hair. He appeared of medium build, brown eyes to complement his hair. Pale skin and a lean frame. But on the whole, nothing particularly extraordinary to look at. At first glance at least. But a closer eye saw more. Sleeveless tunic above dirty black trousers, even in the winter, he didn't take a chill. A normal man could never attain that calmness in the cold. And his eyes. Brown they might be and average at a glance, but stare into them and a person could see all the wildness of the great north contained in his blood. An untamed nature that couldn't be taught or even learned, but rather a heritage one inherited by blood. There was also a hardness to Philip, the sense that he was not a man to cross. A single long look at him could tell one as much, from the calloused brawlers knuckles to the few scars that could be seen on his arms and face.

Eyes turned to Azir at Philip's question. What indeed would it entail? They all knew whom the only one of them was who could gain audience with the Shade King. The vampire's face darkened, and his regal features took on a hounded expression.

"No. I will not do it."

"Why?" Beathan asked. "Just an introduction, mate. S'all we're askin' for."

"Yes, why not?" Philip echoed the fairy, suddenly seeming glad to be questioning Azir, even if it meant a reversal of his initial position.

"Because I may not be as welcome as you assume." Azir's eyes slid to Alayna's and she knew what that worried expression was.

"But nobody but us knows about that, Azir." Alayna said.

"The woods in this region have ears and eyes, and all of those report back to The One Who Rules. I would not be so certain of our secret." Azir paled slightly as he spoke.

"What secret?" Philip demanded, and Alayna winced slightly at his tone. Jealousy was on the edge of his heart at every turn these days. It was hard having to defend herself at every turn. *Yet you did kiss Azir*, a voice whispered far back in her mind. Could she really blame Philip?

Azir broke from his concern to take a moment to gloat. "Ah, yes, to what little secret could our dear Alayna be referring?" He tapped a finger thoughtfully on his lips in mocking emphasis. "There are just so many secrets." Azir smiled and winked a darkly twinkling eye at Philip.

Philip's face flushed as he read between the lines and he took an angry half step forward. Alayna rushed to head off another fight.

"The Alchemist," she interjected sharply.

"What?" Philip turned her way in confusion.

"The Alchemist," she repeated. "We came upon him as we escaped the menagerie. Azir killed him. Tore his throat out." Alayna knew she should feel some sort of disgust at that last statement but could not. Instead, a warm satisfaction was left. What did that say about her?

"But he was under the protection of Dracula," Beathan spoke ponderingly.

Azir smiled again with false bravado, even though there was a sickly cast to his face at the memory of defying the vampire king's orders. "Exactly fairy. While our one-time-Collector over here was crashing about in the midst of the menagerie for no good reason, I was the one actually protecting Alayna. And doing it at personal cost I might add."

"You never told me," Philip muttered in Alayna's direction.

She swallowed. He would find offense in this she thought sadly. "It never really came up. Besides I promised I wouldn't say anything."

"You promised him." Philip stated the obvious to himself as he turned these knew pieces of information over in his head.

Beathan was eyeing Azir from across the fire, a prospective gleam in his eyes. "If any man deserved death, The Alchemist was atop the list," he nodded approvingly to the vampire.

"I do not need your approval, Fairy," Azir responded haughtily.

Philip was finally wrapping his mind around events. He spoke slowly, as if thinking out loud. "So you're worried to gain audience with The Shade King because you're afraid he might know of your transgression?

But you don't really know that he knows. You're really just scared. Frightened of something that is only a possibility, not a certainty."

"I am not afraid!" the vampire shot back venomously. "Just cautious."

Philip shrugged at that statement as if the distinction was of no consequence, or perhaps didn't exist. Azir's eyes tightened in anger.

"Well, there you have it. We can't do this anyway because the vampire is afraid of his own kind—worried, sorry." Philip was clearly not sorry. Alayna's eyes narrowed. What was he aiming at, trying to get Azir riled up?

Azir's face mottled with rage as Beathan chuckled slightly. "I am no coward, Collector. I was there with her in the menagerie. Where were you?" the vampire shot back. It was Philip's turn to grimace in frustration.

"So, seems we're at a bit o' an impasse. No real options other'n the one at hand, but the only one able t' make it happen, ain't willin' t' do so." The fairy trailed off sourly as he stared into the flames.

"There really is no other option, is there?" Philip said slowly, as if admitting it to himself for real, for the first time.

Alayna shivered slightly despite the fire. The cold night air bit at her nose. She thought about it, wracked her brain for another solution. But nothing came. "I think it is," she finally said, so long after he spoke that most didn't realize she was answering him.

Alayna turned to the vampire. "Will you at least consider it?" Azir opened his mouth to object, but she spoke before he could. "Just think on it. Please. For me?" The vampire closed his mouth and gave her a curt nod before walking away from the fire to stare moodily into the steadily lightening grey of morning, slipping down through the thick canopy of branches overhead.

CHAPTER FOUR

Dawn crept quietly into the air. The others had lain back down to sleep some, but Philip hadn't slept at all. His mind just kept turning over and over upon itself. He searched for answers, any excuse not to entertain the idea of an alliance with the vampires. And yet, nothing came to mind. No alternatives were left to him other than to give up his plan or ensure certain death on himself and the people he cared about. Neither of those options were acceptable. That left the plan with the vampires. It was something that at the very least needed to be explored, but it didn't mean his stomach wasn't roiling at the thought of working with the night-stalking bloodsuckers.

The deep chill of the winter's night in Transylvania hadn't abated, but Philip needed no cloak as he lifted himself off of his bedroll and trudged over to sit on a log staring moodily out into the woods. Azir still hadn't spoken to any of them since their last discussion and Philip couldn't say he was disappointed. The vampire's overly proper pronunciation of every single word set his teeth on edge. Alayna still lay curled on her bedroll, cloak pulled closely about her. Her strawberry hair poked out from beneath the hood, a stark contrast to the grim landscape around them full of browns and whites. Beathan was stirring but Philip turned away and continued to stare at their surroundings. He wasn't in the mood to speak to anyone just yet.

His thoughts retraced the past year or two, trailing backwards in time to match his moodiness. Retrospection had its place, but the way Philip felt right now, he knew it would take him nowhere good. Not so long ago he had been a sailor, on a ship, with a partner he loved and trusted, and a cargo hold full of dangerous creatures. Everything had changed.

A hand touched his shoulder and he looked up to see Alayna clutching her cloak about her to ward away the chill. Wisps of her hair straggled across her face, but if anything, the messy imperfection only accentuated her features. She was quite simply, gorgeous. Nobody in their right mind could deny it. She smiled tiredly down at him, yet Philip felt a wedge between them that hadn't used to be there.

"What are you thinking about?" she asked fondly. "You've got a faraway look to your eyes."

"I was thinking about James."

"Your former partner," she murmured to herself pensively.

Philip nodded, though there was no need. Alayna had heard about as many stories as Philip had to tell of his old friend. "He'd likely be ashamed of me."

"For what?"

Philip looked at her askance. "Come on, Alayna, don't do that. You know he wouldn't have condoned what we plan on doing—attacking the Guild and working with the vampires."

"Things are different now," she said.

"Are they? I don't know. Maybe I'm different. Maybe things haven't changed at all, only I have."

"Maybe," Alayna responded. "I know for certain I'm different than I once was, and I won't apologize for it. Life changes, we change, and the world changes around us. There's nothing wrong with that."

"You're probably right." Philip quirked his mouth up in a half smile.

Alayna sighed. "I didn't know James. I've only heard you speak of him. But I cannot believe he knew what you now know of the Guild. If he'd seen what we have seen, experienced what we have experienced..." she trailed off, shuddering.

Philip reached up and grasped her hand. Sometimes it was easy to forget what she had been through, culminating just over a week ago. Other times, like now, the haunted look in her eyes at the memory of the menagerie gave her away.

"Perhaps, you're right." Philip shrugged uncomfortably. "But it still doesn't sit right with me. "James was a Guild man through and through.

He wouldn't have given up on it. He likely would've had some noble, idealistic notion of trying to change it from within."

"Well, maybe he could've tried that, maybe even succeeded. But you don't have that option. Do you know what I heard you called at times in the menagerie, when they didn't know I was listening—by Collectors and creatures alike? 'The Renegade.' You are not one of them, Philip. Not human." She said the last bit rather pointedly. "People have different options available to them."

Philip grinned and lifted his sleeveless arms in the winter air. "I haven't forgotten." He winked. "Perks of troll blood."

"Ugh, sometimes I wish you could share that with me!" She sighed, shivering slightly.

Philip pulled her down onto his lap suddenly, holding her close and smiling even as he kissed her. She giggled in delight and returned the kiss. Thoughts of darker subjects were lost for a brief moment, before the pall set back in. It happened when Azir rolled out of his own blankets and let out a scornful snort at the sight of them canoodling. Like swallowing a rock, the noise brought Philip back down to earth, all the awkwardness of the past weeks at the forefront of his thoughts again.

Alayna took his cheeks between both hands, palms cool and perfect against his face. "I'm not with him. I'm with you. You know that, right?" she murmured, staring into his eyes.

Philip stared back, not knowing exactly what was the right thing to say. He wanted to communicate his fears and worries. But would she see those as too much insecurity, or worse as an annoying jealousy?

"Philip, did you hear me?"

He nodded reluctantly.

"Well?" she asked.

"Well, what?"

She sighed in exasperation. "Well, what do you have to say?"

He cocked his head slightly as he gazed at her, colorful hair framing her pale face, slightly exotic features just labeling her as non-human to anyone who had eyes to see. Thoughts raced through his head, all the things he wanted to say. Yet, all that came out was a pitiful grunt followed by a weak statement.

"It just doesn't always feel that way, I guess," he said.

She sighed again, but this time with just a hint of sadness in the sound, and all his worries clamored to confirm his worst fears. "I'm yours," she repeated. She kissed him for emphasis, and it was enough to assuage his fears for now. However, they came rushing back as soon as her lips left his and she started to speak again.

"But—"

"But what?" he interjected.

She stared at him solemnly. "But I do care for him, and you'll have to come to terms with that. Regardless of what you think of him, he was there for me when nobody else was—I know, I know, you thought I was dead. I'm not blaming you. But it doesn't change the fact that I was on my own until he got himself caught trying to rescue me."

Philip swallowed his frustrated retort and jerked his head in some semblance of a nod to signify his agreement. He didn't have to like it, but he couldn't deny the truth. While he'd been criss-crossing the countryside for months, lost in the mind of a troll, trying to catch and eat anything that moved—namely Beathan—Azir had been right by his beloved's side, coaching and counseling her through the fighting pits. It set his teeth on edge, and yet Alayna might be dead without the hybrid vampire, so what more could he really say?

"Just—" he broke off before finishing.

"Just what?"

"Just…think of how you would feel if the roles were reversed, Alayna." Philip gazed seriously into her eyes. He saw pain there, and regret. Her eyes shone.

Alayna swallowed. "I know, love. I can understand how you feel." It wasn't exactly an apology. But he wasn't sure he deserved one. It was a difficult situation. He was nuanced enough to understand that.

"It might help, if you discouraged him a bit at least. There's no denying he's under the assumption that he can win you over eventually— if he doesn't think he's done so already." He shot her a quizzical, searching look. There were things they hadn't spoken of, questions he wasn't sure he wanted answers to.

Alayna had the decency to blush, and the guilt in her eyes all but confirmed his fears. Yet, again, he found himself with questions he couldn't ask. He didn't want to know the extent of Alayna's guilt.

And she didn't volunteer the information. She just pulled him close and kissed him again, fiercely this time, as if to prove the fire of her love for him. It convinced him—for now. Things would shake out the way they would shake out.

"Are we alright?" she asked. It was her turn to sound concerned.

Philip smiled. He loved her, there was no question of that. He wasn't sure if he could ever let her go, even if he were to want to.

He nodded to her. "We're alright, love. Although, you can't blame me for wishing he wasn't around all the time." The final words came out in a half-mutter.

She shrugged. "Well, we do need him to get an audience with the Shade King."

"Yes, we do." And just like that Philip's mind was occupied with more agonizing thoughts debating the merits and morality of their tentative plan.

————

WITHIN A FEW HOURS Alayna had convinced Azir to go forward with the plan, and Beathan had pushed back against Philip's own second thoughts. They broke camp, following Azir's lead since he was the only one who knew where the Shade King could be found.

"So, where are we headed, mate?" the fairy asked.

"A bit further through these woods, and then you will see," responded the vampire.

Philip snorted in disdain. The vampire always liked to hold back information—he was like the fairy in that way, only Beathan did it out of an enjoyment of mischief and fun, whereas the vampire liked to appear mysterious. It set Philip's teeth on edge when either of them did it, but especially when it was Azir.

The vampire pursed his lips in annoyance at the noise Philip made and shot him a dirty look before conceding the information.

"There is no guarantee where The One Who Rules is at any given time. He circulates between a number of locations and a number of different countries even. However, most often he can be found at Bran Castle. A favorite lair of his and his people."

"Don't you mean 'your' people?" Philip asked acerbically. Azir ignored him.

"Bran Castle? Where have I heard that before?" Alayna asked.

Philip shrugged. "I'm not sure. I've heard of it. It has a nasty reputation, but I don't remember speaking of it with you."

Azir mimicked Philip's reaction. "Maybe in the menagerie. Someone in the pits or the cages might have mentioned it. Or maybe one of our captors said something about it to one of the others in passing. Either way, our dear Collector here is correct. It is not a place for the faint of heart. And it is especially not so for outsiders."

"So we're likely t' die then, eh? Is that what ya' mean? Nothin' new there, that sounds about normal!" Beathan quipped with a laugh. The fairy's comment brought a smile to Philip and Alayna's faces, but Azir's visage only darkened. The vampire really was frightened. Philip wasn't used to seeing him this way. On the one hand he enjoyed it. But on the other, it did not bode well for their futures.

They trudged on, with tired feet and heavy legs. Their long night and lack of sleep not helpful to them as they made their way through the dense forests on the rough-hewn trail along which Azir was leading them.

CHAPTER FIVE

Alayna wished they would both shut up. Philip and Azir had been bickering incessantly for the last half-day and it was driving her insane. At first, she'd tried ignoring them, then she'd focused on Beathan and tried to engage the fairy in some meaningful conversation, but it hadn't lasted. At first the fairy had been game enough for a chat, but he seemed to enjoy the interactions between Philip and the vampire as much as he did his conversation with Alayna, treating the two men like a comedy, even prodding their trivial disputes with carefully worded barbs and cleverly instigative comments that only Alayna seemed to realize were designed to prolong their arguments.

The fairy snickered up his sleeve as he listened to Philip and Azir debate yet another meaningless detail of their plan. "What's that, eh?" He turned his roguish face toward Alayna.

"I said, do you ever think of returning to Ireland?"

The fairy shrugged. "There's plenty o' reason t' return home t' me fair isle, there is, but plenty o' reason not to, as well. I got a few unsettled debts an' a handful o' angry enemies waitin' there for me. No, I'm not goin' back there. Not quite yet. Now why, ya' goin' on about that anyway?"

It was Alayna's turn to shrug. "Just curious, I guess."

Beathan shook his head, dirty-blond locks swinging in the cold breeze. "Can't avoid those two forever." He jerked his head toward the bickering behind them.

"Who said I was?"

Beathan leveled a flat look at her. "Please, Lass, I'm no babe in swaddlin'. I know when a gal's torn between two men. It's like me ma always says: 'A body with eyes for more than one, soon has eyes for none'."

"I'm not torn!" Alayna answered more sharply than she intended. "I'm with Philip, and he knows it."

"Does he now?" The fairy raised an eyebrow.

She nodded curtly. "At least he should. I've said as much."

"It's not always the sayin' that matters, Lass," Beathan shot a wry smile her way.

Alayna shrugged her shoulders uncomfortably, avoiding the implications of that statement. "I just wish they'd stop bickering so much. It's driving me crazy!" She let out a sigh of exasperation.

Beathan chuckled. "Better entertainment than some journeys I've been on."

"I don't know how you stand it." She rolled her eyes.

"I just pretend they're a mangy dog an' a stray cat fighting over the same scrap o' meat. Reductions like that tend t' make the world more whimsical."

Alayna squinted behind her at her two companions that were at each other's throat. It might not work for her, but at least it was worth a try. If nothing else, imagining the two of them as whiny little beasts was comical.

They walked, setting a quick pace—all of them were at least partially non-human and could rely on greater stamina than most humans. When the midday break came, they huddled in their cloaks—well, all except Philip who was impervious to the chill—and sat on a couple of fallen logs in a small clearing off the side of the trail. They ate their meager rations in a quiet daze of restfulness, even their non-human bodies tired eventually when called upon to traverse rough terrain, especially considering what they had all been through lately—Alayna most of all. Her time in the menagerie had taxed her physically more than she would admit out loud. When they rose to start again on their trek, Azir took the lead and the rest of them followed.

Alayna fell in beside Philip this time, hoping to thaw some of the ice between them lately. Well, perhaps not ice, but awkwardness, certainly. "A wish for your thoughts, love?"

Philip managed a smile, although he didn't look at her when he answered. "And are you a djinn now?"

"It's only a saying, Philip. I'm just wondering what you're thinking?"

This time Philip looked at her with his signature grin, and the wildness in his eyes set her heart racing. "A good thing you are not, love, they can be a nasty sort. Every wish they grant is accompanied by three unforeseen struggles associated with it. Some of them cruel and most of those issues dangerous. No, best steer clear of djinns if you can."

"I thought you spent most of your time in the Atlantic when you were with the Guild?" Alayna shot him a confused look. She thought she'd known most of his history.

"You're correct, I did. It was Martin—Astori, I mean—I learned about them from him. Second hand of course, but he spent lots of time in that region of the world so I took his word as true." He grimaced sadly at the mention of Astori.

Martin Astori, his one-time leader and former mentor. Killed by Philip's own hand the night Astori's mad-hatched plan had succeeded in converting Alayna from human to Elfas by work of magic. The secretive magician had almost reignited The Great Transformation, attempting to forcefully change humans to supernatural against their will, as had happened decades ago during the first Great Transformation. It was lore now, but some still remembered. Luckily this time Alayna had been the only victim. Philip had stopped Astori, with the help of Beathan, of course. Not every race of beings was as neutral as the Elfas. Alayna shuddered to think what would have become of the Atlantic Coast if unsuspecting humans had been converted into vampires, werewolves, and who knew what else against their will.

Alayna placed a hand on his arm, knowing how painful it was to think of the betrayal of his former mentor. She squeezed gently before retreating her hand back within the warmth of her cloak. The afternoon sky was covered in clouds, what could be seen of it through the forest canopy at least. It was a chill day.

"Stephen," Philip said out of the blue.

"What?"

Beathan and Azir walked ahead of them, engaged in lively banter that they both seemed to enjoy. Alayna looked at Philip again in question.

"You asked what I was thinking about earlier. I was thinking about the boy, Stephen. Well, I suppose he's not really a boy now, is he," Philip mused.

"Do you miss him?" Alayna asked curiously. He didn't speak much of Stephen.

"He was a lively sort. A good lad." Philip smiled wryly. "He was only with me for a short while. But still, a good lad."

"So why are you thinking of him?" Alayna asked.

Her part-troll lover shrugged his deceptively powerful shoulders. "I suppose because I was thinking of James the other day, so it's natural that Stephen should follow. I guess I'm just wondering where he is. Or how he is for that matter. It's a dangerous line of work, Guild work."

Alayna made a sad little smile. "Well you taught him well, as best you could." Philip nodded grimly and they walked on into the deepening shadows of the afternoon.

The trail they followed under the guidance of Azir flirted in and out of existence. Sometimes a game trail, sometimes a larger woodcutter's path, other times it winked out of existence and the hybrid vampire led them through game runs and open meadows without a trail in site. But they placed their trust in Azir and soldiered on, even as they grew weary.

It was as they were tramping tiredly through just such a one of those sheltered meadows that Beathan drew a quick intake of breath and nervously flung a hand up.

"Stop!" the fairy whisper-screamed, concern showing clearly on his face.

Everyone followed suit, even though the vampire rolled his eyes at being told what to do. Philip tensed as he paused, coiled like a viper ready to attack, and Alayna took her cue from him. Beathan didn't scare easily, and while it wouldn't be fair to call his gaze a look of fear, there was definitely worry creasing his brow.

Alayna gazed around the clearing at which Beathan was staring intently, his mischievous fairy eyes darting every which way as he tried to scan their entire surroundings. The meadow was completely enclosed by forest, a small swath of open sky above them, which at nighttime might have given sight to a full moon. It only showed dismal wintery greyness above. The green grass of the meadow was wild and rich, watered by seasonal rains and somehow, surprisingly unburdened by a lack of snowfall. That was odd since most of the forest had plenty of snow. But the strangest sight of all, one that Beathan had clearly noticed first, was the few small circles in the grass a few yards across in diameter. Some of the circles were a rusty red color, with tiny mushrooms growing within the grass; others had an almost scorched look to them. The four of them had unwittingly walked across two of these circles without paying proper attention. Azir was standing inside the very edge of one as they paused.

Alayna was growing nervous herself now. What was this place? Her eyes scanned around them like everyone else. She saw that even a few leaves on the trees at the edge of the clearing had that scorched look, as well. As if fire had caught and burned recently, but only on specific leaves and without spreading.

"Beathan, what is it, mate?" Philip asked quietly.

The fairy held up a hand for silence and cocked his ear. Against the suddenly solemn mood, Alayna was forced to stifle a giggle at the look of frustration on Philip's face. Her love hated being in the dark about things, and Beathan loved to hold knowledge back as long as possible, usually for dramatic effect. However this time, as she swallowed her laughter, she could clearly see it was not the case. The fairy really was listening for something. Philip seemed to notice this also and shrugged away his frustration. Only Azir seemed stuck in his annoyance, and unable—or unwilling—to pick up on the mood.

They remained unmoving, waiting silently for Beathan to speak or act, for what seemed like a long few minutes. The fairy's cocked ear listened for something unknown to them. Finally, after minutes of silence and stillness, Beathan seemed satisfied and his tension lessened.

Beathan shook his head slightly. "Sorry, I was a wee bit worried for a moment there. Thought we might hear somethin' that we most assuredly do not want t' hear." Relief plastered across his face at the silence around them in the wood.

"And just what exactly was that, Fairy? What was so important that we had to stand here waiting?" Azir grumbled grumpily.

Beathan opened his mouth to answer when he froze again. Out of the stillness, a faint sound drifted across the meadow from the northern edge of the woods, the direction in which they were heading. It was a tiny, keening cry. No, it was a burbling brook of a wailing song, wafting in and out of cadence. It was an ethereally beautiful melody, combining all the wildness of nature and beauty and freedom into one powerful and bewitching song. It had a strange note of fear attached to it, as well. And it froze them all in their tracks, immobilizing them, paralyzing them with its symphony of flickering sounds.

Beathan swore venomously, real fear entering his voice. He managed one last word, even as his jaw ceased to function for the moment and slacked open in a mesmerized fashion.

"Iele!" It was the last sound the fairy made.

Philip and Azir mimicked the fairy's slack-jawed appearance, while Alayna fought to throw off the fog drifting over her mind at the beauty of the song.

They stood there for what might have been minutes or hours, but before she knew it, twilight was descending. Or had it always been descending. Was this just the natural state of existence—an endless twilight realm? Incorporeal forms began swirling and dancing around the edges of the meadow. Alayna struggled to make logical sense of what her mind couldn't process. And all the while, the music lilted through the glade, its tune seeming to whisper in between the very trees themselves, making a mocking mist of her mind.

The forms at the edges of the meadow darted in and out of the trees, visible, then hidden, over and over again. She watched as their circular, swaying dance moved closer and closer, like the noose of a rope tightening around a neck. As the forms drew closer, they began to coalesce, to lose their insubstantiality and become solid as they merged. The firmness lent a strange sense of terror to their imminent arrival at where Alayna and her companions stood frozen in the middle of the glade. The newfound corporeal appearances were an inexorable indication that something bad was about to happen, something real, something tangible, and Alayna was powerless to stop it.

She cast her gaze around frantically. Philip was off to her side, with Azir not far away. Beathan was still the furthest away, having been the one in the lead. All three of the men were still frozen. Azir's eyes were blank, the nothingness that comes from a deep dream. Beathan and Philip's faces gave her a bit more hope. Philip's eyes would fade in and out of consciousness as the siren song worked its magic upon him. Clearly, he was fighting it, but for some reason he was unable to remain awake and alert like Alayna. Of the men, only Beathan was close to full consciousness. He had the occasional glazed over look of the other two, but for the most part his eyes bore a wild look of fear that she did not often associate with the fairy. Whatever he knew of these beings, it was more than Alayna, and it did not bode well.

Alayna continued fighting the mist that threatened to swallow her mind, as the waif-like female creatures with tangled, disheveled hair flitted ever closer, their nakedness seeming to be almost a pure connection with the land around them. As she fought the fog, Alayna could finally make a count of the beings. They were fully solid now and Alayna could see that of all the dancing, insubstantial forms of earlier, only three remained. They coiled ever closer in their primal movements. Coiling, coiling, closer still they approached.

Horror akin to what a rabbit must feel like in a snake's scaly grasp bit at Alayna's gut. Was this how it would end? Dead by the hands of some nasty fairy-folk she'd never even heard of before? Iele, is that what Beathan had called them? It could be since that was the last thing Beathan had said before going silent. Alayna thrashed physically at her bonds, the song's ropey chords immobilizing her where she stood. Philip had fully succumbed now. She hadn't seen him awake for some time. What was time anyway? It was difficult to keep straight with this twilight world playing around inside her head, wreaking havoc with her brain. The song lulled her, told her to quit fighting, just as the others had succumbed —Beathan had finally gone blank now also.

Instead she fought harder than she'd ever fought before. Alayna gritted her teeth, relishing the small, simple movement that she managed with her jaw, while the rest of her stood stiff. She railed against the magic bindings of the music, willed herself to reach a weapon. A crossbow, a knife. Just move a finger, she pleaded with herself. She hadn't survived the menagerie and the fighting pits for it to end like this.

Nothing happened.

She wilted in defeat, though her body hung stiff as it had been since the song began. And still the beings circled closer. They were taking their time, clearly in no hurry, not an ounce of fear or concern on their faces. Terrible, beautiful, primal faces. They were some fairy-kind that Alayna had never encountered. She gave up. Alayna was the last one fighting, and what could she even do? About to fully surrender to defeat, Alayna had one final thought. A gambit that might work, and even if it didn't, what more harm could it do?

She let her eyes glaze over, let her mind go. Alayna relinquished control of her consciousness to the music, let it take over and lull her, let it croon her to the precipice of sleep. Except for a sliver of her consciousness. As Alayna teetered on the edge of a twilight dreamland, she held on to one tiny shred of her mind, her identity, her existence. She was still awake but only barely.

The beings were among her companions now, their pale fingers caressing and touching as they sang and skipped. Yet, Alayna had let her mind go, let her eyes go blank, so she could only vaguely see them, and only had a sense of their presence. She could feel them though, and as a set of fingers traced her face, a hot sensation accompanied it, like fire ghosting too near to her skin. No more wondering about what scorched the leaves and grass bits in the meadow.

Alayna held on to that last bit of her consciousness for dear life. Not knowing when the right time would be, for what exactly, she wasn't even sure. Alayna gathered her will as she could hear the song begin to quiet and then fade. The voices stopped as the beings stopped dancing, and the echoes of the otherworldly music began to whisper out of existence.

Something in Alayna's gut told her that this was the only chance she'd get. The magic had wooed her companions into the dreamworld, and nearly done so to her, as well. If it started up again, she wasn't sure she could retain any scrap of her mind. The struggle to remain conscious had already worn her down. As the very last echo of the song disappeared, Alayna gathered all the strength she had left, tapped into her inner core of strength and desire to survive and willed herself to move.

And move she did. Like a prisoner breaking free of shackles, her arms burst into action in a flurry of movement. One hand reached a knife and the other found one of her miniature crossbows. The bow was up in a heartbeat and had loosed a bolt before the beings even knew what had happened. The arrow flew true and struck the face of one of the Iele, piercing her through the eye in dramatic fashion. She wailed as she died, even as Alayna swung cat-like around the stiffened body of Beathan to drive her belt-knife into the heart of another of the beings. Two dead and one to go.

The remaining Iele, keened her rage, facing up to charge Alayna and avenge her comrades. Alayna flipped the knife in her grasp, slippery as it was from blood, and cast it end over end toward the final being. It struck the Iele in the arm and while not a killing blow, it seemed to be enough to dissuade the final creature from continuing the fight. In a rush of speed, almost as if it could glide across the meadow, it darted away and back into the darkness of the forest, screaming its pain, grief, and rage as it went. Its cries echoed eerily in its wake and Alayna shivered as she stood guard carefully, to make sure it didn't return.

Alayna kept her eyes on the forest even as she walked around the tight group of her companions, prodding arms and torsos, hoping for signs of wakefulness. It did not come immediately, but when it did, it was Beathan who first seemed to cast off the magic of the music that had imprisoned their minds.

"Where are they, what's happened, lass?" he exclaimed in worry.

Alayna shrugged almost nonchalantly and pointed to the ground. "Two dead, and one gone."

Beathan shook his head in confusion and then winced, looking more miserable than a man with a hangover. "How? It shouldn't be possible."

Alayna heard a muffled noise from Philip but when she checked, he wasn't fully awake yet. "Why? What were they? What do you know of those creatures?"

"Too much. And yet, not enough," Beathan trailed off, then began again when Alayna indicated rather impatiently that he should continue his explanation. She was in no mood for his dramatics. "Belong t' the fairy kind, they do. But at the same time, not, eh?" He looked at her like she should understand.

Alayna just shook her head. "Out with it, Beathan."

"They're called Iele—o' sometimes nymphs o' dryads. They frequent many different parts o' this continent but can be found most often in these regions. Dark, secretive, they're rarely seen an' not always hostile."

Alayna snorted in disbelief. "Really mate? I saw the look on your face when you'd realized our predicament and I saw what they could do. There's no doubt in my mind we'd be dead right now if I hadn't fought them off."

"Oh, most assuredly we would be. No ifs about it. Alls I meant was that they can be friendly—leastwise, friendlier at times. But not in our case. The minute we crossed into their territory an' traipsed our way across one o' their wee dancing circles we were doomed—o' we should've been." He indicated the scorched circles in the meadow.

Alayna cocked her head and looked at them more closely. "What are these?"

"Remnants of former dances, echoes of their former songs, seared into the consciousness of this land—their land," Beathan lilted in his Irish brogue rather mystically in Alayna'as opinion.

The fairy continued. "They aren't necessarily evil, but they do have a temper t' be sure! Their dances an' songs are sacred t' them. Precious, like little else in this world is t' them. An' they don't take too kindly t' folks witnessing it, o' tippy-toeing across the leftover marks o' their sacred dances." He indicated to their scorched or rusty red circles in the meadow.

"So all of this, we almost died, just because they're territorial and we accidentally walked across something sacred of theirs?" Alayna exclaimed incredulously.

The fairy shrugged. "S'not that crazy when ya' think about it, lass. Many a species o' being is right protective of what's important t' them. We may not understand it, may not agree with it, but they had their reasons."

Alayna sniffed in disdain. She was in no mood for Beathan's philosophical approach. At that moment, Philip shook himself out of the delirium and slumped to a seat in the meadow. Alayna rushed to his side and crouched down.

"Are you alright, love?" she asked.

He nodded a shaky yes and turned his eyes upwards to Beathan. "Iele?" It was a simple question directed at the fairy. He must've heard Beathan yell it before they'd lost consciousness. Beathan nodded a response.

"We should be dead," Philip muttered.

"Look t' her for answers," Beathan jutted his chin toward Alayna. "How did ya' manage t' shake free o' their bewitchment?"

Alayna shrugged. "I'm not really sure. Better question might be, if I could, then why couldn't either of you? You both have more practice and training in this area of mental control and resistance."

Philip shook his head. His eyes seemed to be clearing, but she could see the same grimace on his face that was on the fairy's, like some kind of magical hangover had its grips on them. "No love, the Iele are known to have one of the most powerful magical abilities of persuasion that we are aware of." He'd instinctively switched back in the 'we' of Collector-mode while describing a species of creature to her, he forgot who he was now whenever he began to instruct. "The Guild rarely even has us hunt them down because they're just not worth the risk. You're likely to lose more men than what taking them is worth—besides, they're not a risk to highly populated areas since they only live in the depths of the wild and only attack to avenge the trespassing on their sacred spaces." He glanced around as understanding of what happened occurred to him as he saw the scorched rings and red and mushroomed circles in the glade.

Alayna nudged him gently to continue. He pulled his gaze from the meadow and back to her face, as Azir finally slumped to the ground in wakeful moaning. The magical hangover seemed to hit him hardest. Perhaps because he'd stayed under the spell longer than any of the rest of them.

"So why were you immune to their magic?" Philip mused.

"I wouldn't say I was immune, it nearly got me." Alayna responded.

"Still, even managin' t' break free at all is near miraculous," Beathan added. "The Iele have a right nasty reputation. Not many a person can escape."

Alayna shrugged uncomfortably. "I'm not special or anything," she muttered. Not quite sure why she was embarrassed.

"I don't agree with that at all." Philip grasped her hand and smiled at her as she pulled him to his feet. "But we've seen you have greater success with resistance to mind control in the past than you should have based on the limited training you've received. The vampires in the forest, on the way to the Alchemist's." He prodded her memory.

"True, true," Beathan mused along. "You shook off a vampire's crooning rather easily. Could have somethin' t' do with your mental capabilities as an Elfas. The gestalt consciousness an' all..." He waved his hand vaguely as he mentioned what he didn't fully understand. He was alluding to her people's ability to share consciousness as a race when they wished it, and even to share consciousness with people close to them even of different races. Philip was often one she could do that with. Or had been able to.

"Could we please quit speculating and get out of here?" Azir spat acerbically. He was on his feet again, and with murder in his eyes. Perhaps he was annoyed that for some reason the elfas part of him hadn't been resistant to the Iele's song like Alayna had been. Maybe because it was diluted with another half, while she was pure elfas.

"We should get out of here," Philip agreed quickly before grimacing as he did. He continued on, "the one that's still alive isn't likely to come back, but it's best not to take chances."

They all agreed and walked on through the full night even though they were exhausted. As they left the meadow and entered the woods, Alayna glanced back for one final moonlit glimpse of the two pale bodies blotched with red that she left in her wake. Her body count was growing. This time strangely, as much as she'd disputed Beathan's initial philosophizing, she couldn't help but feel a certain sadness at the dead behind her. They were off to try and free the world from its thrall to the Guild, and yet the very people they were trying to protect were the ones who'd attacked them and forced her to kill them. She wiped an odd tear from the corner of her eye and steeled her heart again. More would die before this was done. Maybe even her.

CHAPTER SIX

The following days were a blur—in the sense that nothing of note happened. Philip and Azir traded barbs and Beathan, lacking for any other entertainment, spurred them on. Alayna found herself receding into a contemplative shell. More and more her thoughts would turn toward her time in the menagerie. A scent or sound here, a sight there, and the memories were triggered, which sent her spiraling back into that hell, so much so that sometimes she felt like she could still smell the stench of unwashed bodies, could still taste the blood in her mouth after biting her cheek while being tortured. Alayna shook her head to clear it. She was safe—well, as safe as one could be when searching for a vampire stronghold. She was never going back to captivity. She'd die before she let that happen again.

A hand grasped hers and she looked at Philip, worry dampening the wildness that usually raged within the pools of his eyes.

"I'm fine, love." She squeezed his hand in reassurance. He nodded his acceptance, doing her the courtesy of not pressing the issue. Whatever gulf had formed between them, whatever bridge they were trying to cross to get back to where they had once been, he could still read her. He knew when she was alright and when she was not.

"S'been four days since we left the clearing with the Iele, mate. We any closer to findin' the wee prince o' the vampires?" Beathan smirked as he shot the question Azir's way, knowing how it would rile him.

Azir's nostrils flared. "You would do well to rein in your tongue, fairy. We are close indeed. And this close to Bran Castle the woods have eyes... and ears." He gazed around the forest ominously.

"Touch too much drama for me. Spare me the performance," the fairy said and winked at the vampire. "I've never censored meself before, and I'll not start now."

"Still, Azir's probably right. If we're this close, we should start exercising more caution," Alayna said.

Philip shrugged, his plain yet somehow rugged face, framed by a shock of shoulder-length brown hair, was determined and unconcerned. "If we're close, then they likely already know we're coming. If they haven't attacked us yet, then it's because they don't want to—or have been told not to."

"The Collector is only all too correct," Azir said, his nose seeming to turn up at echoing Philip's words.

Philip shared a look with the vampire. "I know my way around a nest."

"We prefer coven."

"Do ya' now? I always thought it was a swarm. Ya' know, like mosquitoes."

Azir rolled his eyes but didn't deign to answer. "Well, if they know we're coming, all the more reason to be careful, right?" Alayna voiced again.

"What more can we do, love? It's a risky venture, we've already established that. Heading into a nest of vampires—even when in the company of one—is always ill-advised, let alone without all the usual trappings. We've only got a few stakes and no garlic, no running-water that's been bottled. Asking for more caution in an already half-mad adventure is like saying we should worry about something we can't change. We do what we always do: stay sharp and watch each other's backs. Anything more is just wishful thinking."

Did he have to make it sound so grim? Alayna shuddered at the thought of becoming a vampire's meal. She'd met more than one who'd wanted to bleed her dry. She fingered the tip of her stake, having pulled it free from the sheath at her belt. Well, she would not go quietly into any cook pot, metaphoric or not.

———

AFTER TWO MORE DAYS THEY reached their destination. As the ground began to slope upward Azir paused and motioned for them to do the same. "We'll clear the tree-line soon and then it'll be only a short way farther, all within eyesight of the castle."

"So this is it then?" Alayna murmured nervously. All her posturing about their plan and moving forward with at least a temporary alliance with the vampires had seemed like a good idea back then, with the menagerie and Helmsted still fresh in her mind. But in the cold light of morning, it looked like a pale version of itself; a recipe to get them killed.

Azir nodded. "It is a good thing, my dear, that we camped a few miles back and decided to approach in the morning. It may not be much, but I will take any advantage we can get."

"If we have to fight our way out, at least we know there's safety outside," Philip concluded.

"Look at the two o' ya', practically finishin' each other's sentences." Beathan nudged Philip in the ribs with his elbow. Alayna stifled a laugh, as inappropriate as the time was for humor. The fairy certainly pushed his friends to the limit. It was lucky he was so loyal, and so good in a fight. Otherwise, they might not be as tolerant.

Philip and Azir simply pretended they didn't hear the fairy. Alayna sighed. Would this feud between them ever end? She knew it was partly her own doing, but they needed each other, all of them—at least they did, if they were to have any hope of accomplishing their current venture. Couldn't the two of them suppress their emotions for the time being?

They approached on weary feet through still-dew-wet grass. The trees indeed ended as the hybrid vampire had said, but they did so much closer to Bran Castle than she had expected. They were practically on top of the fortress already. It was blocky and crude, yet bleakly beautiful in a way. It jutted up from the top of the hill on which it was built, rough-hewn rock formed sheer walls and narrow windows and one main gate dotted its surfaces. Any attacking foe would have their work cut out for them if attacking the castle, even with the advantage of numbers—let alone just four of them.

"Good thing we aren't attacking?" Philip whispered to her as they stalked closer, not for the first time causing Alayna to pause and wonder if sometimes their mental link went both ways instead of one, if in fact he could read her mind sometimes. No. He was just attuned to her, knew her so well he could anticipate her thoughts. It sent a warmth through her, that thought.

They walked quickly and quietly to the main gate of the castle, an iron-bound oaken double door, thick enough that it must have weighed as much as a mountain. They stopped in front of it. All four of them casting glances at the others.

"So do we just knock then?" the fairy asked with a roguish cast to his face.

Azir shook his head in annoyance. "I told you to keep a civil tongue when we enter. No jokes!" Beathan put up his hands in apparent acceptance. The vampire continued, "They will already know we are here. We have no course but to wait."

The silence between them stretched from moments into minutes before a noise finally crept its way into the daytime air around them. They heard a grating sound as a smaller door within the larger oaken gate was shifted open. A pale hand slithered out beckoning them inside as a few wisps of smoke sheeted off its skin in the morning sun. A hiss and the hand retracted inside the cracked doorway.

Philip looked to Azir, surprisingly waiting for him to take the lead. The hybrid vampire whose strange roots allowed him to walk in daylight without fear of the sun casually stepped inside the doorway as if it was the most normal thing to do. Alayna knew the attitude all too well. When going into battle, never show weakness. Let your enemy think they gave you no cause for fear. Azir had put on his armor.

―――――

ALAYNA LET Philip and Beathan go inside next before following last. She slipped through the darkened doorway and into a strange courtyard. There were canopies in place, letting through only the smallest traces of light to filter in and hit the ground. The vampire who had beckoned them in slipped quickly across the canopied courtyard to the opposite side where true darkness awaited. The body, the shape of the vampire, the way she moved looked familiar to Alayna. It tugged at her memory.

With Azir in the lead still, the four of them walked through the protected courtyard as another vampire shut the door behind them. It closed with a sinister click. Trapped. That was all Alayna could think for a moment. I won't be captured again! Her inner voice rising near to madness seemed to chant over and over again. She had to soothe herself in the grimmest way possible, by reminding herself that they were more likely to be eaten than imprisoned.

"Welcome to the fortress of the One Who Rules," a silken voice said to them. It was the female vampire who had let them enter. As they entered another darkened doorway on the other side of the courtyard, the interior was awash with torchlight. While Alayna knew that vampires could see perfectly well in the dark, the torch-lit corridors of the fortress lent an eerie, menacing atmosphere much akin to what she imagined the entrance to a cavernous hell-mouth might appear.

The vampire turned around and Alayna let out a hiss of recognition. It was the vampire who set upon them with her companions in the woods, and then again as they had reached the mountain cabin of The Alchemist.

"Salynksa," Azir nodded his head cautiously and courteously in greeting.

"Azir." Her lip curled in disdain as she looked at him. "Just when I thought you couldn't get any lower in your actions, you appear in the company of these three—enemies who killed one of ours not long ago. A half-fairy, a Collector, and his bitch lover." She practically spat the last few words out.

"Former," Philip countered, unperturbed by the vampire's venom. He had seen his fair share of fights and didn't startle easily.

"What?"

"Ahem, well me mate o'er here was just sayin' that he's not a Collector no more, lass. He's gone rogue, actually. A complete renegade he is," Beathan ended with his signature smirk. Salynksa just stared at him until his smile faded.

"My companions are necessary in these trying times," Azir answered fluidly despite the delay.

"And what trying times are those?" Salynksa asked, only seeming to be halfway curious.

Azir cleared his throat and spoke confidently. "I would be happy to discuss just that with the Shade King."

"You think you're getting an audience with the One Who Rules?" Salynksa asked incredulously. The surrounding vampires—and Alayna was nervous to see that there were quite a few of them, at least ten or more—snickered condescendingly at their leader's question.

Azir's eyes went flat. Alayna knew him well enough to know he hated being humiliated. She could also see by the dark glint in the female vampire's eye that she was attempting to do exactly that. Alayna hoped the hybrid could hold his temper. The odds were not in their favor. Alayna fingered the wooden handle of her stake.

Salynksa noticed Alayna's hand move to the wooden weapon and stepped past Azir to close the distance between her and Alayna. "Want to try me again, Elfas. Last time it ended too quickly."

"If I recall, it was you running from me last time."

Salynksa snorted in disdain although her eyes betrayed her flames of indignation at Alayna's dig. "Only at first. And from him, not you sweetling." She glanced at Philip whose body had tensed, ready for action the moment he saw Alayna squaring off with the vampire.

"Besides," Salynksa continued, "we caught up with you again. And if I recall, on that occasion it was you and yours cowering behind little old twinkle-finger's defensive charm, not us." Beathan smiled appreciatively at her mention of his magical arts.

"Back away, vampire, or you'll regret it," Philip growled, low and menacingly.

"I can handle myself, Philip," Alayna said sharply, only somewhat disappointed in herself for speaking so bitingly to him.

Salynksa sidled even closer to Alayna as tensions in the room balanced on a knife's edge. "Someone thinks highly of themselves. Think you'll stand a chance against me?" she crooned scornfully.

Alayna thought about all that she'd endured. The many fights in the pits, the training with Philip, the tactical tips from Azir, the dangerously rough edges to her soul that she could only barely conceal. Salynksa was in for a rude awakening if she thought this Elfas easy prey.

"Don't test me, sweetling. I won't kill you. I'll just cut you up real nice, nice enough to have a quick sip, and then toss you in a dungeon, somewhere nice and dark and damp, to await my pleasure." The vampire cocked her head as she watched her words strike home.

Something in Alayna snapped. All her hopes from earlier for Azir to contain his rage flew out the window. Just the mention of being captured again, held against her will, sent all reason disappearing in a rush into the ether around her. She would not be a prisoner again!

Without waiting, harnessing the element of surprise, she lashed out with a closed fist and sent Salynksa sprawling to the ground in a heap of pain, clutching her face. Alayna didn't stop there. She leaped atop the vampire and smashed fist after fist into the vampire's face. A brutal, primal delight welled up in her at unleashing all this pent-up anger, confusion, and fear. It was like being in the pits again. Almost.

The corridor erupted around her, but she focused only on the combatant beneath her. She vaguely saw in her periphery rushed movement and shouted insults, threats, and commands before arms wrapped around her and hauled her off her victim.

"Easy love, easy," Philip murmured as she thrashed in his arms.

Salynksa climbed to her feet quickly yet moving a bit more gingerly than usual. She hissed her displeasure. "I'll kill you for that."

"Now, now, Salynksa. They are with me. You have your orders concerning me, don't you?" Azir said hurriedly, despite his clipped and proper accent.

"I don't care," Salynksa raged, and yet his words did seem to give her pause, as she flung up a hand to the ten vampires who had encircled them and were tightening around them like a noose. The vampires paused.

"We want to see *him*," Philip said calmly, still holding on to Alayna.

"You cannot just walk in and demand an audience!" The vampire almost sounded afraid as she said it.

"Be easy, Salynksa, they may have their wish," a voice suddenly interjected from the deep shadows down the corridor. It was an old voice, paper dry and yet at the same time damp, like blood dripped across an ancient scroll. It was full of cruelty, despite its calm tone. And it was confident, oh so confident, secure in the knowledge that this was its domain. And it ruled here with absolute finality.

CHAPTER SEVEN

S alynksa looked afraid now as she bowed her head in acquiescence. "As you wish, Master."

Philip fought the urge to swallow, his mouth suddenly devoid of moisture. In all his many years with the Collectors Guild, he'd never actually spoken with anyone who had seen the being before him and lived to tell the tale. The Shade King was practically a bogeyman to Philip's former kind, and no amount of training or tactics could prepare a person for a meeting with the lord of the vampires. He went by many names—the Shade King, the One Who Rules, Dracula—the current Dracula that is, it was more of an earned title than a singular being. All incarnations of his title named him someone, something, to be feared more than almost any other.

"Well, Renegade, we finally meet." The voice seemed to crumble from the darkness, just beyond Philip's eyesight, exuding an almost reluctant curiosity. Only a dark form loomed behind the wall of vampires surrounding them.

"Is it really a meeting if I cannot see your face?" Philip mustered his voice, and somehow managed to sound calm and assured even as his heart clenched. It wasn't fear. Philip didn't look for death, but neither did he exactly fear it. No, this was some kind of primal reaction within him to an ageless terror, more a revulsion to evil manifesting itself in his body, than an emotion in his mind.

The dry voice chuckled. "Oh, but I can see you."

"Show yourself," Philip challenged.

Movement could be heard as the form receded back into the depths of darkness beyond the reach of torchlight. "Salynksa. Bring them to the room." And then he was gone.

Salynksa looked visibly relieved to have direct instructions from her master, and she breathed a heavy sigh of relief. Philip could only imagine what mistakes might cost a person in this realm.

"Looks like you're getting the audience you wanted after all, day-walker," she said to Azir with a knowing smile. It was a cruel look, anticipatory, and devoid of pity. What did she expect to occur in 'the room'? Azir's face took on a sickly cast as he tried to muster his confidence, shorn by simply the voice of Dracula.

They followed Salynksa down the narrow corridors of the castle, surrounded on all sides by the escort of vampire guards. In short, they were going nowhere without a fight. Not that Philip had expected anything different when they'd embarked on this venture. Seeking out the Shade King had always been foolhardy at best. It was unwise to think they'd accomplish their aims without substantial danger—from enemies and their potential allies.

Bran Castle was a fortress to its core. The narrow passageways would make for close quarter fighting, where the greater numbers of a besieging foe would not overwhelm defenders. Murder holes were crafted into the ceilings or floors however you looked at it, so that defenders could launch projectiles or pour boiling liquid down on unsuspecting attackers. In short, it was quite defensible and not just inside the castle. It was on raised ground, adding height to the walls, making any exterior enemy think twice about attacking. Philip would have hated to lead an army against it a century or two ago. But that wouldn't be necessary here. Language would be their weapon—he hoped. Better to convince the Shade King to lend an ear to their plans rather than resort to violence in a desperate escape attempt. And the further into the castle they went, the more unlikely that hypothetical escape became.

Surprisingly, however, they did not travel down into the bowels of the fortress like Philip would have expected. Instead they trekked upwards, following stairwells one after another until they had to be near the top realm of the fortress. Tapestries lined the walls, and any exterior window was covered with draperies creating the darkness necessary for vampires to survive. A few cracks here and there let in a thin ray of light from the outside, eliciting brief grunts of pain from their captors as they walked through them.

Before long they climbed a final, short stairway and entered a wide room, circular in nature—the interior of a turret. More light than Philip expected was allowed to enter the room through gaps in the drapes along the windows. Philip strategically placed himself—and his company, by stopping Alayna and Beathan with a hand on their shoulders—within the shine of one of those gaps, letting the sun wash over his face as protection. Dust motes swirled in the rays, and the room had an almost airy quality to it. Divans and chaises dotted the edges. Like an unused but once-loved family room. Except it was not unused at all.

A raspy chuckle filled the air as Philip stopped his companions in the sunlight. All eyes were drawn to the throne-like oaken chair in front of him. It was large, but not raised off the ground. Well made, but not extravagant. It oozed confidence and class while somehow remaining just a subtle indication of wealth. The laughter died out and nobody echoed it. The shape of a being was still enshrouded in darkness, unable to be clearly viewed—whether because of the lack of sunlight directly hitting the throne or because of some other, more sinister and mystical reason, Philip wasn't sure.

"Do you think a few rays of light will protect you, Renegade?" the voice from the shadows asked mockingly.

"Do we need protection?" Philip countered stoutly.

"All in my domain should seek protection. Whether by me... or from me," the voice responded, dropping to a low, throaty growl at the end. Philip swallowed involuntarily.

"Nice place ya' got here," Beathan piped up from just behind Philip and slightly off to the side. "Not exactly what I imagined though, I must admit."

"What, you thought that because we are children of the night, that we would be sequestered away in some cave somewhere, waiting like grubs for twilight to return?" the One Who Rules answered scornfully.

"I think he just meant, it's not exactly what we are accustomed to seeing in regards to a vampire's lair," Philip interjected as politely as he could, hoping to forestall any of the fairy's antics—antics that more often than not turned folks against him sooner rather than later.

"Well, I have a few hidey-holes out there in addition to this castle, and I visit them from time to time—when it suits me," the Shade King said slyly.

"Makes sense," Beathan answered blithely, "occasionally it's good t' know where t' run. It's like me ma always said: 'if ya' never learn t' run an' hide, ya'll deserve however 'tis ya've died.'"

Philip clenched his teeth in annoyance. He wanted to deal with the Shade King. He was fairly certain Beathan would only antagonize him.

Sure enough, the shadow on the throne seemed to lean forward and answer softly, menacingly, "Does it make sense, Fairy?"

Silence stretched for a few long moments until Azir cleared his throat uncomfortably. "Master—"

"Why are you here?" the shadow interrupted, suddenly brusque.

"We need your help," Philip answered.

"Do you now?" the voice answered and this time its pleased tone was accompanied by a number of titters from around the room.

"...And you need ours," Philip concluded with as much force as he could. The titters were replaced by spiteful hisses.

Again silence. "And why would you say that?" the Shade King asked very softly. Philip knew he was treading on delicate ground. Dracula was a title that a vampire didn't inherit like human monarchs, but rather earned. And keeping the title, especially for any great length of time, required strength. And intimidation. Dracula couldn't afford to be seen as weak in front of intruders.

"I have ruled for nearly four hundred years," the voice rasped. "Do you think I did so by listening to the counsel of one from the Collectors Guild?" Anger laced the edges of the comment. Philip would have to be very careful indeed.

"Former," Philip responded with his own hard edge, much more forceful than his inner caution had told him to proceed.

"Excuse me?" the voice whispered from the shadows.

"I said I'm formerly of the Collectors Guild, but no more."

"That...remains to be seen," the Shade King murmured pensively, his barely controlled aggression from a moment before seeming to have receded for now.

The shadows around the oaken throne roiled as the One Who Rules moved within them, and finally parted as a hand stretched forth and beckoned Philip to come closer. The hand looked old, but strong, the flesh un-weakened by time. Pale flesh, but there was a purplish-bluish midnight hue to it somehow, as if the skin itself has somehow sucked into it all the marrow of a starless night. A few veins in particular carried this color to the extreme.

"Come closer, Collector."

Philip stepped a few steps closer, willing himself to show no fear. He'd faced down vampires by the score, wendigos, and fauns of all kinds. He'd tangled with a Black Annis and lived to tell the tale. He had seen worse than one ancient bloodsucker. Or so he tried to tell himself. All of his instincts were at a fine point. Reluctantly he had to admit—if only to himself—that he understood just why Azir seemed so frightened of Dracula. Yet, Philip willed himself to stand firm.

"Pray tell me, why do I need your help?" the Shade King asked after a pregnant pause. The rest of the room was silent but for the quiet, tense breathing of everyone who was watching and listening. Philip knew his answer was important. He had to be convincing. Their lives likely depended on it.

"We have a common enemy. I, a renegade, and you leader of a cohort of creatures long despised and hunted by the Collectors Guild. We have much in common," Philip began.

The shadow on the throne snorted scornfully. "Hunted? We do the hunting here, Collector. In this land, my desire is law, not some pitiful cabal of human weaklings in the west. I fail to see what we have in common."

Philip grimaced. Not a good start. "I simply point out that the enemy of my enemy is my friend—or as close to friends as we are ever likely to become," he continued, breathing as calmly as possible. Vampires could sense weakness; a killer instinct of theirs, the ability to hone in on a physical—or emotional—weakness and exploit it. Philip couldn't give Dracula that advantage. "Could we not be of service to one another?"

"Again I ask you, what service could you possibly be to me?"

Philip sighed a deep lungful of breath. It was time to cut to the chase. Pretty words and courtly phrasing would get him nowhere against a being like the one he needed to convince. Besides, he'd never been particularly great with words.

"I want to take down the Collectors Guild. There is something broken inside of it," he stated plainly, bluntly.

A titter of interest echoed through the tower room. Dracula finally seemed to stir on the oaken throne-like chair in front of Philip. The shadows whispered as he did. "Go on, Collector."

"You may rule this land with an iron grasp, but how far does that power truly extend?—no need to answer me here and now, it was a rhetorical question." Philip held up his hands to show there was no offense meant. "But truly, beyond your borders, your kind are indeed hunted by those whom I used to serve. I killed or captured hundreds of your kind over the years. I gave them a stake through the heart." This time the muttering in the crowd was bitter and angry. Philip ignored it.

"Yes, for all your power and posturing, you dare not extend your sway over the rest of the continent. Bound by the night, you barely make it from one cave to the next when you try and leave the shelter of your deep woods and dark castles, and when you do, you're cut down by people like me, by Collectors trained to fight against you, taught to withstand whatever mental caresses you rain down upon their minds. Between them and the sunlight you can hardly call yourselves powerful." Hard, black eyes stared at him from around the room. Philip almost wished he could see the face of Dracula to know for sure how his words were being received. All he got from the throne was silence.

"Yet despite all that, despite your plight, you're still the strongest, most organized, widespread, and dangerous group of beings other than the humans. You're the only ones I can turn to with my request for aid."

"You have my ear, Collector. You may continue," Dracula said silkily. Philip glanced at Alayna and Beathan. They nodded their support for him.

Plain words. Again, those were all he had and perhaps they were best. "There is something rotten inside the Guild. Some wrong, deep down to its core—not every single one of them—," Philip amended quickly, thinking of the lad Stephen, or his old partner James, "but many, perhaps even most. And certainly among all those who occupy positions of power. I want to strike at the council of leaders who rule the Collectors Guild, the ones making the decisions. I want to destroy them and let whatever might rise from the ashes as a result, arise."

Philip paused for breath, shaking slightly at voicing such a dangerous wish out loud in front of the ruler of the vampires. His insides cringed at what he was doing, yet it was necessary.

"You more than have my interest now, Collector," the Shade King said almost lustfully, "can you imagine what my kind would be able to do without the might of the Guild to keep us in check?"

Philip swallowed. Part of him was terrified to even contemplate such an outcome, yet it was that very idea which he knew was the bait to get Dracula to have interest in an alliance. Without the Guild, vampires would spread like a disease across the continent. It was a concern, but one for another day. A man could only deal with one issue at a time, and right now, Helmsted, the Collectors Guild, and all it stood for was front and center in Philip's mind.

"Indeed, it is something to consider." Philip forced himself to agree with the king of the vampires, even as he quivered inside at the thought.

"But how would you accomplish this? Even with our aid it will be difficult. You are only four, added to our numbers," Dracula murmured, almost talking to himself.

Philip let him think for a moment, there was no rush now. He had the king's interest. They were safe—for the moment. He was infinitely glad that Beathan and Azir had quit talking and that his three companions were letting him lead the discussion. He had the experience with the Guild, and other than Azir's relationship with the vampires as one who was sometimes among them and sometimes not, Philip was the one with the most experience.

Feeling like the pause was enough, Philip answered the question, "It's all about the leadership. Strike at the head and the rest will scatter—or at least be left in such disarray from the power void that they won't be able to recover any time soon."

Dracula leaned forward again, his excited intent almost bringing him forth from his shadows. "But again I ask you, how will you be able to aid us?"

Philip was taken aback. "Do you really not see?" he asked, almost biting his tongue to get the words back in his mouth. He had not intended to sound so condescending.

"Enlighten me," the Shade King said softly, menacingly. With that one thoughtless comment, Philip had likely eroded whatever goodwill or patience he'd built up in the past few minutes.

Philip spread his hands, and stepped slightly forward, feeling the cool air on his hands and arms as he moved them. He realized he'd been frozen nearly still as he had been talking. "I was a mid-level Guild member. I have valuable information. I spent my time more recently on the opposite side of the Atlantic, but before that I spent years training and learning my craft on this continent. Why do you think the Guild was so desperate to catch me, to get me back? The Renegade who got away, with so many of their dangerously vulnerable secrets locked in his mind."

"So, with our strength in numbers and your vital information exposing them, you hope to decimate the Guild you once served?" The king finally saw to the heart of the deal Philip was proposing.

"Exactly," Philip said.

"But you still fail to mention how you plan to strike at the Guild leaders, even with my help. They cannot all be gathered in one place, ripe for the taking."

"Again, exactly," Philip agreed. "The council is spread across the continent. They rarely meet, and when they do it is almost never all of them together. This is to prevent the occurrence of exactly the sort of attack we are proposing. But a series of calculated strikes at outposts they thought safe and secret; let it be known that it is I, the Renegade, who is hitting them. They'll realize the danger. If I can strike at others, why not them. Hit a few more outposts, and then a few more, slowly and with the right timing, it should be just enough to put them on edge, then send them to flight, to gather in numbers where they think themselves strongest. I'll force them all together for the first time in decades." Philip clenched a fist as he lost himself in the answer.

"*We.*"

"What?" Philip asked.

"If I agree to help, then not you, but we will force them together," the voice from the shadows purred. Philip felt a little sick.

Philip made himself nod. "London is where it'll all end then."

"Your passion is... convincing," Dracula said thoughtfully, his intrigue clear in his voice.

"But?" Philip voiced the implied, hesitation.

"But how do I know it is not a trap? History between our kinds is long and fraught with violence. I'll need more proof of your trustworthiness."

"Do you really think he'd lie to you? That he would come here, risk all this, all of us, and be lying?" Alayna finally spoke up. And Philip grimaced internally. He could practically feel the Shade King's attention narrow down to a fine focus on the one person Philip least wanted him focused on.

"Wilder gambits have been played before, girl," the Shade King said disdainfully. "As I said, I'll need more proof. A test of your will to see this through if you will." Philip could hear the smirk in the vampire king's voice and his insides dropped. Something bad was about to happen.

"What did you have in mind?" Philip asked carefully.

"A test of life. A chance of death," the Shade King answered cryptically.

"Riddles now, mate?" Beathan spoke up, with a derisive snort.

"Plainly spoken then, a trial by combat," Dracula said with a hint of a sneer in his voice.

Philip swallowed. "No."

"It was not a question," the menace was back. "Either one of you fights, and maybe we strike a deal. Or you all die."

Philip took a deep breath. There was no way out of this. "Fine. I agree. Who am I fighting?" He could practically taste the resignation in his own voice.

"Oh no, no," the king crooned, "not you, Collector. You noble types never value your own life enough. The only true test of your commitment in this is if you are willing to risk a comrade's life for your aims. Perhaps, the fire-haired one?"

Philips teeth clenched in anger at the amused tone coming from the shadows. "No." he said again firmly and forcefully.

"But you just agreed to my terms, now you are backing out? Tsk tsk, not good for trust, is it?" The room tittered.

"She's not fighting, not this time," Philip said his only anger mounting. She's been through enough already, he thought.

Alayna put a hand on his arm. "It's alright, Philip, I can do this. I've faced worse in the pits."

"That's what I mean. You've faced enough of this. You don't need to do it again. I'll get him to let me fight," he whispered back to her even though she seemed confident enough. Unafraid even. She really had changed.

"I'll do it," a voice said from slightly behind them.

Philip and Alayna's heads swiveled. Beathan was standing there, head tilted to one side, cock-sure grin on his face, and yet somehow also managing to look serious.

"No!" this time it was Alayna's turn to object.

"Enough lass, I said I'd do it, an' I will. Enough now." The fairy's face had become completely solemn.

"Done. I accept these terms," Dracula said and a throaty chuckle emanated from the darkness on the throne.

CHAPTER EIGHT

"An' just who shall I fight, Oh Shadiest of Kings?" Beathan asked with a flourishing bow.

"A captive of ours. A beast that settled a little too near to our castle and attacked any and all indiscriminately. It even killed one of our own. We simply cannot allow such actions to go unpunished."

Beathan waited for the Shade King to give more of an answer. When none seemed forthcoming, he prodded further. "A name t' this beastie o' yours?"

"Capcaun." Beathan could practically hear the smirk in Dracula's voice. That didn't bode well. He swallowed. Well, he'd been in tight spots before. Dracula beckoned one of his subjects toward the throne and began issuing muffled orders. The subject in turn beckoned another vampire and sent that one running off with a task, while he continued conversing with the king.

Alayna squeezed Beathan's arm reassuringly and he flashed her a quick grin. But Philip's face was a grim mask.

"I don't know much about the creature, but what I do know isn't good," Philip said in typically blunt fashion.

"An' just what is a Capcaun?" Beathan asked. Philip's worry was infecting the fairy and he nervously scanned the crowd of satisfied vampires around the edges of the room. His light-fingered nature made him look instinctively for items he might be able to lift, as he often did when his nerves began to unravel. One vampire had a moonstone bracelet hanging loosely around a thin wrist. Child's play to take that. Beathan's gaze roved on, noting rings, and pouches, decorated belts, and bejeweled necklaces. As a whole, these vampires nearer to their seat of power were a wholly more ostentatious lot than Beathan was accustomed to encountering. Azir certainly didn't dress like they did.

Philip answered his question, pulling the fairy's eyes away from his imaginary picking of pockets. "It's a strange creature. Solitary and known to be extremely violent."

"Wonderful," Alayna muttered, sour with worry. Beathan felt warmth at their concern. It almost distracted him from his own.

The former Collector continued. "They've been seen in different types of forms—disparate accounts of the number of arms and legs, even heads they possess—lacking the consistency of form of most creatures. But to simplify matters, they're more or less an Ogre, often with a dog-like head." He grimaced, a common facial expression for Philip.

"What is it, mate? What aren't ya' tellin' me?"

Philip sighed. "One of the only things that is indisputable between accounts of the Capcaun is that they eat people."

"That is nothing particularly new," Azir muttered, finally speaking after long minutes of silence. "The world is one giant buffet of food for most beings."

Beathan watched as Philip shot the vampire a withering look. "That may be true, but some of us find it particularly distasteful to eat people." Azir shrugged at the response, looking undisturbed. Beathan forced down a chuckle at the irony of Philip's statement. His friend was conveniently forgetting that he'd lost his mind for about a month not too long ago and had spent the majority of that time trying to eat Beathan.

"What?" Philip asked quizzically, noting Beathan's grin.

"Nothin' mate, continue."

"Well, as Azir pointed out, many creatures eat others, but the unsavory reputation that Capcauns get is not for the fact that they eat people. But rather the fact that they almost always attempt to start eating you before you're dead."

Alayna made a slightly overly dramatic retching noise as what Philip said sunk in. Beathan was inclined to agree with her.

"So, what... that means it's fightin' tactics will likely include a few maneuvers where it'll try an' get its jaws aroun' me throat?" Beathan asked.

"At the very least," Philip answered seriously, "maybe more than a few. It's described as ravenous. Maybe you can use that against it. Anticipate its moves, or..." The former Collector trailed off as he realized he was stating the obvious. Beathan knew how to fight. In fact, the first night they'd met, years ago in a rundown neighborhood in New York, Beathan had gone toe to toe with the non-human Collector and stood his ground just fine.

"I'll be fine, I know how t' fight," Beathan said as he clasped his friend's shoulder. Philip nodded his agreement, only looking just a little bit like he was trying to convince himself with his nod.

The vampire who'd been sent out on the errand reentered the room and information was relayed to Dracula, still enshrouded in his darkness on the throne.

"It appears that all is ready. If you will follow me, please," the Shade King said with mocking formality.

As he stood up from the throne, they finally got their first real glimpse of the vampire that had ruled for centuries over the rest of his kind. Shadows still encapsulated him, but as he left the chair and stepped through the sizzling rays of light from the windows, Beathan and his companions caught a quick sight.

Midnight hues dappled the parts of his skin that were visible and not covered by the black robes he wore, but not in a way that evoked a sickly appearance. On the contrary, it was almost beautiful. Beathan was forced to admit to himself that he was almost mesmerized by the pale yet somehow night-hinted skin of the old vampire. He made himself breathe. The vampire's features were simple, and yet not. Alien in an ancient way, as if tracing back to roots long forgotten in the annals of men and other beings. Narrow features, sharp features, and those eyes, dark eyes.

When Dracula's eyes passed over him, Beathan could practically feel the weight of that gaze. Involuntarily he found himself holding his breath again until that gaze passed. However, as weighty as that gaze and as oddly attractive as the appearance—the ultimate predator—those eyes betrayed not a hint of beauty. Dark and pure black they reflected ages of immense cruelty, like all the pain and suffering in the universe soaked up into the empty space between two stars. No, nobody could look at those eyes for more than a moment and still feel any hint of attraction to the supernatural being.

Beathan and the others followed behind Dracula as he and a few of his right-hand lieutenants led the way out of the tower and down the stairs. The rest of the vampires followed behind. Beathan hated the way it felt to be followed by vampires. There was something definitively unsettling about it.

Down steps and through hallways, they followed in silence. No one in their party questioned where they were going, and none of the vampires, and especially not the king, volunteered that information. What did it matter, really? A fight was a fight, wherever it took place. They arrived deep down in what must be the bowels of the castle; torches were ensconced on walls creating a flickering orange light. Beathan tried to limber up as they walked, stretching arms, and checking the charms at his fingers, wrists, and neck. He had a few secrets that he could count on, ones that likely the vampires didn't know about. He smiled slyly.

Right as they stopped, a young-looking vampire stepped a little too close to Beathan and wasn't paying close enough attention. Quick as thought, Beathan slid a hand along her finger and pocketed the white gemstone ring on her smallest finger. He quickly deposited it in his own pocket before anyone was the wiser.

It felt good to steal something, just to put his itchy fingers to rest, if nothing else. He loved Philip and Alayna but traveling with them seriously curtailed his ability to maintain his primary craft—that of a thief. Beathan let out a calming sigh and smiled. The first genuine smile he'd let free in a while. The act of thievery had steadied his nerves. Somehow, he wasn't so nervous anymore. Oh, there was still the faint fluttering of a butterfly somewhere deep in his belly, but no more than usual in a dangerous situation. Mostly he just felt ready. Almost excited for the contest of wills that he was about to begin. He'd fought before, he could do it again. He'd survived this long, hadn't he?

A distant roar echoed through the corridors of the castle. Another, this time closer. Beathan felt his pulse quicken. His breath became shallower and faster intakes as he felt his excitement grow. Murmurs of anticipation filled the chamber as the on-looking vampires also vocalized their eagerness for the event to begin. As the roars grew closer still, Beathan casually limbered up and took in the room around him. Rough-hewn flagstones lined the floor. They did not fit together perfectly, leaving creases and gouges in the floor, dips and rises where filth and grime had collected. Uneven footing. Perhaps that could be an advantage —fairies were known for their nimbleness, and even as a half-breed, Beathan was no exception. The walls of the room were carved from the plug of rock on which the castle sat. They had descended deep under the castle, into the earth itself. The light was a flickering orange hue, as it had been during the entirety of their descent.

"Hmm?" Beathan asked.

"I said are you even paying attention to me?" Philip growled under his breath.

"What? Oh, not really mate. Just lettin' me nerves settle a wee bit by takin' it all in, ya' know?" Beathan indicated the room and the vampires in it that he had been observing.

"You don't appear very nervous," Alayna said almost suspiciously.

"Well, we all have our faults." He winked at her, while Philip rolled his eyes.

Azir interjected himself into the conversation. "You should be nervous, fairy. Capcauns are not to be taken lightly."

"I'm sure I've faced worse," Beathan said flippantly, thinking of the wendigo he and Philip had faced that night in New York.

"That as it may be, I would not like to see you fall today. Focus would be best," Azir retorted solemnly.

"Sentimental, Vamp? I'd not have expected it from ya', but I appreciate it all th' same," Beathan clapped the hybrid on the shoulder.

Azir's serious gaze locked in on his own. "Your survival is imperative to the mission—and likely our ability to leave this castle with our lives. I was most certainly not being sentimental."

Beathan snorted. "You and Philip are so solemn, so serious. Practically mimickin' each other right now." He glanced over to see Philip clamp his jaw closed. Likely the former Collector had been about to echo the vampire's words before Beathan had called them out on it.

Alayna stifled a giggle as she looked at the two resistant companions who couldn't stand each other. "That's the spirit, lass. A laugh never hurt a body's chances o' winnin' a fight." He winked again.

And then the time for talk was suddenly over as the Capcaun entered the chamber. It had to stoop to get through the doorway and it was muzzled and led by a chain looped around its neck. It fought its captors every step of the way. There was clearly no lack of rage in this creature. The vampires in charge of corralling the creature forced it over to one side of the room while all the spectating vampires gave it a wide berth. Guards stationed nearest to the creature held long spears with viciously barbed spear points. They looked ready to the state of almost being frightened. Rare for a vampire. It almost made Beathan lose his blood rush. Almost.

"Fight, fairy, and survive. Survive and we can talk more. Lose, and well... you'll be dead." The Shade King shrugged his shoulders theatrically, playing to the small crowd in the room, feeding them the entertainment for which he had clearly—or at least partially—engineered this showdown.

Beathan rolled his shoulders to loosen them, checking his jangles and charms, even as he rolled his own eyes theatrically. He could put on a show also. "Let 'im loose, kinglet. I've faced me fair share o' beasties before." Beathan shook his arms, idly loosening his shoulders, and turned from Dracula toward the Capcaun, but not before he saw Dracula's mouth tighten in annoyance. Well, if he did die today, annoying the king of the vampires was at least one good thing he had done before he returned to dust. With an ironic laugh he stepped toward the beast across the room from him, anticipation filling his body as air filled his lungs.

The vampire guards loosed the chains from the creature and the ogre roared its fury. Lightning quick, it swatted a vampire guard, sending her tumbling into the crowd with a stunning blow, but not before the other guards stabbed it a few times with their long, wicked spears. Not enough to injure it, just a course correction to shepherd it back toward the middle of the room. Toward Beathan. And to rile it up he thought wryly. Just his luck.

The Capcaun stepped toward him and Beathan took it all in. It was a large creature, with hunched shoulders just to keep it from bumping the low ceiling of this underbelly castle chamber. Dog-headed, it was about as ugly as one would expect of an ogre, even of the canine variety. Sharp teeth and pointed, wolf-like ears. The face was covered in thin, patchy hair. However, it was the body that was the most intriguing. It was like a tale of two creatures, mashed up, and forced to fit into one body. Half of the ogre was robust and full, muscled and toned. It had one powerful arm and one powerful leg, which was the arm that had swatted the vampire guard with such vicious speed a moment earlier. But the other half of the creature looked almost emaciated and shrunken, as if all the nutrients of its kills had gone to one half over the other. Fur on the thick half was matched by hairless skin on the gaunt side. Although clawed fingers adorned both hands. Claws that could do some serious damage.

It howled its cry again and charged. If it couldn't escape the circle of spears keeping it down here in the bowels of the castle, then at least it could vent its fury on something else, someone else—Beathan. The canine ogre moved with a sort of jerking lope, as if its unmatched sides of its body couldn't quite move together in any unison. Yet that didn't keep it from being fast. Oh so fast! Beathan made sure to keep the initial swipe at the vampire guard firmly in his mind as he barely ducked under the flailing, clawed fist of the beast as it completed its first pass.

Beathan danced lithely around, keeping his feet moving, ready to react, ready to run and squirrel away from the ogre at any given moment. The thing quickly lumbered forward once more and yet again Beathan dodged. He heard the catcalls and jeers from the vampires. They wanted a fight; they wanted a bloodbath. He was depriving them of it. From a distant corner of his mind he heard Philip and Alayna and even Azir shouting encouragement and hints and suggestions his way. But there was no time to pay attention to them because the beast was coming his way again, and this time with serious intent in its glossy black eyes.

This time Beathan didn't manage to completely avoid the attack. He ducked, but the creature was fast. It sliced open a gash almost a hand's length long on his shoulder. He winced in pain and looked on with revulsion as the canine maw sucked the fairy blood of its claw. Vampires cheered their excitement, and despite the pain of his wound and the threat to his life, Beathan felt his blood pump and his muscles swell in excitement of his own. Time to take the attack to the Capcaun.

Beathan slipped a couple of daggers free and danced in close to deliver a few brutal slashes of his own. He drew blood also, but the beast was quick, and it recovered fast enough to keep him from cutting too deeply. But blood was blood and the fight was even. Beathan found himself grinning from the contest, dirty blond hair bouncing loosely around his ears as he bobbed and weaved, dodging the Capcaun's attacks.

The beast closed the distance and jabbed the slender arm toward Beathan, feinting, while following up with a positively killing blow with its meaty side. Luckily Beathan saw it coming and dodged again, but not without flinging one of his own hands up as he did, lopping off one of the Capcaun's clawed fingers as it followed through. The beast shrieked in rage and pain, as the crowd murmured with more anticipation. The vampires cared not who bled, as long as they bled freely. The Capcaun stalked around Beathan in a circle. Losing a finger seemed to have added some caution to its fight. Beathan cocked his head at it and grinned.

"Well boyo, are ya' ready t' finish this?" he taunted toward the enraged, yet careful creature.

It threw back its wolfish head and howled, slamming its strong arm into the rough-hewn wall, sending bits of rock and gravel down to litter their dueling ground. Blood dripped from its hand, just as blood dripped from Beathan's shoulder, making its way down to his hand, making his grip on the dagger slick. He'd have to focus. Dropping his blade now would likely mean death.

The Capcaun put both forehands on the ground and charged forward in a strangely ape-like stance. Beathan flicked a few of his charms and accelerated his speed. In a flash he leapt above the charging creature, landing on its back, slamming one dagger home into the creature's back, and the other into the side of its neck. It screamed in what Beathan hoped were death throes. It thrashed and spun, twirling Beathan around dangerously, as he clung on for dear life to the knives implanted in the ogre. Blood gushed from the wounds and made the handles even more slippery. And with one final, massive shake it flung Beathan off of its back and into a nearby wall.

Beathan nearly plowed into a vampire as he struck the wall, the bloodsucker scampering to get out of the danger zone. Beathan shook his head groggily after striking his head on the stone. The Capcaun, unfortunately, was somehow still upright and alive. In fact, it was charging his way again, perhaps a little more slowly and more painfully itself, with Beathan's blades in its body, but with enough power and intent to likely finish off the half-fairy.

Beathan urged himself up, tried to scramble to his feet. He made it up to his hands and knees before realizing it wouldn't make a difference. He turned instead to another course of action. Desperately, and at the last minute, as the Capcaun closed the distance Beathan muttered the words and flicked the jangle to activate his defensive charm—the same one he'd used at the Alchemist's cabin not so long ago. He prayed it would hold up —or rather his will and energy would hold up long enough for him to clear his head and maintain the defensive charm.

Above him, the beast reached Beathan and with a ferocious rage it hammered downward with its strong arm, but to no avail. It hammered unyieldingly on an invisible barrier. It roared in frustration, the dagger planted in its neck still causing blood to spurt. The Capcaun's slender arm snaked out and scraped hungrily over the barrier. It bit and clawed and chewed at the charm, but it couldn't break through. Beathan slowly made his way to his feet and stared into the eyes of the ravenous creature as it scrabbled away at his magic to no avail.

It was slowing. Beathan thought of letting the charm go, of attempting to finish it off, especially as holding the defensive charm—

even with his clearing head—was growing more difficult with every drop of blood that left his shoulder, but something told him that it was just a matter of time. Blood pumped from the beast's two major wounds, especially the side of its neck. If Beathan could maintain his barrier's strength against the onslaught of the Capcaun for long enough, then he might actually be able to outlast the ogre as it simply bled out. It was certainly losing some of its pace and power as it moved. Yes, that was the best, safest, course of action.

He ignored the booing of the vampires as he decided to let the beast weaken itself unto death. Beathan fought down the desire to loose the charm and deliver a killing stroke once and for all. His Ma had always taught him not to be an idiot. Not to fight fights he couldn't run, lie, steal, or magic his way out of. And so he gritted his teeth and chose the safer and smarter route, he held onto the will necessary to keep the charm up and let the beast batter itself out. And soon enough it did. The blood pumping out of its neck didn't slow and after a few long moments the beast delivered one last slumping blow to the invisible barrier before keeling over and bled its last, its blood filling the dirty cracks and grooves between the flagstones of the floor.

When he was sure it was dead, he dropped the charm, stepped forward jauntily and plucked his knives out of the dead creature's body. "Done is done now, eh?" he asked the Shade King.

In answer, he heard a raspy chuckle from within the shadowed shroud around the king of the vampires. "A deal is indeed a deal. We shall talk further of our plans."

Beathan felt a shiver at suddenly realizing he'd played a vital role in this new alliance.

Our plans. It chilled his soul. Deals with devils rarely played out well.

CHAPTER NINE

Philip breathed a huge sigh of relief as the Capcaun finally collapsed after battering itself to death on Beathan's defensive charm. For once the fairy had made the smart maneuver and played it safe. They would need to make similar decisions as this endeavor progressed. Life couldn't become just one wild gamble after another. If a person wanted to achieve much, they needed to take risks—but calculated ones. Philip wasn't interested in a suicide mission. He planned to live to see the outcome of this joint venture with the vampires.

Alayna and Azir cheered when the Capcaun hit the ground finally, while the vampires hissed their annoyance at the fairy's survival, especially in such un-dramatic fashion, but Philip ignored them. He stepped hurriedly up to his friend's side, stabilizing the half-breed as he stumbled with fatigue. Philip knew just how wearying it was to sustain the defensive charm, especially when the user was injured. That brought Philip's attention to the cut along Beathan's shoulder.

"Just a scratch, mate," Beathan muttered with exhaustion and squatted down.

Philip inspected it all the same and while the fairy had lost some blood from the rather long cut, it was not overly deep. In this case, Beathan wasn't exaggerating too much. He would likely heal just fine, and quickly—if the wound were tended to soon. Philip looked up to ask for help, when he saw two vampires heading their way, bags in hand.

"We are sent by our lord to tend to this one's injuries," the first vampire said as if he couldn't care less whether Beathan lived or died. Philip put a hand up protectively.

"Treat him well, or you will answer to me." His hand made a fist. Alayna was crouched down beside Beathan, whispering in his ear, while Azir was engaged in cautious conversation with another vampire not far away.

The two medicinal bloodsuckers showed the first sign of care for their victim as they brushed past Philip and squatted down next to the fairy. Their eyes flashed, whether with annoyance or fear Philip wasn't sure, and the second vampire said, "We have been commanded to attend to him. If we do not treat him well, we will answer to far worse than you, Collector."

And that was enough for Philip. These vampires were arrogant and overly confident, sequestered away in their protected castle. They didn't know what he was capable of, didn't yet fear Philip. But they feared the Shade King, which was enough to ensure that Beathan would get fair and decent treatment. After all, they were allies now.

Allies.

The word echoed soundlessly in Philip's mind as the thought came. What had the world come to that he could actually say he was an ally with none other than Dracula himself?

"Well, it's not actually confirmed yet, love. He said we'd speak more."

Philip was startled out of his reverie by Alayna's hand on his shoulder and realized he'd been speaking his thoughts out loud.

"Might as well be, what reason has he still to deny us his cooperation?" Philip poised.

Alayna shrugged, her red-gold locks bouncing with the movement. "Who can read the mind of a demon?"

Despite his previous statement, Philip was forced to agree. The king of the vampires was indeed a difficult one to read, and his reputation was far from anything that could be referred to as simple. Vicious, cruel, but equally cunning, Philip would need to stay on guard to ensure the Shade King didn't back him into a corner or outwit him somehow.

He turned to gaze at the vampires offering ministrations to the fairy. They were treating the wound with some sort of balm after stitching it up. Beathan was wincing and whining and making all sorts of theatrical claims and threats as to their lack of care for his pain and what he would do to them in return. The two vampires—male and female, with the classically pale, yet dark features so common to their race—were ignoring the fairy as best they could. Their mouths formed thin lines of frustration and annoyance every time Beathan gesticulated wildly, melodramatically driving home one of his points or threats, while almost tearing a stitch free each time he did.

Philip hid a grin, despite their predicament in the midst of enemies, Beathan was doing what he did best—tweaking noses. Philip laughed and nudged Alayna to look, as well. "Look, every time he makes a threat or begs a question as to the pain they're causing, he throws an arm in the air."

"So?" Alayna asked puzzled.

"So, every time he does, he comes close to popping a stitch, and their heads nearly land on the chopping block," Philip chuckled in answer. Alayna still looked at him like she didn't understand. But before she could ask for any clarifying information another voice chimed in.

"They were commanded to tend well to Beathan's injuries. If they do not manage to do that, and to do it well, they will be punished. The One Who Rules is not a lenient king. Likely, our fairy friend has managed to figure that out and knows exactly the type of harm he puts his tenders in each time he moves so wildly." Azir had rejoined them after finishing the conversation he'd been engrossed in with one of the more friendly vampires in the room—if that description could be used at all.

Philip made to open his mouth to make a snide comment but then closed it silently, remembering the way Azir had cheered when Beathan's opponent had finally fallen. It hadn't entirely been the cheers of someone worried for his own hide, but more that of a reluctant comrade. Someone who had perhaps grown to care for the half-fairy, even if it was against his will and full of regular annoyance. Beathan had that impact on people. Perhaps it was time to give Azir a break. Philip had no illusions that they'd ever like one another, but they were working together and that was simply the way it was.

Another vampire approached them. "If you will follow me, I will take you all to the quarters of the One Who Rules. He wishes a private audience." The messenger's voice was a sibilant whisper. Her narrow features and dark eyes could have blended into a crowd of vampires with hardly any difficulty.

"All of us?" Philip asked quickly. Regardless of promises and expectations of care, he wasn't keen to leave Beathan alone in a room full of enemies.

The messenger nodded. And then turned and walked out of the room, expecting them to follow. Philip looked to Alayna and Azir and then made a jerking, beckoning nod with his head to the fairy who had noticed the interaction. Beathan quickly freed himself from the ministrations of the healers with a thump of his chest as he stated how healthy he felt—one last chance to tear his sutures, which elicited worried winces from the vampires tending him—before joining the rest of them as they walked from the room and followed the vampire messenger.

Eyes followed them as they left, but no bodies did. A group of vampires hoisting the dead beast onto a trolley cart—to be lugged off to some refuse pit no doubt—was the last thing Philip noticed before they were in the corridor and making their way back up through the keep. One step after the other, they made their way upward through the darkened interior of the fortress. When they finally reached high enough to have windows in the walls, drapes covered those windows allowing no direct sunlight into the castle. It had to be daytime still, enough hours hadn't passed since they'd arrived this morning for it to be anything less than maybe midday at the latest. Philip was anxious to get the alliance settled and then make their way out of the castle and into the forest while it was still light out. He didn't trust the Shade King, regardless of whatever test they'd passed by having Beathan fight the Capcaun.

The messenger halted in front of an old ornate door. Three knocks, more symbolic than waiting for an answer, and then they entered. It was a room full of tapestries on the walls, a desk and chair as if for study. Windows with drapes that could be easily tied back if wished. Philip wondered if the windows were for gazing at the stars, or for something else. There were strange rumors of potions from the late Alchemist given to the Shade King for temporary ability to withstand the sunlight. Rumors it had led to a desire by the king of the vampires to see the sun whenever possible. Either way, that time was at an end thanks to Azir. Yet another thing Philip was forced to admit he was grateful to the hybrid vampire for. The Alchemist had deserved to die. Philip only wished he'd been the one to kill him. Azir had risked his life to kill the wily old scientist since there was a protection placed on the human by Dracula himself. It would be best if that information didn't come to light. Philip told himself that it wasn't because he wanted to protect the vampire. No, it was simply so as not to endanger their newfound and tentative alliance.

The Shade King was draped over a chaise on one end of the room, lazily eating something that could only be described as a frozen ball of blood. Others of the same kind seemed to be clustered together in a bowl on a stand near the chaise, like a bowl of grapes—bloody red grapes. Philip looked away in disgust.

"Mmm, this one is from the south, I believe. The great continent below ours," Dracula murmured as he chewed through the frosty blood-grape. "I have an attuned and delicate tongue, you see."

Philip grimaced and the rest of them kept their silence, staring the king down. The Shade King waved nonchalantly at the messenger. At the dismissal, the vampire left the room and closed the door. They were alone with the king. Four on one. And yet the Shade King still stared at them with complete unconcern in his eyes. It was unsettling to be taken so lightly. Philip couldn't remember the last time a potential enemy had felt so utterly comfortable in his presence. It made his shoulders twitch, as if he were just waiting for an unseen dagger to plunge into his back. But no, there was no secret attack coming; they weren't left exposed in any way. It would do well to remember the Shade King was simply that confident in his own abilities.

They stared at each other for a moment longer, both waiting for the other to speak first. Philip resolved to wait him out. It was an audience the king had requested, so he could speak first. The Shade King had somehow dropped the shadows cloaking him from earlier. The midnight-mottled, yet pale skin of his hands attracted Philip's attention as those fingers drummed carelessly on the arm of his chaise.

"You are quite lovely, my dear," the vampire said suddenly, startling Philip from the near mesmerizing drumming of the king's fingers. Had it been a trick? Philip berated himself silently for losing focus so quickly with such a simple little mental trick from the king. The king glanced his way and smiled knowingly as if he knew exactly what Philip was thinking. Philip gritted his teeth.

"Thank you," Alayna replied courteously but brokering no real gratitude.

"So cautious, all of you," Dracula murmured with open hands and a grin. "We are allies now. Be at ease. Sit," he indicated a few armchairs in the room, arrayed near his own. Philip and his companions did as they were asked.

"Are we?" Philip asked.

"Hmm?" the king feigned inattention.

Philip gritted his teeth again in annoyance. It was all part of the vampire's ploy. "Are we actual allies? Was one duel enough to prove my resolve?"

"So brutish and to the point. No idle conversation? Tsk, tsk."

"We simply wish to know where we stand," Azir murmured his support for Philip, surprisingly.

The king's eyes narrowed finally as he looked at the hybrid. And not for the first time Philip wondered if he didn't already know about The Alchemist. "You know where you stand, Daywalker. You are a useful tool to me." Even a few days ago Philip would have relished the casual dismissal in the king's tone as he spoke to Azir, clearly not deeming him important enough to entertain much of his thoughts. But for some reason it bothered Philip now. He did not want any of them toyed with by the Shade King.

"Enough." Philip said simply, bluntly.

The king turned his gaze to Philip, mouth retaining its casual smile, but those eyes, they were devoid of any empathy and they bored holes into Philip's own. The king knew what Philip meant by his statement.

"So touchy, you all are. So boringly lacking in even the merest hint of tete a tete." The Shade King's mouth soured slightly in boredom.

"Sorry to disappoint. Only Beathan here is a fan of wittiness and banter, and as you can see, he's a touch indisposed at the moment. Your doing." Philip glanced at Beathan who was actually looking rather pale and exhausted from his bout with the ogre. Philip felt another pang of guilt for not having been the one to fight the Capcaun himself.

"Ah, I see," Dracula sighed. "It shall be a bitter alliance between us then?" The inflection at the end indicated the question.

"So we are allied?" Philip asked again.

A slow smile spread across the vampire king's face. "Mostly."

"What does that mean?" Alayna interjected with impatience while Azir tried his best to worriedly hush her. Azir was startlingly fearful in the presence of his master. But Alayna shrugged off his caution in annoyance, staring defiantly at Dracula.

Dracula's eyes perused her once again and he sighed with desire. His eyes possessed a strange cruel lust to them, which was more than enough to get Alayna to shrink back in discomfort, in a way that all Azir's cautioning hadn't been able to achieve. "At the risk of repeating myself, you truly are lovely, my dear." Dracula's eyes stared agates into Alayna's until she looked away.

Philip forced himself not to lose his composure as the vampire looked his love up and down. "We are waiting on a straight answer. Beathan fought your ogre. I've passed your test of commitment. Is it enough?"

"Is... it... enough?" The Shade King steepled his fingers in front of his face as he paused long and dramatically in between words. "In short, not exactly."

"Why not?" Philip burst out in anger. Had Beathan risked his life for nothing then?

"Forgive me for being careful when dealing with my recent enemies," Dracula murmured with mockingly fake concern. And then his eyes grew more serious. "In truth, I underestimated those other members of your party. The fairy dealt with the Capcaun much too easily. Alas, it was not a sufficient test of resolve." Dracula spread his hands casually as if it was out of his control, and he wasn't the exact person who, in fact, had control of this situation.

"So Beathan won his fight too easily?" Philip asked incredulously.

Dracula winced and wobbled his head back and forth as if weighing the statement and then shrugged. "Basically, yes."

"I don't believe this!" Alayna interjected, recovering enough from his unsettling gaze from a moment ago to find some of her usual fire. "He risked his life. He dueled for nothing other than your entertainment and that's not enough?"

"Ah yes, the reluctant gladiator," the Shade King stared at her inquisitively.

"What do you mean by that?" she asked defensively and Philip prayed she could keep her temper.

"Word travels fast in my domain. I've heard of your recent...bondage."

She swallowed and was about to retort, but Philip cut her off. Better to keep the focus on himself. He was uncomfortable with the king's interest in Alayna.

"What else do you need?" he asked Dracula.

The king chuckled. "Always so short and to the point."

"It's who I am." This time it was Philip's turn to spread his hands.

"Fair enough, Collector. As further proof of your commitment, there is an... errand I need you to run."

Philip clenched his fists at his sides, willing himself to stay seated and not leap to his feet in disgust. He was no errand boy. And something ominous was coming, he could feel it.

"There is a certain Guild leader—a small outpost nearby—meant to keep tabs on me and mine," the vampire said and placed a hand on his chest modestly. "I need you to capture him and bring him back to me. Alive." He said the last word darkly. "With your knowledge of the inner workings of the Guild, their ins and outs, the best way to enter one of their establishments without succumbing to their tricks, it shouldn't be all that difficult for you."

The lustful gleam in the king's eye told Philip that Dracula knew exactly what he was getting from an alliance with Philip. It chilled Philip to think of what might come after their cooperative attack on the Guild. Philip wanted to surgically execute the leadership, not decimate the entire organization. But was that what the king wanted? Likely not. Philip shuddered to think of the sway the vampires—so organized and plentiful—would have over the continent without the Guild to keep them in check. He'd have to figure out a way to check them too. Otherwise this was all for naught. This was all about making the continent better, safer, not less so. At the end of it all, the Shade King might need to be dealt with.

"Why?" Philip asked suspiciously, as he pulled himself back out of his thoughts.

"I do not need to explain myself," the Shade King said tightly, not used to being questioned.

"Well, I don't do anything without understanding it," Philip said stoutly.

Dracula pursed his lips. "Very well, this particular Guild leader and I had an agreement of sorts. He would procure for me various creatures to do with as I saw fit, and in return I granted him safety, security in my domain, and no small amount of wealth. However, recently it appears he has grown a conscience and no longer wants to participate. I don't take kindly to people reneging on pacts with me," the Shade King finished ominously.

"A Collector? A Guild leader was in league with you?" Philip asked in disbelief. Although why he was so disbelieving after everything he'd seen of the Guild lately was beyond him.

"Come now, you didn't really think that you were the first Collector to come tap, tap, tapping at my door, did you?" Dracula grinned widely, whitely, and for the first time Philip got a good look at his fangs. They weren't straight points like most vampires, but had a slight inward curve to them, like an ancient fang-tooth tiger he'd seen once at a museum in London. Oh, the vampire's fangs were smaller of course, but they retained the quality—something primal—that elicited thoughts of a time long past. It made Philip shiver, and he hated himself for feeling fear.

"Creatures as currency?" Alayna muttered angrily. "The Guild is disgusting." Her comment brought Philip crashing back to reality. She reminded him of everything she'd been through, and exactly why he was so set to eviscerate the Guild leadership. What she had endured in the menagerie had been unspeakable. It had to end.

"Fine. We'll do it," he said, forcing his voice not to waver as he thought of doing the Shade King's personal bidding.

The vampire's mouth hooked into another mocking smile as if he could again see right into Philip's heart. "Good," he purred. "Does tonight work for you?"

"Tomorrow," Philip countered. "Beathan needs at least a day to recover." He stifled the fairy's weak protests with a raise of his hand. It was as much about establishing some sort of victory in this negotiation as it was to protect his friend's health, but he couldn't explain that to the fairy now. Philip just needed a win, even a tiny one right now.

Dracula nodded. "Done. Tomorrow night it is. I want him alive." His voice was iron. The dismissal in his tone was also clear.

Philip and his companions rose to leave, making their way to the door. It would be good to leave this infernal castle and see the sunlight again, to make camp under the open stars tonight. Anything to get rid of this dirty feeling he felt when dealing with the devil in front of him.

They were almost to the door when Dracula spoke again. "Do not go far to make your camp. I'll send Salynksa along tonight with the details of the assignment."

Philip exited the room, wondering how he'd managed to make himself a thrall to the Shade King. The pit of his stomach churned. This alliance had better be worth it. They had to make the Guild leaders pay.

CHAPTER TEN

The four of them sat around a small campfire staring glumly into the flames. Well, Philip certainly looked glum, as did Azir for some odd reason. Beathan might have just been feeling tired still from his exertions the day before. Alayna, however, would better describe her emotion as frustrated. An alliance with the Dracula might be necessary but running around doing his bidding didn't have to be. Or did it? She couldn't figure out if she was annoyed with their situation or bothered that Philip hadn't managed to find a way to get them out of it.

Oh, she wasn't frightened of fighting a few Collectors; they'd been doing that for what felt like ages now. Had she ever been that sweet country girl from America? That person felt like more than a lifetime ago, like a dream of a dream. No, it was the fact that she hated the idea of somehow being subservient to a bastard like the Shade King. Her time in the menagerie had taught her how to recognize a self-serving egomaniac. Helmsted had been one, and the Shade King was one also. And there was no mistaking how he viewed their relationship.

Salynksa had found them the night before, just as promised. Her haughty tone of superiority and the language she used—no doubt carefully coached by her master—left little room to doubt that the Shade King saw them as tools, as less than. As serving him. It was not an alliance in his mind. He had the upper hand in resources, and most importantly they'd come to him, petitioning for this alliance. In the vampire's mind, that left him firmly in control. Alayna detested it. But most of all she hated that it might be a fair assessment of their situation. Philip had the know-how and inside information that the Shade King wanted. But they needed the manpower to have any hope of accomplishing their ends. And that meant this alliance, or subservience, or whatever it could be called, was necessary.

And so she stared broodingly into the flames with the rest of them. She decided that most of all, she was disappointed. Philip usually thought or fought their way clear of circumstances like this. It felt like Dracula had gained the upper hand awfully quickly. Worst of all, Alayna had a feeling Philip knew. With shame in his eyes he'd look at her, and her inability to hide her emotions—she'd always worn emotions on her sleeve, but even more so since her ordeal in the menagerie. She was more volatile now, mercurial at times, and didn't seem to have any hope of hiding emotions these days. She could admit her lack of control. It was a work in progress. But she felt badly Philip had to see her disappointment, especially because she wasn't even sure it was entirely fair. She didn't know how she'd have done things differently.

"So this Guild leader we're to capture, what do you know of him?" Alayna asked simply to break the silence, even though they'd discussed over and over again everything Philip knew already. It seemed to have the desired effect as eyes and heads brightened and perked respectively.

"Sampstone," Philip breathed like a curse.

"Bad one, eh?" Beathan murmured, still sounding mildly exhausted.

"Bad in some ways, yes. Simply a disgusting human being in others. He was always a sniveling little rat, tattling on anything and everyone when we were younger and in training, hardly more than boys. But he was a climber also. Knew how to grease the right boots and shake the right hands to advance. One of the few Guild members to rise relatively high— to a command of his own post, however small—without having significant field experience."

"A Guild bureaucrat, I never thought I'd see one of those," Azir snorted in disgust. Philip inclined his head in agreement, hardly pausing like he'd used to do when agreeing with the hybrid vampire. Alayna noticed that he'd been settling down a bit in regards to their fourth companion, and she had to admit she was glad of it.

"So a brat as a child, an' a less than admirable man, but I fail t' see what makes him horrible?"

Alayna had to agree with the fairy. She couldn't help but wonder if Philip's personal dislike of the boy was clouding his judgment of the man.

"It wasn't only that," Philip continued. "It was just a... sense. You know when you meet someone who you can just tell would sell your soul for a single coin and not think twice about it. Well, that was how he was. He's always had an angle to play, some leverage or blackmail on someone to aid in his ascent."

"Well, why worry about someone selling your soul when you are planning to go ahead and do it yourself?" The words popped out of Alayna's mouth before she could take them back. The campfire crackled in the silence that followed her statement. An owl cried in the distant night, and a chill breeze rustled the leaves and needles of the trees around their camp.

"This was your idea, remember?" The hurt on Philip's face was palpable.

"I know it was, but I just..." She trailed off.

"You just what?" Philip asked.

"I thought you'd find some way to make this feel more like a partnership and less like a feudal lord ordering his vassals around!" she burst out, finally saying what he'd been reading in her eyes for the past hours.

"That is a bit harsh, Alayna." Surprisingly, it was Azir sticking up for Philip. When had that alliance happened? The world must be coming to an end. Azir continued, "I warned you all, that this would be a bad idea. I argued against it. But you have hitched your wagon to his now, and he will not take kindly to you reneging on anything he perceives as a deal struck. The only choice now is to see this through."

"But this feels different, worse somehow," Beathan muttered. "Are we sure we want t' do this? Killin' an evil Collector is one thing—I've no love for them, ya' know that. But capturin' an' turnin' them over to be the plaything of a sadistic bastard like th' Shade King is a whole other level o' twisted."

Alayna swallowed as the fairy put words to what she'd been feeling— that buried emotion she'd been trying to put more concrete words to other than that vague feeling of disappointment in Philip. "Agreed," she seconded the fairy with a nod, while Philip just sat there miserably quiet and Azir rolled his eyes.

"Do we really want t' do somethin' we can't come back from?" Beathan asked.

"We'll have the manpower, with the vampires assisting. We'll be fine," Philip answered.

"I didn't mean literally, mate." Beathan shot Philip a cautionary look before speaking further. "It's like me ma always said: 'Don't sell your soul unless ya' get enough out o' the bargain t' buy it back again an' then some'."

"You don't think this is worth it? That the Guild doesn't need to be brought down?" Philip challenged.

"I think he's just saying that we have to make absolutely sure of our course of action. We don't want regrets plaguing us for the rest of our lives," Alayna said.

"Did you all ignore what I said earlier? There is no backing out now. In the One Who Rules' mind we have as good as committed ourselves already. There is no turning back," Azir huffed in frustration. And Alayna did have to admit that the vampire knew the king best.

"There you have it." An icy determination settling onto Philip's face, replacing the glumness, as he once again wound up agreeing with the vampire. He didn't exactly look toward Azir in any kind of support, but neither did he grimace at their agreement, as he'd been wont to do in the early days of traveling together.

Alayna was shaken from her thoughts by the arrival of their enemies —or rather allies now, she was forced to admit. Salynksa and a contingent of vampires slunk into the flickering light of the camp with sinister smirks on their faces.

"Dangerous to light such a bright fire in these woods," Salynksa said wickedly, a challenge glittering in her black eyes.

Philip, however, didn't rise to the bait. With a sigh he just responded, "Should we be frightened of a few meager bloodsuckers come to keep us company? Besides, our alliance should keep us safeguarded against attack. Or am I mistaken?"

A long look passed between them, before the vampire acquiesced. "You are not mistaken."

Again, Philip took no joy from the small victory. Instead he just looked tired. Exhausted really. Alayna was worried for him. However, Salynksa wasn't finished yet. "You are protected—for now. But others before you have been protected and gone on to fall to the fierce fangs of our kind, regardless of limits imposed from above."

"Is that a threat?" Alayna asked, blood rushing to her face. She had unfinished business with Salynksa.

"Just a warning, Elfas. The Alchemist was found not long ago. His throat ripped out. He too had the protection of the One Who Rules. Look what it got him." A simple statement. Matter-of-fact. Did she know Azir had killed the scientist? Did Dracula know? Not likely, otherwise Azir would probably be dead by now. Unless, he was waiting to pay the favor back in kind, once this alliance had run its course.

Alayna chanced a glance at her vampire friend, but Azir held his cool through the reference to his vengeful kill of The Alchemist. Azir had been off-kilter ever since they'd set their course toward Dracula and this alliance, but today he seemed his normal acerbic self. It was good to see him back to his usual ways.

"Gods, you really are boring, Salynksa," Azir said, as if to punctuate Alayna's thoughts. Azir cleaned one fingernail with a fang, nonchalantly as if he had not a care in the world.

Salynksa hissed in response and was about to lash out before Philip put an outraised arm in between them. "Enough." Again that exhaustion. Alayna would have to keep an eye on him.

"You do not command me, human." Salynksa's eyes flashed dangerously and her coterie readied themselves to attack.

"I know I don't, Salynksa," Philip responded calmly, using the vampire's name for the first time, "but we are working together tonight. Or had you forgotten?" A flash went through her eyes again. This time it was not anger, but fear. Fear at failing a harsh master.

"I have not forgotten," she said quietly into the darkness.

"Good. And don't forget, I'm hardly more human than you are, however I might appear." Philip bared his teeth in a feral manner and Alayna saw the vampire look at him, really look at Philip for the first time—all their past interactions had been verging on violence, in contrast with now. Alayna saw Salynksa take in Philip's visage: his plain face and shoulder length brown hair. His sleeveless tunic despite the cold. His average frame, not a large man, but never to be called small. And Alayna saw the caution bloom in Salynksa's eyes. Not at his physical attributes, but rather at what all of his plain appearance could never hope to hide. The determined set of the jaw, the way his body didn't react to the cold, and most importantly the wild, raging north contained within his feral eyes. The completely inhuman nature of those eyes gazing back, uncompromising into the vampire's own eyes.

Alayna watched with satisfaction as Salynksa swallowed, watched as understanding dawned on the vampire that should she cross Philip he would unleash all the unyielding power of a hybrid part-human, part-troll upon her.

"We are allies. Tonight," Salynksa reiterated, this time her quiet tone was more conciliatory than Alayna had ever heard from her.

"Good, then let us be on with it. Lead the way." Philip motioned for her and her vampire followers to set their course into the dark cold night.

———

THEY JOGGED SILENTLY, deadly, through the night, hell-bent on their mission ahead, on those poor Guild souls who likely had no clue what sort of a viciousness was about to rain down on them. And Alayna couldn't help but wonder—allied as they now were with the king of the vampires himself—whether they really were representing a hellish new coalition for the world. No, this wouldn't last forever. They'd clip the Guild's wings and then deal with the Shade King later. She made a promise to herself. If she didn't, she'd likely vomit from how sick the thought of this partnership made her. And she'd been the one to submit the idea.

The raiding party reached the outskirts of the small city—hardly more than a large village really—with barely any of them winded or needing a break. Alayna, in particular, had lungs that could run for days on end. Vampires, fairies, and assorted hybrids and half-breeds could almost keep up with her, as well—courtesy of not having human frailties.

Philip held up a hand for them to stop, within earshot of the village, but still beyond the circles of light, pooling from windows—lamps and candles for the few late night townsfolk awake at this hour.

"In and out. No fuss about it. Minimal casualties if possible," Philip ordered.

Salynksa shook her head wickedly. "Our kind said nothing of such rules. We give no quarter to our enemies. And make no mistake, the Guild is exactly that. I'll disembowel any who get in my way and will expect nothing less from my people." A few of the vampires chuckled sinisterly around her.

Philip swallowed, a bit of a sickly cast to his face, but he had no rebuttal. They were well and truly in this now, about to carry out a joint attack on a Guild outpost with vampires sent by Dracula himself. Expecting a lack of casualties would be naïve at best, dangerous at worse. He nodded tersely, agreeing, and Alayna felt a twinge of pain at his pain, and guilt at being the one to set them down this course. But there wasn't long to delve into that emotion because Salynksa was issuing orders—having been the one to scout the outpost and having dealt with Sampstone in the past on behalf of the Shade King. The vampire quickly arrayed her people and their companions.

There wasn't much to the plan. It was a small outpost, with hardly more than a few Collectors guarding it. An all out assault was all that was needed to set the first Guild domino toppling. Philip and the rest of them nodded their agreement as Salynksa outlined the plan. "Rush the door—you can smash it down?" She inquired of Philip. He nodded brusquely. "Smash and grab. Kill whomever you like and eat who you want. But most of all, we get out with Sampstone alive. Master wills it," she finished, malice and delight mixing on her lean face.

Nods all around and then they were swiftly rushing into the muddy streets, violence waiting at their fingertips. Alayna ran, the cold air rushing against her, pushing her strawberry-blonde locks against the sides of her head as the hood fell back. She ran so fast she outpaced most of the others—such was her body's capability. But Philip must have pushed himself to run his absolute fastest and keep up with her, because as they reached the large building, he was right by her side.

Without slowing, Philip bulled into the great oak door with his shoulder. It shuddered and cracked at the edges but held. Just barely. The others were upon them in seconds and as Philip thrashed his body into the door once more, it burst inward with barely any resistance. Shouts of dismay, alarm, and confusion met them as the Guild members on watch had unwisely fallen asleep.

It was a small outpost, especially for a dangerous area of the world such as this, so close to Dracula and one of his primary haunts. It was no surprise that the compound was swarmed over in minutes. Vampires bled Collectors who scrambled to find stakes. Philip engaged with a man who was armed and ready but stood no chance against a half-breed with the power of the north coursing through him.

Philip slammed one fist into the Collector's upraised arm and all protection the man hoped for evaporated. He fell in a twitching heap as Philip's fist continued its course and collided with his face. Salynksa and Azir cornered a man who wet himself for fear of facing two vengeful vampires with nothing but a single stake. Alayna would have felt sick if she hadn't been confronted by her own Collector. He snarled something mostly unintelligible except for the final word, his sentence ending in 'bitch', and threw himself at her. Enough time spent fighting alongside Philip and Beathan, and then skills honed in the menagerie alongside Azir, left her more than his match. Alayna sidestepped a swipe and brought her knife up inside his guard, finding his heart very quickly. He died with a shuddering sigh. She told herself it was a mercy. Better a quick death than the wailing, painful deaths of the remaining Collectors at the hands of their feeding allies, the vampires. Alayna forced back the urge to vomit. It was all worth it. It had to be. These men were part of a corrupt organization, one that had used and abused as many beings as it claimed to protect.

She saw Philip slip further into the small building, down a darkened corridor. No doubt searching for the true target of the mission, Sampstone, while the vampires feasted behind him. Alayna followed.

She caught up to him and whispered, "Not much resistance."

He grunted a half laugh, half sigh. "Insane really, considering how close they are to Bran Castle—regardless of whatever protection they might have thought they had. It's enough to make you wonder if someone in the Guild actually wanted to eliminate Sampstone. As if they gave him worthless recruits to lead."

"Well, their wish is our gain," she murmured as they stepped further into the darkness on silent feet. Only the sound of screaming could be heard from behind them and the faint squeak of floorboards beneath their feet.

"If I remember him, Sampstone will be hiding. He was never a fighter."

Alayna sniffed the air, trying to catch a whiff of something, anything that might lead them to their prey. But all she smelled was stale, spilled ale, and dusty unswept corners. This place smelled like an old inn more than anything else. She let Philip take the lead. It was his old Guild, his former acquaintance they were hunting.

Then she heard it, the muffled sobbing prayers of a man who knew the end was near. They stopped in front of the door at the end of the corridor where they had been searching. Bedroom by the looks of it, as they swung the door inward, its hinges creaking as they did.

Nothing. A bed with more finery than she would have expected a room in this place to possess. A stand with a mirror, washbowl, and all sorts of scented oils and herbs. Someone really liked the finer things in life.

There, a closet at the back. The whimpering continued. They stopped in front of the door, Philip and Alayna making no more efforts to conceal their approach. A puddle of liquid seeped under the door. Whoever was in there had soiled himself already. If it was indeed Sampstone, then Alayna couldn't help but feel disgusted. Cowardice wasn't necessarily grounds for being handed over to a bastard like the Shade King, but it didn't inspire any confidence to the opposite.

Philip casually swung the door open and Alayna peered at the man inside. Moonlight shone through the window of the room, lightly casting its illumination across the man crouching in the closet.

"Sampstone," Philip said by way of greeting. The Guild member was unlike almost any other Alayna had seen. By and large, most Collectors appeared to be cut from the same cloth; strong, physically fit, soldiers, warriors trained to fight and die for a cause they believed in. This man was soft. He wasn't obese exactly, maybe not even fat, but there was a doughiness to his frame around the middle and chest, and in his arms and face that belonged not on a soldier of the Guild, but rather on a pampered noble man from the generation prior. His hair was slicked back with some kind of oil as if even at night he took pains to look his best. The rank scent of more than one of those oils upon his body mixed with the piss at their feet causing an unpleasant smell to offend Alayna's nostrils.

"Philip!" Sampstone exclaimed, hope initially blossoming on his face then fear again as he realized just who and what stood before him. A rebel. The Renegade, as people had taken to calling Philip. "What are you doing here?" Samptone quavered.

"We're looking for you," Philip said a little too quietly. Alayna wasn't sure if his tone was masking anger or guilt.

"Don't kill me, please." Sampstone held his hands up in a beggar's pose.

Alayna sniffed in disdain. Even in the menagerie, in the fighting pits, and under torture she'd never abandoned courage so easily as this.

Philip stared at the man impassively for a moment. "Even knowing who you are, what you were like as a youth, I still can't believe you were dealing with Dracula." He shook his head.

Sampstone blanched, whether at the name, the accusation, or both, Alayna wasn't sure. But then out of nowhere the Guild man summoned an ounce of courage and spat back, "Looks like I'm not the only one!"

Philip's impassivity only deepened to something that Alayna could only describe as iron disregard. Sampstone saw the same thing in Philip's eyes as Alayna, causing him to cower in fear. He seemed to regret his words. "Please, I have money. My... dealings as you called them. They brought me wealth. I can pay you. Just get me out of here."

"What did you do for him?" Alayna inquired.

"For whom?" Sampstone hedged cautiously as if trying to figure out how much depth there was to their accusations. Continued wails from the other room punctuated the night and the Guild member cringed at the sound.

Alayna laughed harshly. "The Shade King, that's who."

"Oh, him. Right. Well I gave him things—people, creatures. I guess you could say I was a procurer of sorts. Things to play with, exotic creatures to drink. People to try and convert if he pleased." A vampire's bite couldn't transform a person against their will. They had to accept the bite, choose to become a vampire. Alayna pitied the playthings Dracula must have bullied into considering the conversion.

Alayna hadn't thought Philip's face could grow any harder. "But then you stopped?" Her mate filled in the gap.

"Y-yes, the Guild caught wind—some rat likely squealed to them," the cowering man suddenly looked vengeful despite his cowardice and Alayna could imagine him doing the terrible things to which he was confessing. "They began paying notice, watching more closely until I had to stop. I told him—t-the One Who Rules—that it was just for a bit, just a little while. Until things calmed down. You work for him now, don't you? You must if you're here on his behalf. You could put in a word for me, Philip. For old times' sake." The hope that had flashed in his eyes upon initially recognizing Philip was back. Flickering, and fearful, but there.

Philip just shook his head. "Flesh-peddling. I never thought that even you would stoop so low. The Guild is a ruin now. Even those who were monitoring you more closely have missed too much for it to count."

"Flesh-dealer," Alayna muttered quietly, repeating Philip's words. She fingered a knife. She'd been peddled previously—sold to the menagerie. The man deserved everything that was coming to him.

Sampstone seemed to feel the conversation slipping away from him, saw the anger in their eyes. "Please," he begged one more time.

"I don't work for Dracula, Sampstone—not exactly, that is. But I'm taking you to him all the same. Alive."

Philip hauled the whimpering man to his feet with Alayna's help. The Guild member soiled himself again as they did.

CHAPTER ELEVEN

Beathan surveyed the mass of seething, feeding bodies around him. It took all of his will power not to scamper from the room. Watching a pack of vampires drain the life from an entire room full of people was enough to chill even his Collector-hating blood. He swallowed.

Azir looked up from the throat of a man he was sharing with Salynksa. Bits of blood and gore dripped from his teeth. The vampire smiled and for a moment Beathan couldn't be blamed for nearly forgetting that Azir had been his traveling companion for quite some time now. Beathan returned the gaze. No fear. Vampires were predatory and they didn't react well to people acting like prey. Salynksa lifted her maw from the dying man's throat, as well, and stared at Beathan. Beathan could swear she was gazing at his throat, not his face. He forced himself to put on his jauntiest grin and a throw a wink their way before he turned and walked outside, back into the night.

The cold air hit him bracingly and he ran his hands through his dirty blond hair before realizing he still had the blood of one of his own kills on them. He was making a mess of himself. The few remaining strangled moans from inside barely penetrated the air around him. The night was silent otherwise, silent in the way a whispered prayer hopefully fended off a violent onslaught. It was like the rest of the collective village was holding its breath, hoping against hope that the violence meted out to the Guild outpost wouldn't reach their doors. The silence reached, stretched and was so quiet as to almost appear overbearing. Beathan found it oppressive and was even about to reenter the outpost despite the way the feeding vampires made him want to retch. Fairies were notoriously mischievous and definitely not above a good bout or two of general wickedness and debauchery from time to time, but no part of him was downright evil. It was hard to make the same case for those bloodsuckers inside. Beathan felt a stab of guilt realizing his companion —his friend?—Azir was one of them, but was rescued from exploring that thought to its depths by the arrival of his other two companions beside him.

Philip and Alayna dragged the man who could only be Sampstone between them. He was apparently dead weight, his heels clipping the cobblestones as they looped their arms through his. He was blubbering quietly, a sort of muted, weasely terror before Philip muttered a curse and a threat under his breath and the man fainted completely.

"Mission accomplished then, eh?" Beathan said quietly.

Philip nodded solemnly. Alayna didn't respond at first. "Inside, such... frenzy. Is it always like that?" The disgust on her face was plain.

"Usually, although I can't claim to have witnessed a feeding like that many times in my career as a Collector."

"Not a pretty sight, lass. But it's who they are, in their natures." Beathan wasn't sure if he was trying to convince himself or her so he fell silent, matching the night. There was still a bone-deep exhaustion in his body from the duel only a short day ago now. He needed sleep, not a run back to Bran Castle lugging their human cargo between them.

"We'd better get a move on," Philip murmured, thrusting his chin back the way they'd come. Beathan went to grab the Guild member's feet. He was heavy as a dwarf who'd glutted himself on stone-pies and goldmead for a week straight. Heavier than he looked, to be sure. There was fat on this one, alright.

"Shouldn't we wait for—for them?" Alayna asked and Beathan was nearly certain she'd been about to ask about Azir, not the whole pack still inside.

"He'll be busy as the rest," Philip answered, his mouth twisting in distaste.

And so they started the trek back to the Dracula's fortress, lugging Sampstone between them. The terrain was rough and apparently Beathan wasn't the only one who was tired. They stopped frequently, each of them cursing the Guild man's heavy body at different times. Sometimes Sampstone woke, and other times he lapsed back into a terrified stupor or unconsciousness. It was a wonder he'd ever managed to become a Collector, let alone a low-ranking bureaucratic leader within the Guild.

They reached a small set of boulders within the woods and collapsed in a heap atop them, letting the Guild member's limp body crash to the floor. They were all tired, not just from fighting tonight, or duels in Dracula's castle or the menagerie's pits, but from months—in Beathan's case years—of trying to scrape and claw their way clear of Collectors Guild control. Philip put his hands on his head, the weariness showing on his face as Alayna slid off her rock and sat on the cold ground, leaning back against the boulder.

"Does it ever end?" she asked.

"What's that?" Beathan turned his face toward her.

"This—the fighting, the struggle."

"It's what we're fighting for, isn't it? The whole point of this dangerous alliance?" Philip answered. "The hope that we chop off the Guild's head and find a way to exist without having to look over our shoulder the rest of our lives."

"So it's not about vengeance, then?" Alayna directed a hard look at her lover, and Beathan couldn't quite tell which response she wanted—to hear Philip say it was, or that it wasn't."

"It can be more than one thing at once, can't it, love?" Philip replied obliquely.

"Freedom. This is about freedom—of all types," Beathan added.

They sat in quiet for a while, resting and letting the night shroud them. "We should get going again," Philip finally said.

And just like that, quicker than Beathan would have imagined possible for a fatter-than-average Collector, Sampstone was up and sprinting into the trees, running as fast as his fleshy legs could carry him. He must have regained wakefulness and waited for a moment that he thought was opportune to make his dash. Or perhaps he'd simply been guided by desperation.

Philip groaned but lunged to his feet and Alayna and Beathan followed him, gaining ground on the Collector without any difficulty. Fear might have given him legs to run, but he was no match for their supernaturally powered bodies. They caught up to him in no time and encircled him until he stopped.

Sampstone raised his hands in the air, tears leaking from his eyes, the terror-filled eyes of a cornered animal. "You don't have to do this. Please. You're not—none of you are vampires." His tone verged into desperate pleading.

"You're coming with us. Like it or not, it's happening," Philip said with grim determination. "We all know you're not innocent here so don't play like you are."

Again Sampstone surprised Beathan, like his mad dash to escape, his blubbering mess of a face changed from terrified to vitriolic in a heartbeat.

"You're no better, Philip. You're just a rebel bastard who's allied himself with a demon king that feeds on the flesh of our kind!"

The words hit home, Beathan could see they had as he looked at Philip's face, but still the former Collector stepped forward with an implacable resolve. "Be that as it may, this is still happening."

Skittering his feet this way and that, Sampstone finally made a dash again, sprinting straight for Beathan as if he marked him as the weakest link of the three. Perhaps he was right, because in his exhausted state Beathan didn't feel up to matching blades with anyone. Luckily, the Collector had no blades, they'd checked him for them before transport. He lumbered toward Beathan with an animal fury contorting his face, the last chance, the last hope for a man who knew death hovered just around the corner for him.

Beathan set himself and braced for contact, but the rushing body of the Collector was not all that hit him. As Beathan wrapped his arms around him to bring Sampstone to the ground, he felt the smashing impact of something hard and rough and jagged bash into the side of his head, even as he managed to pull the Guild man down. Sampstone must've scooped up a rock as he ran and held it in reserve as a last wild attempt to fight his way to freedom. The whimpering man was surely full of contradictions. One moment crying, the next fleeing, then fighting with a craftiness nobody expected.

Beathan rolled out from under the weight of the Collector, shaking his head woozily. Sampstone fought to regain his feet but was quickly smothered back to the turf by Philip and Alayna. Alayna struck him viciously in the face and Beathan heard the crunch of breaking bone. Likely Sampstone's nose.

"You bitch! You Elfas whore!" Sampstone spat out through the blood pouring from his face. "I wish I'd sold you to the Shade King!"

Philip leaned in close and grabbed the sides of Sampstone's head. "Watch what you say, Sampstone."

But the man was caught in a frenzy of pain and fear and anger. He rattled off a list of all the things he wished he'd done to Alayna both himself and the people he'd have sold her to. Some of it was sickening, some downright evil, and all the while Philip's warnings for Sampstone to silence himself fell on deaf ears.

"I'd have tied you up for my men's use. I'd have given you to a hundred Draculas if I could, just to see you wail!" Sampstone was still screaming viciously.

Beathan only had a moment of warning, saw the knuckles on Philips hand whiten slightly as they grasped the Collector's head, before his friend lost composure and quite literally crushed the man's head in his hands like an egg. The pop of cracking skull, like a bursting, bloody bubble filled the night air and then Philip let the dead man's head drop back to the earth, staring in disgust at his own hands.

"Why did I do that?" Philip mumbled to himself. But there was a strange light in his eyes that made it hard for Beathan to tell if his remorse was genuine or feigned.

"What have you done?" Salynksa's hard voice sounded into the night from behind them. She, Azir, and the rest of the vampires had finally caught up to them.

"What he should have done," Azir answered the vampires' leader harshly. Philip's eyes gleamed in momentary agreement with the vampire before he addressed Salynksa with mock regret.

"He tried to escape. He attacked Beathan and nearly killed him."

A slight exaggeration, although Beathan's head was still decidedly woozy and trickling blood. A rough few days for him it had been.

"That is no excuse," Salynksa barked angrily, fearfully. "The One Who Rules does not tolerate failure."

Beathan saw Philip swallow. "It just happened, it was an accident."

"It was no accident, Collector, and you know it." Salynksa turned and stalked back into the night, disappearing with her vampires in tow.

Beathan sidled up to Philip, as his friend gazed after the disappearing allies. "Well, was it?"

"Was it what?"

"An accident."

Philip glanced guiltily at Alayna who had slumped down in exhaustion again, sitting next to Azir who still had blood around the edges of his mouth. "I don't know." Beathan raised an eyebrow in question. "Truly I don't. I was angry, yes, at what he was saying, and then he hit you. But..."

"But?" Beathan prodded.

"But for all that it still felt like it was too much. I didn't want to hand him over to the Shade King. This felt like an excuse to act and maybe get away with it."

"Ya' call crushin' a man's skull a mercy killin'?" Beathan asked incredulously.

Philip just stared at him relentlessly until he was forced to agree. If even half the stories he'd heard of Dracula were true then Philip had just saved an evil man from an even worse fate, regardless of whether he deserved it or not.

THE SHADE KING WAS LIVID. All sense of calm and composure, the smirking menace he exuded during their first meeting was gone. In its place was a volatile and incredibly dangerous vampire. No wonder Salynksa had yelled at Philip in fear upon discovering Sampstone was dead. Although the man hadn't been under Salynksa's charge, the mission still had technically been under her command, therefore the failure was hers.

"Why have you brought me this corpse? I don't drink carrion." Dracula gestured with one hand in disgust at the body of Sampstone laid out in front of his throne, crushed skull and all. Philip really was a force of nature sometimes. Beathan had even seen some of the lesser vampires eyeing the dead man and then eyeing Philip nervously. They knew he was likely the only one capable of such extreme power and ferocity. There was a grudging respect in their gazes.

"Delivery as requested," Beathan spoke up and waved a hand with a flourish.

Dracula snorted in disdain and ignored him, focusing instead on Philip. There was no questioning that the former Collector was the unofficial leader of their little company, but still, it dug at Beathan to be dismissed like that. He was a thief, a rascal, but also a showman, and any showman worth his stones hated irrelevance as much as anything else. Beathan stifled his twitching fingers. He'd show the Shade King, he'd steal something from the all-powerful vampire himself. The sheer pettiness of it would satisfy the fairy as much as anything else. Then the king would see who was trivial and who wasn't!

Philip addressed the vampire king. "We brought him because you asked for him." Calm and composed the way Dracula was not.

"I asked for a living Collector. I wanted Sampstone alive." Menace filled his words, and implied threat. The room fell silent as the surrounding vampires watched to see how their leader would deal with his allies' failure to comply with his demands.

"We don't always get what we want," Philip responded, bluntness and simplicity infusing his statement. He continued to stare the king down placidly. Beathan wondered how many people other than Philip could manage to stare at Dracula so calmly. Beathan wasn't even sure he could hold his nerve if the Shade King looked at him the way he was now looking at Philip. The darkness around the king billowed and moved, like a storm building up a front.

"Salynksa says there was no need for you to kill him. She said it was an unnecessary and direct disobedience of my command."

It was Philip's turn to look like he was chewing rocks. But surprisingly it was Azir who spoke, Azir who was so unusually timid around Dracula compared to when they were traveling with just the four of them. "He was well within his rights to do what he did, Master. It was the right thing to do." Azir almost managed to finish saying what he was saying without flicking a glance toward Alayna. Almost.

"Ah yes, silly insults, and impotent threats," Dracula sneered. I've heard all about it from Salynksa. Unrequited infatuation doesn't merit disobedience, Azir. You would do well to remember that." Dracula looked between Azir and Alayna who were both beet red for different reasons, and chuckled. "And Azir," now the Shade King's voice dropped low and dangerous, "it doesn't do to lie to me. It wouldn't be the first time a human has turned up dead against my orders."

He couldn't know, could he? Beathan's heart thrummed. If Dracula had figured out Azir killed The Alchemist against his explicit wishes it would likely be the end for the hybrid vampire. Azir blanched as if the same thoughts that were rushing through Beathan's head were coursing through his own.

Luckily Philip was thinking fast and interjected. "Whatever anger you might be feeling, we are not under your orders. You seem to need a reminder that we are in an alliance." There was a threat in Philip's words, a quiet dignity and pride in his stance that snapped Dracula's full attention back to him. The air was sucked out of the room as a few audible gasps echoed quietly. Nobody spoke to the king in such a manner. Beathan would wager if a vampire did, they quickly lost whatever it was that made them a vampire. Alayna smiled as she looked at her mate.

Leaning forward, head tilted like a snake, the Shade King perused the four of them, Philip most of all. "Too true," he conceded finally, and then his mask of calm was back again, his face almost portraying a false joviality that made Beathan more uncomfortable than the rage.

"This wasn't what you wished, but he's dead all the same, the outpost wiped out, and we," Philip indicated the four of them, "have hopefully proven our commitment. Call it incompetence if you like, but not a lack of resolve." His face soured at the words.

"No, never a lack of commitment on your part, I can see that now," Dracula mused. "But oft times incompetence kills more quickly than stupidity. I do not suffer fools in my company."

They stared at each other for what seemed like forever, neither blinking, neither breaking the gaze.

"Does the alliance hold?" Alayna voiced, seemingly out of boredom. Although the tenseness in her body, coiled and ready, proved that the tone was feigned.

"But of course it does, my dear, I will lend my mighty hand to your cause," Dracula turned away from looking at Alayna to fixate back on Philip again. "And so, tomorrow our planning begins."

CHAPTER TWELVE

Philip tossed and turned all night. It didn't help that they had accepted rooms in Bran Castle until the planning phase was complete. Being in the heart of vampire territory, within the very walls of their fortress, set Philip's spine tingling. But the alliance was real now, official and firm in all parties' eyes. If ever they needn't worry about attack from the bloodsuckers, it was now. Rather, Philip slept fitfully specifically because of the alliance. They were much too far down that road to turn back now. Men dead, an outpost sacked, and most crucially promises had been made. Yet, there was no denying that Philip's uneasiness kept him awake. It would probably be like this until their objectives were accomplished and the two sides of the alliance parted ways again. And there was no question that they would part ways at some point. This was a product of necessity, and once the need was gone, Philip and his companions would sever all ties to the Shade King. They'd likely have to cut and run the first chance they got.

Dracula, no doubt, had something up his sleeve once the Guild was well and truly hobbled. Philip got the sense that the ancient vampire didn't like loose ends, or the sharing of any type of power. Philip couldn't allow that to happen. Couldn't check one continental power that was out of control, just to allow another, quite possibly worse power to fill the void. It was a problem for the future, however. One dilemma at a time.

Alayna rolled over in the bed they were sharing, and her hand slipped across Philip's chest. She snuggled into him, unaware that he lay awake. Her hair splayed across his chest, rose-gold even in the shadows of a room ensconced in night. He smiled at the sight of her. A bit of drool slipped out of the corner of her mouth and he resolved to tease her about it the moment they awoke in the morning—if he ever managed to sleep that was. She was hard in all the right places, but soft in times like this. These were the moments that he'd missed the most. Times alone, just the two of them, as it had been just after New York, and Astori, and Alayna's change. He loved his friend—Beathan was a heart-companion by now, no question about it. But traveling in groups and camping under the stars often left little room for privacy. Philip enjoyed seeing her restful and asleep, and doing so lulled him in turn, a yawn wracking his mouth, his eyelids drooping. The distance that had formed between them was slowly starting to evaporate. The more he saw that whatever might have happened between her and Azir when they had been separated was a thing of the past. The ease in her presence was returning and accentuated at times like this. Oh, she was different, there was no question of it— harsher at times, a bit more reckless, and with a hair-thin trigger. But down to her core she was the same, and so was he. They'd find their way back to that loving existence that had so blissfully encapsulated their time together in the north, before Beathan had been captured, and when they'd been forced to run. Before The Alchemist, and the menagerie. Before Helmsted. The thought of Helmsted, that Guild legend, leader of a rogue band of Collectors, high in the Guild Council, set a chill of icy rage through his veins. He would make her pay, for everything, but mostly for what she'd done to Alayna.

But not now. Now he'd sleep. Yawning again, Philip forced his mind blank and closed his eyes. Sleep came gradually, slowly, but it finally came.

———

"YOU ARE a treasure trove my friend. Your mind is solid gold. It's just a pity it took you so long to come to your senses and turn on the Collectors Guild." Philip cringed inwardly as the Shade King called him friend. A sign of how far he had fallen—or maybe a sign of simply how many dark twists and turns life could take.

Dracula had his cordial face on today, almost jovial at times, but it was most definitely a charade. Philip couldn't forget the anger from yesterday when the vampire's plans for Sampstone had been foiled by Philip bringing him dead instead of alive. He couldn't ignore the looks of fear that the vampires directed their master's way. Dracula—the One Who Rules in his people's minds—was worshipped by them, feared by them. He was great and terrible. He was practically a god to them. But not to Philip. To Philip he was a sadistic bastard, one putting on a friendly face while he was getting what he wanted, but one that Philip couldn't wait to pierce with a stake. And the glint in the Shade King's eye, the dark promises that it held, told Philip that it was the same for his enemy-turned-ally. Dracula caught his gaze and seemed to read his mind, a cold smile playing on his lips.

"I'm glad you find it useful," Philip forced himself to respond. He'd been feeding the Shade King the locations of outposts, some hidden and some not, all morning, and the vampire had been drinking it in, lapping up the details like a glutton drinking in his last glass of wine. "There's a reason they've been chasing me—us—so hard this last year. I'm their worst nightmare."

Dracula eyed him up. "You are indeed."

"So, now we've given you all this information, what do we do with it?" Alayna asked.

"We start hitting targets," Philip answered, looking to Dracula for confirmation. When he didn't see disagreement he continued, "We attack enough minor outposts to raise the alarm. I want them to know we're coming." His voice rumbled into a growl. As much as he hated the Shade King, he loathed the Guild and what it had become, what it had done to people he loved.

"Isn't that the opposite of what we want?" Azir questioned, brow furrowed.

"Not exactly, mate, the outposts are just a distraction, just a way t' coax 'em, herd 'em." Beathan's eye was always keen. Strategy of a thief, mischievousness of a fairy, all rolled into one.

"It'll sound the alarm for the council members, so to speak. If it's widespread enough it'll let them know it's an all out attack. If we are successful with our coordinated attacks, we'll get the leaders where we want them. Probably London," Philip finished what the fairy had started.

The Shade King's eyes narrowed in anticipation. "Yes, once they know we're coming, with all of our coordinated strength and knowledge, they will huddle so very close together for as much protection as they can possibly muster. Until with one final, lethal assault, we strike!" The vampire's voice was a croon that turned to a shout as his palm smacked the old oak table around which they were sitting. Azir and Alayna started slightly. Philip ignored the theatrics while Beathan just rolled his eyes.

Dracula grinned toothily. "We all get what we want then."

"I'm not so sure that's the same thing," Alayna muttered. Philip agreed silently.

They wrapped up the meeting since there was not much else to say. Most of Philip's information and brain was revealed for the vampires to use. He'd held some of it in reserve, just in case the vampire tried to break their alliance, but truth be told it probably wasn't enough. He was at the mercy of the Shade King now. It all depended on how much the king of the vampires wanted to ruin the leaders of the Guild. Luckily, from the gleam in his eyes as they hashed out the plan, Philip was fairly sure that Dracula wanted that, and wanted it very badly indeed.

The four of them filed out of the room as a service vampire brought a goblet of dark red liquid—some kind of bloodwine no doubt—for the king's midday meal. Without a word they parted ways, they'd reconvene again that night, and the next day, and the next for as long as they deemed necessary to make sure that this strategy proceeded without a hitch.

Philip let Beathan and Alayna exit through the door first, talking quietly, while he hung back and grabbed Azir by the arm as they walked through the door.

"What?" Azir said a touch angrily as he looked down at Philip's hand on his arm.

Philip let go. "I just wanted to...thank you."

Azir's frown turned into a smirk. "For what?"

"For backing me yesterday when I described Sampstone's death to the Shade King."

A curt nod was all Philip got at first, although all smugness left the vampire's face. Finally he answered as they walked behind their two companions, keeping their voices quiet. "I heard what Sampstone said about Alayna—to her. You did the right thing." The hybrid's often-silky voice was iron.

Philip felt a strange softening in that moment toward Azir. He didn't like him; there was no use in denying it. He'd spent too much time killing vampires and watching people be killed by them to ever really get past that. And there was no denying that Azir coveted what Philip had with Alayna, thought he might in fact possess it someday. But, despite Philip's feelings, they both wanted to protect her, both put her first, both would kill and had killed for her.

Philip clasped the vampire's forearm, an overture of peace—well, more like a truce really, the end of which Philip wasn't certain when or if it would arrive. But for now they were companions, comrades, if not exactly friends.

Azir looked at the hand on his forearm for a long moment before clasping it back. His eyes said everything, showed he'd processed through something similar to Philip.

"Are you two done bonding yet? I'm hungry," Alayna shouted from down the hallway where she and Beathan had stopped to wait for them. A sly smirk was on her face as she watched them.

Philip and Azir dropped their grasp quickly, a tinge of embarrassment on both faces. But there was no denying the moment had happened. Suddenly, Philip felt much better about their circumstances, about the outlook of this mission, and their joint survival. One extra, capable set of hands that he could really trust could make all the difference.

CHAPTER THIRTEEN

The next few days were spent covering and recovering the details of their plan for the next month. It was enough to bore Alayna to tears. She was built for open forests and starlit nights not sitting in rooms with her enemies and rehashing a plan that was already fairly straightforward. Once Dracula had mined Philip's brain for locations of secret outposts and hidden prisons and what other knowledge Philip possessed from his time with the Guild, it was really just a case of assigning those locations to different groups of attackers and then turning them loose. Oh, there were dates and timetables to plan also, but in general—at least in Alayna's opinion—the continent was going to resemble more or less one giant melee for the next month. She almost pitied the Collectors who would bear the brunt of this coordinated assault. The vampires had always been organized and had a large-scale operation. They'd always had the manpower, but now they had the final crucial piece: information.

That didn't mean the vampires were going to be doing all of the heavy lifting in this assault. No, Philip had insisted that their company partake, and do their fair share of combat. Alayna didn't mind, though, a bit of action would do her some good. This gloomy castle filled with people who'd as soon drink her as talk to her, was pushing her to her edge.

"Won't be long now, lass," the fairy said with a hand on her shoulder, as Philip and Azir hashed out yet another seemingly insignificant detail with the Shade King.

Alayna rolled her eyes and shrugged. "At this point we'll be here til the new moon."

Beathan chuckled and his eyes softened. "We're different, Alayna. Not built for castles an' enclosed spaces. Fairies an' Elfas share a lot o' common traits. We're built for th' wild."

"Philip's got troll blood infused in his veins. He's a hybrid also. And Azir used to be an Elfas like me. Shouldn't they be going stir crazy like us?"

"Ah, but Philip spent the majority of his life in the Guild. He's disciplined, more used t' suppressin' his instincts when need be. And Azir, well, companion or not—a hybrid vampire is more vampire than anythin' else—these're his kind, not ours."

Alayna sighed. "I just want out of this castle. I want to run. I want the wind on my face and the scent of pine in my hair when I'm done."

"The north calls," Beathan mused thoughtfully. "Soon enough, soon enough."

"But will we ever see home again?" Alayna asked. And she didn't mean America. Her Elfas home was not across the Atlantic, but rather in the untamed northern stretches of this continent.

"Me fair green isle calls me name. I'll see her again," Beathan said with utter confidence. Alayna didn't feel the same certainty. This was bound to be dangerous. She'd spent days listening to Philip and the king plan these attacks. Enough attacks and assaults that even the most cavalier of warriors would think twice about mortality.

Alayna shook off the doomful thoughts. "Care for a run?"

Beathan looked to the end of the table where the others were still plotting. "They won't even know we're gone," he said with a wink.

They slipped out of the castle into the winter air and ran. Alayna suddenly felt like she needed it more than anything in her life. Needed the ability to move, to sprint, to spring forward freely, especially since she'd been placed in a cage. Beaten, tortured. But mostly caged. She would never be caged again.

And so they ran.

THE FOLLOWING days were much of the same, until finally Philip and the Shade King agreed that plans were as final as they could possibly be. Then it was a flurry of readying themselves to go. The vampires didn't keep much in the way of normal food in store, so their group spent a couple of days hunting, tracking, and gathering in the nearby forests for food to replenish their supplies. Then it was reserved farewells made to their tentative allies and they were on their way.

"How can you trust that Dracula will follow through on his end of the deal—keep to the plans, that is?" Alayna asked Philip as they trekked through the snowy landscape.

"He wants this as bad as we do. He'll keep his word. Besides, I've withheld one crucial piece of information until the last." Philip had an unusual smirk on his face.

"If I know him, at all, he will not have liked that," Azir said with a wince and a shake of his head. "It is a dangerous game you played with him."

"Dracula doesn't have to like it. I don't care if he is hundreds of years old and the most dangerous and powerful vampire around. He's not getting the location of the London complex—Guild headquarters—until I say so. Keeping that information to myself insures my—our—involvement in this plan until the end. We don't want to become expendable."

Alayna nodded as she thought through it. Smart of Philip. Without holding that piece back, the Shade King could kill them and simply enact the plan on his own. She said as much, to which Philip gave a feral grin and a very Beathan-esque wink.

Their path led them north and west into the heart of central Europe. They picked off Guild outposts as they went. Always small ones first, often with only a handful of people manning them. Alayna's miniature crossbows saw more action than they had in quite some time and for that she was grateful. The itch to move, to fight, to do something—anything —that had consumed her final days in Bran Castle began to lessen. Collectors were not easily subdued and each outpost they hit carried with it the threat of death, but at least they were doing something. And with every dead Guild member, and every blow they struck at the Guild, Alayna felt a tiny bit closer to paying back what had been done to her.

They always let one member alive or sometimes just conveniently left a by standing witness to carry tales of their exploits back to the council members that led the Guild. Those people near to rural outposts had a keen sense about them, instincts that city folk simply didn't possess. Decades ago, the Great Transformation had hit rural areas harder, supernatural beings had been created overnight. Superstitions and caution were second nature to those country folk. They took one look at Alayna and her companions and just seemed to know they weren't human. The human inhabitants gave them a wide berth.

Philip had them hit the strategic targets that he'd spent so long in planning. They struck specific places at specific times to coordinate with the vampires who they had to trust were wreaking the same havoc elsewhere across the continent as they were.

And so they bloodied their way west a little further, into the mountains. Philip truly seemed to come alive as they reached the foothills of the Alps. A frost entered his eyes, gleaming and vibrant. It seemed to tell the story of his heritage each time she caught his gaze. It was wild and unforgiving, but it still managed to take her breath away, because it was hers.

And he was hers. Whatever space had grown between them during her captivity and his near madness, seemed to shrink. Perhaps it was just what normally happened when two lovers spend time in close proximity, or perhaps it was the fact that Philip had noticeably softened his attitude to Azir, or perhaps it was neither. But for whatever reason, the two of them were almost back to normal, and it lifted her spirits more than just about anything else could.

———

AFTER WEEKS of striking outposts they were all tired. So when Philip's course led them high up into the Alps, into the bitter cold of mountain winter, with its frozen wind and biting nights, it was only natural that they wanted an explanation.

"We've been striking low level targets for weeks now—phase one of the plan. This will have the Guild taking notice. They can't lose this many outposts in this short a span of time and not pay attention," Philip began.

Alayna rubbed her hands together against the chill. "Plus when you add the damage that our vampire allies are inflicting, the cost rises severely." Philip nodded.

"So what's with this trek up into th' peaks? Is there a wee mountain stronghold we mean t' take?" Beathan asked. "Ya' know mate, it really is a bit cold t' take us up so high at this time o' year."

"Not for me." Philip grinned, still sleeveless despite the freezing temperatures. Azir rolled his eyes and pulled his cloak closer around him.

"So...?" Alayna prodded.

Philip nodded, the twinkle evaporating from his eyes. "Right, so we've been a buzzing gnat about their ears. Attracting notice but taking small enough bites as to not garner much of a response yet. But that's going to change."

"A special target?" Azir grunted.

"The Guild has very particular, small-scale, high security prisons across the continent. No, nothing on the level of St. Thomas, Beathan," Philip amended as the fairy's head shot up at the mention of prison. He'd spent a short but brutal time in Guild captivity, along with Azir. It was where they had first met.

"So why are we taking the time to hit a prison?" Alayna asked.

Philip gazed thoughtfully at the expanse of mountains in front of them. They were high up enough that the view was simply stunning. Crystalline peaks and snow-coated tree lines stretched as far as the eye could see. "For so long, people like us have wanted to avoid the notice of the Collectors Guild, but now it's the opposite. We want them to know that we are coming. We want them to sit up and take notice. We want them scared," her mate said, and clenched a fist as his voice swelled slightly. "If they get frightened enough then they'll do what we want. They'll retract, huddle together, for strength and protection."

"London," Azir murmured thoughtfully. Philip nodded.

"Once they're scared enough, once they know we're coming and we're a real threat, then the Guild leaders will cluster together, thinking themselves safer in numbers. That's when we strike, we cut the head of the snake and see what arises in its wake."

"We've been herding them," Alayna mused.

"In a sense, yes. They'll already have begun retracting. There is no way someone like Helmsted would stay exposed and unprotected if she knows we're coming. And believe me, she knows it's us. Trust me, they'll do what we want."

Beathan finally chimed in. "So what's this mate, our final signal flare? Low-level isn't enough? We strike at a hidden, impregnable Guild prison an' we let 'em know once an' for all that if we can hit 'em here, we can hit 'em anywhere?"

"Exactly," Philip agreed, his tone of satisfaction carried with it also a sense of finality. After this strike, phase one would be over and they'd move into the next part of their plan.

"Well, what ya' waitin' for then? Lead on mate!" Beathan said cheerfully with a two-handed flourish at Philip to continue on their way.

CHAPTER FOURTEEN

The prison was another few hours of hard trekking, but Philip wanted to approach in darkness so they took a break to rest and catch whatever sleep they could. Like a soldier, Philip could fall asleep almost anywhere without too much difficulty. But the others didn't have his background. Azir volunteered for the first watch and Beathan did his best to snuggle down in a bank of snow, wrapping his cloak tightly around him and sacrificing warmth for a soft place to lay his head.

Alayna curled up next to Philip. He could hear her measured breathing, but it never verged into that strange, intangible sound that could be so easily identified as sleep. Philip wanted to rest himself but found himself speaking quietly despite it.

"Are you alright?"

She wormed her way a little bit closer as she rolled over to face him. "Fine. Just...antsy, I guess."

"We've fought before, is something different this time?"

"No, not really. It's just every time we hit another outpost, I feel less and less."

Philip thought he understood. "You're worried about the numbness."

Alayna gave a muffled snort into his chest. "Is it so common that there's a recognizable name for it?"

Philip nodded before he realized her eyes were closed. "Yes," he said simply, "soldiers experience it all the time."

Alayna sighed. "It's not only the numbness really. Yes, I feel less and less each time I kill another Collector, but..." she trailed off.

"But what?" he whispered, prodding.

"Well, I feel less empathy, but I also feel generally less satisfied. Like something is missing, or something isn't enough. Does that make sense?"

Philip waited a moment, thinking his way through his response. "You know, when I originally proposed this, you all thought it was only about revenge. And it was, to be sure. But it was also exactly what you just verbalized. After seeing what Helmsted had done at the menagerie—to you, but also to all the other beings and creatures—I realized that striking her down wouldn't be sufficient. I had to do something more, something that would be—" Words had never been his strong point so he just fell back on simplicity. "Something that would be enough."

He felt Alayna nodding into his chest again. "I'm glad you understand. I was starting to think something was wrong, the way I was feeling less and less. Like the menagerie broke me." Her voice was small, vulnerable.

"Some scars go deep and take time to heal. You have to be gentle with yourself Alayna and allow yourself that time to heal. However long it takes. And I'll be with you every step of the way."

She pulled back this time, gazing into his eyes, a small smile on her face. She kissed him deeply then pulled back again to speak. "I'm glad. I'm glad you came for me in the menagerie, I'm glad we're doing this together. I'm just...glad. Glad you're in my life."

And it was at that moment, all the separation between them that had been edging away little by little since the menagerie, evaporated. She was his and he was hers. He didn't care what that awful place had done to her, or who she'd bonded with, who she'd been forced to rely on. In fact, he was grateful to Azir for being there, to help her when he was half mad with grief and no help at all.

They fell silent then, sleeping in shifts until nightfall. When the sun finally set, Philip roused them and set them on their course upward. Every step felt loud as snow and ice crunched underfoot. It was a steep track, but carved into the mountain, old and used by the Guild over the years to bring their few prisoners up and down as needed.

"What's this place called, anyhow?" Beathan asked between breaths, gasping for air like all three of them other than Philip. The air was thin this high up, and cold, burning lungs more than it would have at sea level. For all except for Philip, that is. The troll part of him was used to it all—the cold, the air, the climb. He'd felt more and more invigorated with each step they had taken up into the peaks. The Alps might not be his homeland, but they were close enough.

"No name really," Philip responded to the fairy, "just a number. Number 3."

"Mean anything?" Alayna gasped for air, as even her Elfas stamina wore thin this high up.

"St. Thomas is number 1, and everything else after that is just given a number." Philip shrugged.

"So are you telling me that we are about to surprise attack the third highest security prison the Guild possesses?" Azir asked flatly.

"Scared?" Beathan quipped with a grin.

"Never," Azir responded too quickly. "But I have seen the inside of that hell-hole, St. Thomas, just like you. I have no desire to return."

Philip turned to look at the vampire and saw real concern there. "Relax, Azir. This prison is small and doesn't have the same volume or capacity as St. Thomas prison. Doesn't possess the same evil aura. It's just ranked number 3 because of the difficulty getting in and out. There is only one solid steel door embedded deep into the rocky peak. Even if someone were to brave the climb, traverse the steep path, they'd have no way to get in."

"You tell us this now?" Alayna said incredulously.

"Well," Philip cast her his most roguish face, channeling his inner Beathan, "those attackers wouldn't have me to rely on, would they?"

"You know another way in?"

"Not exactly. But with a little assistance, I should be able to do alright." Philip glanced at Beathan's wrist.

The fairy's eyes came alight with understanding. "Lookin' t' borrow somethin' mate?" he asked with a twinkle.

"Only if you're so inclined." Philip nodded with mock modesty.

"Oh, I could be convinced. The amplifier bracelet, I take it?" Beathan queried.

"That's the one. With it, I should be able to magnify my power enough to get us through the door."

"Apparently the Guild isn't creative enough imagining potential attacks and setting up their defenses, if one little bracelet on your wrist is enough to get you in," Alayna murmured as they paused for breath.

Philip dropped the nonchalance, growing more serious. "It's why I'm a nightmare for them. Most beings like us don't have inside information, don't have a clue what is waiting on the other side of a door at any outpost or Guild prison. I do. I know policy and procedure. I know what to expect, so if I can just think outside the box enough to get me in, then I have little to fear from that point on."

"I'm beginning to see that," she mused thoughtfully.

———

THEY HAD WAITED until it was dark before finishing the trek and approaching, so the night covered them. Philip looked at the moon above, cold and clear, and wished for a moment that it was just he and Alayna, back in the wilds of the north, before anyone had ever started chasing them. Before this endless running and fighting.

Footsteps crunched in the frozen snow behind him. "As soon as we set foot inside?" Beathan queried, unusually anxious as he eyed the bracelet now on Philip's wrist instead of the fairy's.

"As soon as," Philip promised, "and not a moment later. I could probably get us in without it you know, but this will ensure that I manage to do it quickly, maintaining our element of surprise," he shook the bracelet on his wrist, links and charms tinkling softly into the night.

"I haven't fought without it in a long time, mate," Beathan murmured.

"And you won't have to," Alayna reassured the fairy, looking at Philip with the kind of belief and confidence he wasn't sure he deserved.

He swallowed. She'd be fine. She'd fought enough this past year to survive a skirmish. "The door is right around the bend in the path. We'll be there momentarily. Remember, there's not a large force of Collectors inside, but they are elite; some of the Guild's best. We'll have the element of surprise, but don't take them lightly."

"I never do," Azir replied, and flashed his fangs wickedly.

Philip grunted and continued. "I can't say for sure which few creatures are being kept there, but they're likely dangerous also. Try not to kill any creature that isn't necessary." A half pleading note entered his voice and they all nodded their heads in agreement. They didn't want to become the very thing they were fighting against. "But," Philip continued as they were about to make their way again, "do whatever you need to do to protect yourself." Nods all around again.

They rounded the bend, creeping slowly after Philip. The wall of snow, rock, and ice on his left was comfortingly solid and stable compared to the drop off on his right. Cliffside pathways and secret prisons; the Guild never made anything easy. The darkness of the night was offset only by the glowing moon. The whiteness of the snowy cliffs reflected some of that light onto the path, enough to see where there was sure footing. For that Philip was glad. It wouldn't do to plunge to their deaths off the cliff to the path's right simply because of one wrong step.

"There it is." Philip pointed to the door at the end of the pathway ahead of them. Iron and welded into the very mountain itself it was frosted over and dripping with icicles from the hinges and handle.

"Frozen. Tis bound t' make a racket poundin' that thing down," the fairy muttered.

"That's why you lent me your enhancing charm, Beathan. We've been over this. As soon as I start pounding, they'll know we're here. Stealth is over, speed is what matters now."

"We should get on with it then," Azir added, lifting his hands as if to ask why they were still talking things through. It was odd of Beathan to require reminding of tactics so soon after they'd gone over them, but Philip knew his friend was probably just nervous to be without his bracelet for any length of time. It enhanced abilities and that was a powerful gift. It had gotten the fairy out of more scrapes than Philip cared to imagine.

Philip nodded to the vampire, and then spoke to them all. "Let's go."

They sped into a crouching sort of run as they approached the iron door, footsteps now crunching loudly into the frozen night. They reached the face of the entrance and Philip could hear the muttering of men inside, and the grunting of something else far more sinister. He utilized Beathan's lesson from earlier and activated the bracelet with a quick access charm.

Suddenly Philip felt power flood him, more than he could usually grasp. It was like his core had somehow been tapped, as if all the ice in the whole frozen north filled his veins. He roared to release some of that power coursing through him before it ate him up and slammed his calloused fist into the iron door. The sound echoed sonorously through the peaks around them. That surely had woken up any inside, let alone any creature residing in this high-altitude land for miles around them.

The hinges cracked in places, as their frozen state didn't really allow for warping. But the door itself still held. Philip gathered his strength again while his companions urged him on, all the while urgent shouts sounded from inside. Philip's fist crashed into the door again and this time it crunched inward, ripping from the frame, and allowing them to see inside, even though bits still clung to the rocky mountain surrounding the doorway. Philip struck it again, quick-fire and this time it was down.

He turned and flung the bracelet to Beathan as promised and then leaped over the destroyed iron slab, into prison number 3, a war cry on his lips. Shouts of alarm, but also anger, met him as his companions slipped in behind him. Philip crashed his way through one of the Collectors who rushed him, but the man was no match for Philip in his wrath. A fist shattered the man's skull and he was on to the next. He heard his companions dealing with their threats the same way, but elite as this crew of Collectors were supposed to be, they had been caught fatally unaware. Alayna and Beathan slipped through the fighting like the silkiest of serpents, daggers flashing in the faint mixing of moonlight and torchlight lighting their way. Azir tore into throats in a fashion that Philip had somehow become accustomed to, and before they knew it, the battle was won. All Collectors but one were dead or dying. Philip stalked the last man standing, backed him into a corner. He had to admit, the man controlled his fear and snarled a curse. Philip silenced him with a blow to the face. The man crumpled.

"Why didn't you kill him?" Alayna asked.

"He can carry our tale with him when he leaves," Philip answered. Their questioning faces prompted him to continue. "We want the Guild to know of our actions. Just our presence here makes our point. If we know about this place and are bold enough to attack it, then we'll be bold enough to attack anywhere."

Beathan smiled, a vicious glint in his eyes. "Good, let 'em herd t'gether in their little hidey holes from fear." The others muttered their agreement.

Philip appraised the prison as he walked down the darkened corridor. He remembered this place only housed three cold mountain cells. Alayna, Azir, and Beathan were right behind him, the Collector still unconscious on the ground. What looked to be a witch of some kind was muzzled in the first cell, strangely an elfas was in the second—odd since their kind were not normally known for violence; Alayna excluded—and a black mass in the third.

Philip hissed in surprise and concern as he saw the third cell. "What?" Alayna queried. But before Philip could answer all hell broke loose. The witch who must have taken the chance to gnaw through her muzzle during the ruckus of the fighting, spat it out and muttered a cursed spell. Azir, nearest her cell, was struck by the spell and reached as if under a daze to unlock her door. He must have picked up the key from one of the guards.

The witch was out in a heartbeat, flinging more curses and cackling eerily into the night, her spells steaming up the corridor as hot breath left her mouth. Azir, still under the spell of the witch, surprise attacked Beathan, sending him careening into a wall, while Alayna and Philip had turned to the witch. As if seeing her gambit had only occupied two of her foes, the witch redirected Azir, to turn his attention away from Beathan, who was stunned on the ground and collecting his senses. Azir turned to his new goal. The vampire reached the third cell, put the key in the lock, and turned it. Before he'd even opened the cell door, the barred gate burst open, sending Azir flying back to strike the wall and collapse in a heap, all while the dark mass lunged out into the corridor. Only Philip and Alayna were still standing between it and its freedom.

"Good luck trying to chase me with that beastie on the loose," the hag screeched, while hiking her tattered robes and turning her ugly face away from them as she ran on bare feet out into the frozen night.

"Philip," Alayna said urgently motioning for him to look out after the fleeing witch.

"She doesn't matter, Alayna, at least not compared to what she set loose. Smart move on her part—at least it will be if we can stop it. If not, it'll probably catch up to her and prove her gambit too dangerous of a risk."

"What is it?" Alayna asked, fear in her voice as she sensed his trepidation. The black mass took one step toward them, then another. Ignoring their downed companions. It didn't speak, it slunk toward them silent and deadly.

"It's a bogeyman," Philip breathed. "Strong, fast, can take many forms, but its true form is what you're seeing right now—an androgynous, almost shapeless form of darkness. It's said it only takes that form when it plans to do something especially heinous." They took a step backward as the thing somehow, despite its shapelessness, managed to bare inky black fangs.

"Who knows how long it's been captive. It's likely furious." Alayna tried to hide her gulp.

"Get behind me." For once Alayna didn't argue with his command. She, like him, could probably feel the evil emanating from the creature.

The bogeyman let out a barking kind of call and then charged. Philip roared in answer and then gritted his teeth and stood his ground. The bastard would have to get through him if it wanted to get to Alayna.

The clash was titanic, simply put. And it wasn't just the initial impact of their bodies rushing together. Blows rained down on each other and they flung each other into the stone walls of the prison. The very mountain seemed to shudder and shake with each moment they continued fighting. Snarling filled the air and Philip wasn't certain if it was he or the beast who made the noise. Sharp darkness tore into his shoulder and arms, fangs or claws, Philip wasn't sure. He fought back and delivered the type of blows that would have smashed a lesser opponent to bits. And still they held ground against each other.

Damn that witch and her quick thinking. He almost wished the bogeyman would kill him and go out into the night. The rage it was in, it would surely hunt down any living thing and take its wrath out on it, regardless of who had set it free. Philip could feel that much ferocity and anger and pain pulsating in the beast as they fought. But now, it would move on to Alayna before it ever found the witch.

So Philip struggled on, suffering blows, and dealing them with equal measure. He wasn't sure if he'd ever been quite so taxed by a single opponent in his life. He was glad Alayna stayed out of the fray, not just for her safety, but for his own, as well. It took every ounce of control, speed, and strength that he had to dodge whatever blows he could and fight back. He kicked the thing's knee and heard it screech in pain. It tackled him and bit into his back, and contrary to what one might expect, Philip clutched it as close as he could, his powerful troll blood coursing through him, giving him a constrictor-like grasp. Enough so that the bogeyman fought to escape and slither away. They clashed again and again, wreaking havoc on the prison, until they tumbled through the crushed doorway and out onto the path. Under the moon they struggled, closer and closer to the cliff, until they were fighting right at the edge.

They rolled apart and Philip burst forward again with all the quickness and might he could, jumping and putting both feet into the bogeyman's chest in the kind of flying, leaping kick to which he rarely resorted. Perhaps it was the unusual tactics—a brawler relying on something normally out of his range—or perhaps, Philip had simply outlasted the beast. Who knew how long it had been held captive and weakened? But Philip's feet collided with the beast and sent it flying. It snarled as it flew backward, grasping futilely at the feet that had just sent it cascading to its doom. It fell off the cliff and into the night. Philip landed with a painful thud, dangerously close to the edge and the slickness threatened to carry him sliding over the cliff with the bogeyman, but he had the wherewithal to draw his belt knife and slam it hilt deep into the ice, anchoring him to the path, feet just dangling over the edge.

And then Alayna was there, helping pull him back to safety. He took her help gratefully and then collapsed against her when they got back through the door and inside. Beathan was still shaking his head groggily from the attack by Azir. And the vampire was only just coming to himself.

"How long?" It felt like they had fought for hours. But it couldn't have been long if the two of them were only just now rousing.

Alayna cocked her head before understanding lit her eyes. "Minutes," she said with a shrug. Then she flung her arms around him even as he winced, and whispered in his ear, "I was so worried."

As soon as she realized his wince, she pulled back and began tending his wounds. Many of them were deep and needing attention. It was fortunate that Philip healed quickly. A normal man would likely have died by now.

When Alayna had stitched his wounds and tended to the others, when they had shoved the now-awake Collector out into the night— staggering as he went—away to carry the tale of this night to his masters, only then did they hear the sound.

A voice in the second cell cleared her throat and then said. "Please, could you help me?"

CHAPTER FIFTEEN

Alayna couldn't understand how she had forgotten about the last remaining prisoner. She supposed it was because she had been so engrossed in the fight between Philip and that shadowy bogeyman, and then with making sure he didn't bleed out from the wounds he had taken. Still, she felt a twinge of guilt. The being inside was an elfas, and she looked to be relatively young.

Alayna picked up the key laying on the ground where Azir had left it after he'd been cast against the stone wall by the bogeyman. She reached to put the key in the lock and was about to open the cell door when a strong hand stopped her.

"Wait," Philip murmured, his calloused hands staying her own. "We don't know why she's here."

"What do you mean?" Alayna asked.

"I mean, number 3 doesn't usually house innocent inmates."

"Ya' can't know that for certain, mate," Beathan chimed in, while Azir remained aloof and silent, a look of disinterest on his face as he picked his nails. He seemed to have recovered from the blow he'd suffered.

"True, I can't," Philip responded to the fairy, and winced as he moved closer to the cage, sending a twinge of worry through Alayna. He really should be resting right now, accelerated healing or not. "So, elfas, what landed you here?" Philip's voice was harsh but not cruel as he stared at the fair skinned and flaxen haired being in the cell.

Alayna eyed the elfas. She hadn't spent nearly enough time around her own kind—even years after the change brought on by Martin Astori's magic—to be a good judge of their character. The elfas was lithe and lean, just as Alayna was. She had retreated to the back of the pen and cowered against the wall as soon as Philip had stopped Alayna from opening the cell door. She mumbled something too quiet to be coherent.

"What was that, lass?" Beathan asked more gently than Philip had spoken.

"I thought you were here to free me," she mumbled more loudly. "When you started killing the Collectors, I thought maybe, just maybe I'd get free of this hell."

Alayna glanced sideways at Philip and saw his features soften in what could only be called regret. A place like this would have been hard to bear for the weak of will and body. But he remained impassive as he stared at her, before voicing his question again.

"I said, why are you here." Philip cocked his head slightly as he gazed at the elfas. Her features, just slightly exotic enough to be noticeably not human, resembled Alayna's own. It made sense, she supposed.

Alayna heard the elfas swallow audibly before she gathered the strength to stand and answer. "I was taken not far from home. I was careless. I felt safe so close to our lands..." She trailed off miserably. "It wasn't long before I wound up in a prison, then before long they moved me here. I don't know how long I've been here."

"Time has a way o' blurrin' when a body is in captivity," Beathan commiserated. It looked like he'd already been won over by the short and simple story. Alayna could tell by looking at Philip however, that her love still had questions.

"So you didn't do anything to deserve being captured?" Philip probed carefully.

The elfas shook her head and gripped the bars with dirty hands, the first signs of spirit Alayna had seen from her. "No. Do they ever need a reason to take us?" she spat fiercely.

Philip still didn't commiserate. He was being cautious. "I think after the fight you just witnessed that you can't reasonably say they never have a cause for what they do." Alayna shook her head. Still his instincts told him to defend the Guild, even as he set his course to destroy it.

The elfas shrugged uncomfortably, shivering as she did. "I'm no shadow demon, like the one you fought. I'm just normal old me." She must be freezing, clothed in tattered rags, no cloak to protect her from the bitter chill of the mountains. The destroyed and now open door to the prison was doing her no favors. Gooseflesh was forming on her arms. Alayna shrugged off her cloak, removed it of any items of danger or importance from the pockets, and then slipped it through the bars. The look of gratitude and relief on her face was enough to convince Alayna she was harmless.

Philip eyed Alayna questioningly as she gripped her own shoulders against the chill seeping into her now. "What?" she retorted. "It's just a loan until we figure out the truth of her story. Besides, I have you to keep me warm." She snuggled under one arm and saw him smile faintly before he turned his attention back to the girl.

"So, why did they move you here?" he asked.

"From the other prison?" the elfas asked tentatively.

Philip nodded and motioned that she should continue. Alayna was glad of his warmth against her. The night air flooding the prison from the open door was bitter.

"Do they need a reason?" the elfas muttered, almost angrily.

Something about her response tugged on Alayna's psyche. She was about to slow Philip's questions down but unwittingly Philip bulled on. "They usually do, yes."

The elfas swallowed and looked away. Shame. That was what Alayna saw on her face. She glanced up at Philip and saw the recognition, then disgust at what they were both realizing. He opened his mouth, no doubt to retract the question, but the elfas was already speaking.

"I was a reward. They said this was not a desirable posting. Cold. Boring. A dreary place to work and live. I was the Collectors' prize for having to work here. To...do with as they pleased."

Philip spat a few curses, just as Beathan and Alayna herself did. Azir stayed quiet but his face hardened. The plight of this poor elfas was exactly why they were fighting, why they had made a deal with the devil and concocted this half-mad plan to overthrow the Guild. Philip plucked the key from Alayna's hand and was already moving to unlock the door before the words had stopped their quiet echo through the corridor.

The cell door clanked open. The elfas stepped out timidly. Alayna looked at her, really looked, and the evidence of what they should have seen was right before their eyes. Downcast eyes, tattered clothes showing evidence of having been ripped, bruises on her face and uncovered flesh. And the pain and anguish in those eyes, but mostly the shame. Alayna swallowed and reached out to comfort her but stopped short.

The elfas scuttled back as Alayna reached out and threw up a hand to stop Alayna. "Please..."

Alayna raised her hands soothingly. "It's alright. Nobody will touch you. You don't have to be afraid of us." The elfas nodded her head jerkily that she understood. Alayna continued in that same soothing voice. "Do you have a name?"

"Ashei," the girl mumbled. "Like the ash tree, but with a twist." She said it reflexively like it was something someone had said to her often during her childhood. A mother probably.

"It's a beautiful name, lass," Beathan said. And surprisingly she smiled. Or perhaps it was no surprise at all; the fairy had a way of charming folks and the smile Alayna watched him direct toward the young elfas was disarmingly genuine and full of life.

Ashei stepped a few small steps further out into the corridor and free of the cell. Still she seemed unsure, too downtrodden to really know what to do with her newfound freedom.

"Well, this won't do," Philip said, and Alayna winced a bit at his gruff tone, even as the elfas cringed. Philip really needed to learn to moderate his tone better. Philip seemed to realize he had frightened Ashei, and he cleared his throat uncomfortably. "All I meant, is that your state of dress won't do. You're cloak-less for one thing—no you can't keep Alayna's indefinitely as she'll need it back sooner than later. She can't ward off the cold like I can—and being without a cloak in terrain like this can spell death quicker than you'd care to imagine."

"We can take one off of one of the smaller guards," Azir finally chimed in. "A little dried blood never hurt anyone. The clothing other than the cloak might be hard to replace until we get closer to normal civilization."

"I have one change of clothes with me. She can have them. We look about the same size," Alayna volunteered. "I'm Alayna by the way, although you've probably picked that up from what Philip said." She nodded Philip's direction.

They made introductions and the elfas' demeanor changed a bit. She retained a lot of that cagey attitude that reminded Alayna of a small deer ready to burst into flight at any moment. But she smiled occasionally. Even laughed once at a joke Beathan made. She changed into Alayna's spare clothes and for one blissful moment smiled the biggest smile yet at the feel of something resembling clean clothes touching her skin.

"Thank you," she said to Alayna softly.

They did their best to clean up the area, since staying put made the most sense for the rest of the night. The one living Collector was set free with instructions to tell his masters what he had seen. Alayna took a grim satisfaction in the fear on his face as he stumbled out the door and into the cold of the night.

The dead bodies were tossed over the cliff to the same fate as the bogeyman, and Philip lifted the iron door and propped what was left of it against the doorframe. It didn't provide a seal, but it kept any wind out, and the cold that did seep in was kept at bay by the fire they lit. The prison was well stocked if nothing else. A relatively warm night passed, with food in their bellies and one of the few nights of sleep Alayna could remember where they didn't fear attack, since any who would think to attack them in such a desolate area were already dead or gone.

They set a watch and closed their eyes, rotating as needed until the grey light of morning slipped through the cracks in the doorway. They roused themselves and began readying breakfast over the still-lit coals from the fire.

"We should stay one more day and night. The rest we'll get from a safe position could be invaluable," Philip said, the tactically thinking soldier in him coming to the forefront. They all agreed, although Azir and Beathan looked around them in distaste as if wishing they didn't need to stay in the prison a moment longer than necessary. Their time in St. Thomas prison in England was likely a contributing factor. Practicality won out, however, and the company stayed put. They talked, napped, ate, and generally got the sort of rest they hadn't in a long time. When night came again, Alayna found herself overwhelmingly ready for sleep, even though she had hardly done a thing all day. Perhaps Philip had been right. The exhaustion would have caught up with them sooner or later if they continued to push on and mask it. Better to nip it in the bud now, than suffer collapse at a later point.

They slept deeply again, setting watches as usual, but nothing and no one concerned them. They awoke, and this time readied themselves for departure. They ransacked the prison for whatever food stores they could carry and picked up a few weapons collected from the guards the other night before dumping them. And then they were on their way.

"Can I come with you?" Alayna was startled by Ashei's question.

"You want to accompany us?" She stared at Ashei. The elfas nodded.

"It'll be dangerous. Too dangerous for you, likely." Philip answered curtly.

"I don't care. I just don't want to be alone."

"Why don't you go home?—when we're out of the mountains that is," Beathan asked.

Ashei shrugged. "I wouldn't feel safe. And as dangerous as it may be with you, I've never seen anyone fight like you do." She included them all in the statement, but Alayna saw her eyes flicker to Philip. What she meant was she'd never seen anyone fight like Philip. His clash with the bogeyman had been titanic. Impressive to anyone who would have witnessed it. She couldn't blame the elfas for wanting to stay within his protection.

"Besides..." Ashei trailed off for a moment, then gathered her courage to speak on, "I'm just not sure I can go home. Not right now... not yet."

Alayna understood in a heartbeat. Trauma could often cloud the pathway in front of a person. Philip was her home, but even she and Philip had had difficulty rediscovering each other after her enslavement and escape from the menagerie.

Philip opened his mouth to no doubt tell her no, but Alayna put a restraining hand on his arm. "You can stay with us as long as you like. As we said, it will be dangerous. But you are welcome to our company."

Ashei burst into relieved tears and flung her arms around Alayna in a surprise show of emotion. Likely, her first friendly, physical contact with another in quite some time. Alayna clasped her close and hugged the young elfas. She held her until her sobbing subsided into muffled sniffles and the pain and anguish of a desperate captivity began to wash themselves away, purged from her body with tears like a sickness leeched from a wound.

CHAPTER SIXTEEN

Ashei was a contradiction of emotions over the next few days. One moment twitching in fear like a cornered animal at any sideways glance or raised voice—regardless of whether that voice was raised in her direction. The next second she was all bubbly and flitting around like a butterfly with an almost otherworldly innocence and excitement to be free. Free.

Alayna understood her completely. Scars from captivity could take a long time to diminish but nothing could completely stem the wonder that arose from the realization that no chains held you, no bars locked you away from the breath and light of the world.

The terrain down from the mountaintop prison was rough and they took it slowly. Each one of them keeping a watchful eye on their newest companion. She was younger than Alayna had thought at first, likely still an adolescent. If Alayna had been born and raised an elfas—instead of turned into one with magic—she supposed it would have been a little easier for her to estimate Ashei's age. As it was, adolescent was her best guess.

The girl dashed a few yards ahead of the group as their path leveled out for a change. Alayna watched as she came to a halting stop in front of a barren, leafless scrub brush still high above the tree line below them. It should have been devoid of life, this high up and in the midst of the cold of winter. And yet, a butterfly flexed its white wings slowly as it perched on a brown twig. Ashei reached out a finger almost tenderly and giggled as the butterfly easily switched its perch to her warm flesh instead of the cold wood, seemingly sensing the safety of its new resting place. Alayna put out a hand to slow down the rest of their party, allowing the girl a few moments of privacy as she stared in delight at the creature on her finger. With another giggle Ashei wiggled her finger as she lifted her hand and the butterfly took off into a wobbly yet beautiful flight. Another moment gazing after it, then all of a sudden, the girl became aware of the four sets of eyes on her and Alayna could practically see her shrink within herself again. Her eyes looked hollow again, her blonde hair lank and lifeless against her face. Ashei hunched her shoulders as the four of them caught up and then passed her by, before she trudged on behind them in the snow.

It would take time. But if more moments like the one they had just witnessed occurred, then perhaps it wouldn't take overly long for the girl to recover. This was why they were doing this, after all. It was the plight of people like Ashei, bound and abused, that made Philip, Alayna, Beathan, and even Azir willing to risk everything to confront the Guild. Even dealing with Dracula himself.

———

THEY MADE it down out of the Alps and into the lowlands. Winter still clung to the earth around them, but it was nowhere near as bitter as it had been high above. As if in answer to that thought, Alayna heard the wind howl in the mountain passes behind them, yet they were among the tree line now, and mostly protected from its ferocity.

Over the next week they moved slowly, planning out their next moves, resting as they went. They would need to be at full strength for the push ahead. Occasionally, they took small detours from their trajectory, making quick work of small Guild outposts that Philip could recall from his days as a Collector. The outposts were often on high alert, after all the combined attacks from their company and the vampires, but the outposts were still small enough that Alayna and her companions were able to accomplish their missions without grievous injury. Oh, there were a few wounds stitched here and there, but nothing major, thankfully. Each time, Philip sent a scared—but spared—Collector or other Guild member running ahead of them to carry his message, as he had every time before. Whenever, they crossed passes with a youth, a young Guild member in training, he made especially sure that the youth was the one spared to carry the message. They fought with cold calculation, but they weren't heartless. They did not want to become the very thing they fought. Alayna had to remind herself of that each time she relished another Collector kill.

They fought and traveled their way north across the countryside of France, hunting as they went, and stopping at remote inns when they could or camping in a copse of trees near their road. Whenever they stayed at an inn, the common folk could somehow sense their difference, their danger, and stayed well clear of them.

Ashei was skittish still. She was left back during each raid, and kept under close watch when within an inn, hood up, just as Alayna did to keep their more exotic features concealed from humans.

North.

Alayna could practically feel Philip's satisfaction that their path lead north, even if it did skew slightly west. As they patched their strained relationship further, and re-forged whatever part of their bond was necessary, Alayna found herself able to access his emotions more easily again, even speaking into his mind at times as she had once been able to do so easily—a gift acquired from her elfas species.

They made a stop through Paris as they steadily made their way to the coast, angling ever more and more toward their final destination of London. Paris was a place Alayna had once dreamed of visiting, what felt like a lifetime ago, when she was just a mere human with a small patch of land. A dream that then had been far beyond her means to realize. Now, Alayna had crisscrossed multiple continents, and would likely do even more than that—if she survived long enough, at least.

Paris, was beautiful, and elegant, teeming with life, and dirty, all the things she'd imagined and heard in stories so long ago. And yet, it did not appeal. Her nature now, longed for the wilds. For trees not wooden doors. For rocky windswept mountains not cultured stone buildings. She felt the same resignation in Philip as they stayed only long enough in the great city to fell one more, large Guild outpost before making their way to the channel. Alayna was no longer the frail human she had once been. And she never would be again.

As they finished their bloody business in Paris, Philip led their party out from the city as twilight fell. A group of armed guards watched their departure suspiciously. Most people stayed put as night was gathering. Yet all of their party felt more secure outside the expanse of Paris. Well, all except for Beathan perhaps. The mischievous fairy picked pockets left and right, and despite their prolonged stay in the wilderness over the past months, he managed to do so without ever raising an alarm. How he managed to maintain his skills at slight, and deception, and thievery, Alayna would never know.

The guards touched their weapons subconsciously as they eyed the party, as if sensing just by looking at them that they were dangerous. One had only to see Philip's stony expression, to witness the unyielding frozen expanse of the great north in his eyes, to know that he was not a man to be trifled with. Yet, for all that—or perhaps because of that—the guards let them pass unmolested. However, it didn't stop Ashei from nervously thrusting a hand into Alayna's, seeking whatever comfort she might find. Likely, the guards were a stark reminder of the Collectors that had captured and held her. Alayna murmured soothingly and didn't let go of her hand until they were well out of the city and the stars above were beginning to peak through the gaps in the clouds. Alayna didn't have the heart to tell the girl that holding hands in the face of potential danger was pretty much the last thing a fighter wanted to do. A person needed to have both hands free for defense if necessary. But Ashei was not a fighter.

They camped that night in a lightly wooded area and slept more easily. They set their watches and stuck by them, no causes for alarm in the night to bother them.

In the morning, as Beathan was preparing a cold breakfast of dried meat, cheese, and dark bread—foraged from one of the many towns through which they'd passed—Alayna pondered what lay imminently before them. It might not be safe to bring the girl with them much farther. They were almost at the channel.

Alayna muttered a question to Philip through a mouthful of food.

"What?" Philip responded with a grin.

Alayna fought to swallow and asked again a little sheepishly. "I said, what's the next stop?"

Philip nodded his understanding. "One, maybe two more campsites under the stars, but the next real stop is the channel. Our next stop is Calais."

CHAPTER SEVENTEEN

Calais was a relatively grim city as far as cities went, which was typical of many ports across the continent. Beathan wasn't a fan of ports. He loved the ocean. The rhythmic lapping of the waves on a coastline was like some kind of cosmic cleansing of anyone and anything that was close enough to see it or hear it. Beathan didn't often think about forgiveness or feel even a modicum of guilt for his light-fingered ways, but every once in a while it was nice to feel like a person's slate was being wiped clean. For some reason the ocean did that for him.

But not ports. Give him a nice deserted coastline any day. Ports were dirty, smelly, and generally full of the foulest people and places imaginable. Oh, it was easy pickings for his trade; there were more drunken marks wobbling between dockside taverns than one could find elsewhere, but Beathan couldn't help but feel like he needed to turn up his nose as he picked pockets.

"I've gone snobby," Beathan muttered to himself as he palmed a purse into his shabby coat pocket, its previous owner none the wiser.

"What?" Alayna turned toward him with a preoccupied look. Her eyes narrowed as she put things together as she stared at the back of a man walking away from them. "Did you just—?"

"Tut tut, don't talk business in front of the child," Beathan murmured to her quietly, but not so quietly that Ashei couldn't hear from a step away. He winked at her good-naturedly, as if the two of them were in on a secret. He was rewarded by the girl giving him one of her all-too-rare giggles. The fairy was one of the few in their company to ever manage to elicit one of those.

"That's not business, that's robbery!" Alayna hissed indignantly.

Beathan shrugged. "Ya' know who I am. Why are ya' actin' so surprised?"

The elfas seemed to shake herself. "I don't know. Sorry. I guess I'm just a little on edge, this close to the end."

"We all are," Beathan said seriously. Then he tossed her a flippant grin. "Apology accepted, dearie. Glad t' hear ya' feel right as rain about me pickin' a few pockets along the way."

"I didn't apologize for that, I'm not exactly alright with it. I just meant sorry for..." She trailed off.

"Yes?" The fairy waited expectantly.

"For... I don't know, questioning you about it in such a way. In that tone." the elfas finished lamely. They walked further along the docks, Philip leading the way to a ship contact from the old days. One that could secure them passage across the channel to London.

Beathan shook his head and chuckled. "You're a wee mad lass, aren't ya', Alayna? Here we are leavin' a trail o' bodies in our wake this last year, breakin' in an' out o' more prisons an' outposts than I can count, an' you're feelin' guilty about my pickin' a few pockets and liftin' a few purses."

"Well, when you put it that way..." Alayna once again didn't finish her trail of thought. Even she had to laugh lightly at the inconsistency of it. "It's not exactly the same, but I see your point. Just don't get caught. We have enough to worry about as it is, without some angry constable chasing after us." She waggled an admonitory finger at him in mock seriousness.

"Me? Caught? Simply outrageous." He huffed as if more offended than he'd ever been in his life. But anyone could likely see the twinkle in his eye.

Ashei giggled again. "I like him," she whispered to Alayna conspiratorially.

"You might be the only one," Philip grunted in response. Apparently, he'd been paying attention to the conversation from a few feet in front of them.

Philip held up a hand. "Here we are."

They stood in front of a nearly dilapidated old ship. Creaking more than most ships that bobbed at the quay, Beathan wasn't sure it would make it out of the harbor, or through a stiff breeze, let alone across the channel. "Ya' sure mate?"

Philip nodded. He looked at them all briefly. "Keep a low profile. I'm going aboard to speak with the captain. Don't draw any attention." He shot a significant look at the fairy, to which Beathan held up his hands and shrugged slightly, in the widest-eyed innocence he could muster. Alayna and the girl nodded in agreement to Philip, while Azir kept his hood so far pulled forward that even in the cloudy grey light of day one could barely see his features. He'd been quiet ever since entering the city. Perhaps he was feeling the same weight of worry that Alayna had mentioned about being so close to the end.

Well the end might be close, but every end was just a beginning. Even death was just the start of the next great adventure. Or so Beathan told himself when he was given a moment to truly ponder the madness of what they were attempting. Attacking outposts without resorting to secrecy. Hoping that the Guild members would retreat to their holdfast in London. Then attacking them again—a fully stocked, fully manned Guild main complex with who knew what kind of arsenal and armory at their disposal. It might be suicide. Or it might not. He'd survived worse in his time—maybe. At the very least it would be exciting.

"Passage for five?" Philip directed his parting question at Alayna. "You're sure?"

Alayna glanced at Ashei. "I'm sure. She's not ready to leave us yet."

"I'm still not convinced it's a good idea," Philip grumbled. And to be honest, Beathan wasn't either. Taking the girl with them as they'd traveled down from the mountains and north through France had been fine at the time. But here they were, about to sail back to England, toward an all out assault on Guild headquarters. And even if everything came off without a hitch, even their allies would pose a danger to the girl. Ashei's blood would taste as sweet as any to many a vampire. But despite their concerns, Alayna had somehow taken charge of the girl. Philip made most important decisions in the company, but Beathan had seen him defer time and again to Alayna when it came to Ashei. This time it was no different.

"As you wish," Philip said with a resigned shrug, and Beathan heard the girl let out a relieved breath. She didn't understand what she was heading into. Otherwise, she wouldn't be so happy to be joining them.

Philip boarded the ship by way of gangplank and disappeared inside the main cabin. He was gone for a surprisingly short amount of time, only a few minutes, before he reappeared and disembarked under the watchful gaze of a few, hard-eyed sailors, to rejoin them on the quay.

"Well?" Azir asked when Philip was standing in front of them.

"It's all settled. We leave with the tide before first light tomorrow."

"That's it? You were only in there minutes," the vampire probed.

Philip shrugged. The captain is an old acquaintance. And he's in my debt. I ridded his cargo hold of an old poltergeist some years ago. And he never got a chance to repay the favor."

"Well lucky for us, now he can," Beathan grinned. "So where to now? I could eat, ya' know. My stomach is grumblin' somethin' awful."

"Fortunate indeed," Philip responded.

"I'm hungry too, and I'm sure Ashei could eat also," Alayna chimed in.

"I've heard of a wonderful blood den in town, caters to all types. Famous across the continent. A wonderful midway stop between Paris and London." Azir volunteered with a nasty smirk.

"I think we'll pass," Alayna stepped close to Ashei subconsciously as she frowned her annoyance at Azir. Beathan couldn't help but laugh. The vampire was almost as good at drawing a response from people as Beathan was himself.

"Agreed," Philip responded. "But we do need to eat, and somewhere to lay low and rest for the rest of the afternoon, before—"

"Before what?" Beathan asked.

"Before we do the second part of why we're here."

"Which is?" Azir flashed his fangs at being left out of the planning.

"Before we hit one last outpost," Philip stated grimly, and with a decisiveness on his face, the kind of commitment to a fight that made most men turn and walk—no run—away when confronted with it. Philip had that quality about him, the ability to inspire fear and doubt into even the most seasoned of hearts. Beathan was glad they were on the same side.

"Is that a good idea?" It was Azir's turn to be the one speaking with annoyance. "So close to our final destination. Do we really want to alert them that we are already almost there—here, or wherever we are?" He muttered, stumbling oddly over his words, in a way that he rarely did with his precise if strong accent.

"A boxer has to take a swing at his opponent, has to take a few risks, if he wants the opposition to swing back, to overextend and leave an opening," Philip said with a shrug.

"We are not boxers," Azir said through clenched teeth.

Beathan was somehow fairly certain that the vampire was more frustrated with not being involved in the decision-making process, than with the actual decision itself.

"No, but we do need an opening. We need them to take a swing."

"Ah, I see mate. We've been hittin' 'em hard all across the continent. We've got 'em where we want 'em, all tucked away in their London complex hidey-hole. But now we need 'em t' send the footsoldiers out, lessen the actual numbers there," Beathan said.

Philip shot him a grateful grin. "At least someone knows some tactics. It's a long shot, they may read our plan and know we're heading straight for them, they may not extend at all, may keep it all in reserve. But it's worth a shot, and it doesn't cost us anything we haven't been doing already for weeks. The risk is the same as it has been since we left Bran Castle."

"Works for me," Alayna said stoutly.

Beathan and Ashei nodded, although Beathan didn't have the heart to question why the girl was nodding. It wasn't like she was going to be allowed anywhere near the actual fighting. After a long pause, Azir finally nodded his agreement, and it was settled.

Philip rubbed his hands together in anticipation, the banging of ships against the dock, the snapping of rigging and sailcloth, providing a background for their conversation. "Alright then. A meal, a rest, and then nightfall. Tonight we hit our last outpost before it's all over."

———

THEY SPENT the rest of the afternoon and evening in a tavern not far from the outpost they planned to hit. They ate and drank and rested into the night. But instead of finding a room at an inn nearby when it got late, they instead quietly slipped out of the building and slunk through the salt-tanged night air toward their destination.

"It'll just be a few blocks," Philip whispered, his voice carrying through the strange stillness of the night, despite the muted tone and the gentle lapping of the tide against the docks.

Beathan looked around uneasily. Cobblestone streets and brick buildings, mixed with shabby, worn down, wooden structures lined the streets. Something in the air tonight prickled his senses. Some intangible instinct. He voiced as much to his companions.

"Somethin' s'off, I can feel it, mate. Are ya' sure we should be doing this tonight?"

"What do you mean?" Alayna answered instead of Philip, her sharp tone, mimicked by Azir's quick look toward Beathan at the statement. The vampire's narrow eyes tightened even further.

Beathan winced slightly at his inability to describe the sensation that was bothering him. "I can't say for certain. It's just a feelin'."

"Not enough," Azir grunted. He flashed his whites in the night air. "While you all ate and drank tonight, I fasted. I have not eaten in too long. I want some Collector blood on my tongue."

Philip pondered Beathan, his eyes weighing risks and benefits. He was a cautious one sometimes, Beathan's friend, but he was also reckless at times. But usually he wasn't cavalier with the lives of his friends. "You really can't put it into words? Can't quantify what you're feeling?"

Beathan shrugged noncommittally. "It's...like a tightness in th' air tonight. Like th' night is drawn taught as a bowstring. Best I can do. I just feel like somethin' is...off. We'd do well t' be careful, whatever we decide t' do."

Alayna and Philip shared a glance. Beathan didn't mind the two of them having their own communications, silent and intimate. But he chanced a glance at the vampire next to him and saw the sourness on his face that could only be related to the look the two of them just shared.

Alayna shrugged in almost the same fashion as Beathan. "Might as well."

"Might as well." Philip answered with a nod.

"So, we're goin' through with it?" Beathan asked, eyebrows raised, a sense of excitement and anticipation replacing the trepidation he had been feeling a moment before. They were his people now. He'd fight with them, regardless of the when and where. So if a fight was in the offing tonight, regardless of his instincts, then he damn well was going to enjoy it.

He winked at his two friends. "Well, it's like me ma always said: 'If your mate's getting' a spankin' you best find a way to get him out o' it or get spanked with him.' She was big on loyalty an' all, me ma, she was indeed." The fairy shook his head with a little laugh. If she could see him now, taking on the Guild, night after night, prison after outpost, how proud she'd be of him. She'd always despised authority of almost any kind.

Alayna grinned his way. "I'm glad you're not dissuaded from the endeavor tonight."

"Me, lass? Never. Can't let a little thing like danger an' instincts get in th' way o' a good fight," he lilted back in the most carefree voice he could muster. "But," he rounded back again solemnly, "th' girl can't be anywhere near it tonight. She'd be better off waitin' at th' boat."

"Agreed," Philip said immediately. Alayna opened her mouth to argue but then seemed to think better of it. Normal risks were one thing, but if they were going to hit a final outpost this close to headquarters in London, and with a nervous sensation on top of it all, then it at least made sense to make sure the girl stayed out of it.

Ashei put up an argument, but she was quickly overridden and sent back to the ship with instructions of who to say she was and wait with the Captain for their return. If they did return. Beathan's instincts were still buzzing. Tonight would be an adventure.

The four of them prowled through the night for the final few blocks toward the outpost. Beathan kept one hand ready to draw a knife and a few of his more important charms and spells in the forefront of his mind —ready to invoke at a moment's notice should they be needed. Silent as a spider stalking its prey in a web, the four of them rounded a corner and saw the torchlit outline of a building just ahead of them.

It was a squat building, sharing its two sidewalls with buildings that towered a few stories over it. A slanted roof to allow water to runoff into the gutter in front of it. Brown and rundown like the rest of this waterfront quarter of Calais, there were two shuttered windows in the front facing wall, and a rickety door that looked like it was about to fall off its hinges.

A fine mist began to sift down, dampening Beathan's dirty blond hair, but even the slight chill it provided was a welcome change from the snow they'd experienced further south and in the mountains. It reminded him of Ireland. Of home.

"Are you sure about this place?" Azir asked, more than a hint of accusation in his voice. "It does not look like much."

"He's not wrong, Philip. It looks like a stiff breeze could cave in its roof. It's ramshackle." Alayna kept her hood up as she spoke, a glint of reddish gold hair peeking out from one side of the hood.

"It's the right place," Philip confirmed calmly. "Not all Guild outposts are manors and mountain strongholds. Sometimes the dingiest place you can find is the best place to hide an operational base. Slums don't attract many strangers—at least not the type of strangers that are difficult to deal with," he amended. "Ready?" Philip breathed, but the question was just a formality because before they could answer he'd already begun striding toward the front door that was practically hanging by its hinges.

Beathan caught a glimpse of motion down the alley to his right, but when he looked there was nothing there. Instincts. But they were committed now. Alayna and Azir were right behind Philip and Beathan sprinted forward to catch up. Ahead of him, Philip put his boot through the door, and it shattered inward, almost seeming to be more rotted than rickety as the door simply disintegrated as much as it broke.

Shouts of alarm came, but Beathan's former Collector friend was already inside and laying waste. The three of them followed behind and made short work of the five men in the front room. Beathan had no time to see the details of his friends' fights as he engaged an almost elderly Collector, greying at the temples, armed with a club like a constable might be. Easy weapon for close fighting, such as inside a building like this.

The club whistled viciously by Beathan's head, but he managed to dodge the first swing with ease, putting his fist through the older man's jaw with an immediate and retaliatory force. But the old man was a tough one. He simply shook his head to clear it and stumped toward Beathan again. And the dance truly began. The man was quick, and he got a few good lashes in with his club, but he was no match for Beathan's charm enhanced speed and agility. The fairy mostly ran circles around him until he dropped the man unconscious to the floor with a smart rap behind the ear with the hilt of his dagger.

"Why didn't you kill him?" Azir growled, and Beathan looked up to see the others looking at him expectantly, having dispatched of their own opponents.

Beathan shrugged self-consciously. "He's an old coot. Didn't seem fair t' end him like this. Fought well, he did. Maybe he deserves one last draught o' beer before he dies."

"You hit him hard enough to keep him down?" Philip asked intensely. When Beathan nodded his affirmation, he continued, "Good enough for me. Let's go."

They wandered further into the rickety building stepping over the bodies of the men they'd downed, waiting expectantly for the next attack. But none came. No other Collectors came out of the shadows.

"Let's check the cells at the back," Philip muttered, and Beathan could hear his friend's uneasiness. This had been altogether too easy. Even a low-level outpost this close to London should have been better guarded. Shouldn't it?

They walked further back through the edifice, lanterns lighting the interior only somewhat as they were spaced too far apart to really overlap their light cover. Alayna grabbed one and carried it with them, holding it aloft as they went to better light their way. They opened a door in the back—or rather Philip ripped it from its hinges as they didn't want to wait to go back and search the guards for the key. Inside was another dimly lit room with a handful of cells. Only two of which were occupied. One had a small, lithe form next to an even smaller one of the same build, and Beathan's heart clenched at the sight of what had to be a mother fairy and her child, clearly the worse for wear as Alayna held the light toward the bars, illuminating a wearied, downtrodden face, bearing cuts and bruises, arms clutching a little girl close to her.

Alayna stepped toward the other occupied cell and when the light fell on the lean, gangly form, Philip stopped dead.

"Stephen! Lad is that you?"

Beathan craned his neck to see around the two of them in front of him. Stephen. He wracked his brain. He should know that name. A young lad, hardly more than a boy appeared in his memory, on a ship in New York, the day he'd first met Philip, years ago now.

"Philip? Sir, is that you?" The boy warded his hand against the lantern as if he'd been held in darkness for long enough that even its meager light was too bright.

Philip was about to answer when the hairs on Beathan's neck prickled. Then it came. Whatever his instincts had warned him of was about to strike. He turned toward the unguarded door to the cell room at their backs, just as the lad yelled a warning. "Behind you, Sir!"

Beathan saw Philip whirling around just as he was, just as Azir and Alayna did. It was only just in time, as a mass of bodies came boiling through the small prison room door. Thin bodies, gaunt men and women with vacant, desperate expressions began hurling themselves into attack, swinging untrained but angry blows at anything that moved. They grasped the bars of the cell door containing the fairy and her child and began yanking and screaming as they did.

It was mayhem. What was this insanity and who were these people? Beathan fended off a wild swing from one as he saw his companions doing the same with others. Another form slipped through the door, close on the heels of the emaciated people. It was large as a donkey, rangy and lean, like the humans—if they could be called that—who had preceded it. Or perhaps they were like it. Those same instincts that had told Beathan that something was off this night, were screaming at him that this was the source of the attack. It tipped back its head and let out a hooting howl of sorts. It was wolf-like, canine in shape, although perhaps more like a coyote than a wolf. And it was even gaunter than the humans who accompanied it. Ribs pointed through skin that barely concealed it, and thin lips peeled back to expose sharp but worn predator's teeth. It howled again and lunged for the cage holding the fairy, its narrow head and neck slipping easily through the bars, only to be stopped at its bony shoulders.

Beathan blocked another blow and gutted a human with his belt knife.

The thin wolf twisted and squirmed feverishly, and something told Beathan that if it had much longer to try, it would find its way through the bars. The terrified wails of the fairy and her child were enough to wrench his heart.

Beathan killed another fanatic man, with shaggy hair and yellow teeth, even as he saw his companions do the same.

"Philip, the cell!" Beathan shouted in concern. If any of them could get a moment free enough to confront whatever beast it was that had led this attack, it would be Philip.

His concern was met with a terse nod from his friend and Philip smashed his way through the man in front of him and moved to engage the creature. Beathan fought a reckless woman, with more desperation than training or ability. She overexposed herself on every swing and Beathan felt almost sorry to cut her throat. But battle was battle and he wasn't going to risk his life by pulling punches and strikes against this hornets' nest of a fight that these people had instigated.

The cell room was a madhouse. Azir was slaking his thirst by ripping out throats. He was particularly effective considering that none of the people had come prepared with wooden stakes necessary for fighting vampires. Alayna was flung against the wall by one of the larger, less shrunken men who had stormed the room, but she recovered quickly and freed a mini crossbow with one sweep of her hand into her cloak and loosed a bolt from close range. It punctured the man's skull through the eye, dropping him like a stone.

Philip swung a massive blow at the side of the beast that was still struggling frantically to get through the bars. It was almost inside, when Philip's fist crumpled two of its showing ribs. It squealed in rage and fear, and quickly retreated out of the bars to turn and face the new threat, limping in pain as it did so, snapping its jaws. It lunged despite its injury. It got a few good snaps in at Philip's face and hands, but the former Collector managed to ward them off with only a few minor cuts before he stepped forward and grabbed the beast around the neck and wrenched. Beathan could hear the helpless squealing of the oversized but emaciated canine as it writhed to try and free itself. There was the crunching of bone as Philip's grip tightened and then Beathan's friend wrenched again and the neck popped. The beast fell dead to the ground and as it did the resistance in the room broke. Thin men and women wailed and pulled out their hair at the dead creature in front of them. Then they ran screaming from the room.

All but one. One dirty, mangy man, thin as the rest of them stood defiantly in the doorway staring them all down, gnashing his teeth like a wild animal. He was the only one of them that Beathan had seen display any human emotion during the mad, wild few minutes since they'd attacked. And the emotion Beathan saw was anger. Desperate, crazed rage. But the man bottled it, inhaled deeply while staring at them as if marking their scent, and then turned and sprinted from the room, hooting a howl in some twisted mimicry of the dead beast on the ground.

"What the hell was that?" Azir swore vibrantly, sending a few more choice curses after the wailing, retreating foes.

Alayna shook her head, just as Beathan himself was doing, but Philip had a sick look on his face. "Chicheface."

"What?" Alayna asked.

"Chicheface. Or as some would call it the Thin Wolf, or the Gaunt Wolf. It's a legend in these parts. I hadn't heard of a sighting in years. They're of the canine variety of beast—as you can clearly see—and they hunt down faithful wives. Or so the myths say. Although, I had thought they usually target humans not fairies." Philip stroked his face as he pondered the scene.

"And the humans?" Azir prompted with a look of disgust at the dead scattered about the room.

Philip shook his head slowly. "I don't know. None of our records speak of followers."

"It's like it was their god or something," a scared voice volunteered from behind them.

Philip whirled back around. "Stephen!" he exclaimed as if he'd forgotten about the boy in the struggle. Philip gripped the corroded metal bars of the cell and ripped them clean from the frame, allowing the boy to step out. Stephen looked at his former master in wonder and no small amount of appreciation.

"You're probably right," Alayna said to the boy. "That kind of fanatic and mindless attack smacks of some kind of faith or deification. And if that's the case, we might be in trouble."

Philip cocked his head and asked the unspoken question. Alayna simply shook her head slightly in regret. "You saw the look in his eyes as he left," she finished with a nervous swallow of her throat. "We killed their god. When you destroy a person's deity you can expect one of two responses: despair or rage. Let's hope it's the former and not the latter."

CHAPTER EIGHTEEN

Alayna looked at the boy, as Stephen shook hands with Philip, but then pulled Philip into a rough embrace before quickly pushing him away again, as if embarrassed for the show of emotion.

"Am I ever glad to see you, Master Philip!" Stephen half mumbled with a wince as one of his steps seemed to bring him a bit of pain.

Philip ignored the honorific and placed a steadying hand on the boy's shoulder.

As he came further into the lamplight, Alayna was forced to reconsider her thoughts of him as a boy. Stephen seemed to have grown even more in the time since they had last seen him in England, on their way to rescue Beathan from St. Thomas prison. Although she supposed that made sense. Lads of his age were apt to growing in fits and bounds, so long as they were eating properly, which to be honest, she wasn't sure he was. It had also been a couple years, more or less, since they'd last seen him. He had to be, what, fifteen now? And his time in the cell had not been kind. Bruises marked his thin face, a face that was only just beginning to sprout some very patchy fuzz. His aching movements implied that a few blows had likely missed his face and struck his body, as well. She hoped it wasn't anything worse. What had earned Stephen a stay in a Guild prison cell? Last time they'd seen him he'd still been Guild, through and through, despite his aiding their quest to save Beathan.

As if on cue to her thoughts, Philip spoke up. "Stephen, what happened?" Her mate cupped the youth's bruised cheek almost tenderly and shook his head in remorse.

Stephen put on a stalwart face, and to his credit, calmly shook off Philip's hand. When he spoke it was matter-of-factly, and almost with a sense of resignation. They all stayed quiet to hear what he had to say.

"It started not long after I saw you last, Sir. Things began changing. When it was you, and James I was apprenticing with, things just sort of felt...right. Okay, as if we were doing something good. Helping people." His words were simply put, the words of a young man trying to sort out his thoughts on a matter.

Stephen wiped a hand back through his hair as he continued, an exhausted action. "But not everyone in the Guild has honor," his voice hardened. "There was a code before—you taught it to me, Master Philip. Capture, don't kill whenever possible. No torture, no unnecessary harm, and definitely only creatures that were dangerous to humans and actively seeking to harm our kind."

This time Philip did interject. "I'm not a Sir or Master any longer, Stephen. You know that. But continue."

The lad shrugged. "Old habit I guess," and he quirked a smile at Alayna's mate. She was touched to see the fondness there, returned by Philip also. He'd told her stories of Stephen, and it had been clear that he'd missed the lad, even if that had all faded to the background these last years, months, first on the run from Collectors and then wreaking havoc on outposts across the continent.

The lad lost his smile. "It's all different now. We kill as often as we capture, and when we do it's a bloodfest. They butcher as much as they kill. Worst of all is the fact that they'll jail any supernatural being they get their hands on these days. Regardless of the danger they pose." He thrust his chin in a nod at the fairy and her child in the cage beside them. "You can let them out by the way. They won't cause you trouble."

"In a minute," Alayna murmured cautiously, "when we've heard the entire story."

Stephen shrugged again. "Not much more to tell. I began asking questions. Trying to figure out what was happening, why it all felt... wrong. They didn't like that. Shipped me off to this rickety outpost, to apprentice with a master that was as likely to have me clean the piss pots as do something useful. And then they showed up with Kylia and her child," he motioned to the fairy again. "I was tasked with feeding them. I heard their story. Kylia told me how they'd been attacked by Collectors for no reason. Her fairy mate told her to run and she did, while he tried to hold the Guild off. Didn't work of course. Too many of them. They killed him and captured her and her young one. They didn't deserve to be locked up!" he almost yelled angrily.

Alayna had kept a side eye on Philip as they listened. She'd seen her mate's face grow hard as he listened to his former apprentice describe so many of the reasons why he'd left the Guild, and now actively combatted them.

"So Stephen, you still haven't exactly told us why you ended up in the cell," Philip said softly, an unspoken question hanging in the air. The importance of this answer might determine how they proceeded.

"Huh," Stephen huffed, "well they locked me up cause I'm not Guild any longer."

"What?" Philip exclaimed.

"Why?" Azir said at the same time.

The two of them looked at each other in annoyance, but Alayna was glad to see that it really was just annoyance now. Most of the real animosity had seemed to thaw between them.

"I tried to free her. It was the right thing to do," Stephen pointed to Kylia. "Much good it did. We were caught trying to escape. I failed," the boy finished bitterly.

"Let me get this straight. You, a lad, not old enough t' be called a man, risked your life t' free a fairy an' her child. What was in it for ya'?" Beathan cocked his head sideways, as if trying to understand.

Stephen looked at him strangely. "I just told you," he spoke slowly, as if confused and trying to make sure Beathan could understand this time. "She needed help. It was the right thing to do."

A light gleamed in Beathan's eyes, and Alayna could tell in an instant that the lad's pure response had endeared himself to the fairy. "Ya've got a friend in me, Stephen." He reached out his hand. "The name's Beathan. I'm a fairy too, or so I've been told," he winked at the lad. "An' I appreciate those who show me kin, kindness."

"You're related to Kylia?" Alayna asked, startled.

"O' course not lass," Beathan smiled a bit quizzically, "but all us fairy-folk stick t'gether. We think o' each other as an extended family."

His hand was still stretching out toward the lad, and Stephen shook it. Beathan smiled and then let go. The fairy looked to be about to say something else but decided not to and ended up simply clapping the lad on the shoulder.

"Well, I think we've heard enough." Philip turned toward the locked cell holding Kylia and her child. He ripped it off of its hinges and tossed the door aside.

"You can come out," Stephen said with the self-assurance of someone much older than his age.

Kylia came forward holding her young child in her arms. A toddler by the looks of it. Alayna was unable to see if it was a boy or a girl fairy child, because the hair was long—which meant nothing. One had only to look at Beathan's long and unkempt hair to see that—and the child had its face buried in its mother's chest.

Kylia stood next to Beathan, as if silently seeking out the comfort of that kinship Beathan had mentioned earlier. "Thank you," she said delicately. Then she flitted forward and placed a peck on the cheek of Stephen, who blushed furiously. "And thank you. Your bravery will not be forgotten."

"So you're leaving then?" Stephen asked, still a rosy red.

Kylia nodded placidly. "Why would I stay a moment longer in this city of men?" She turned and spoke pointedly to Beathan. "You should do the same cousin. We are not meant for brick and mortar, but for oak, and elm, and moss."

"I have a few more things t' finish," Beathan said with a smile.

Kylia nodded and gave him what was almost a half shrug of sorts, before turning and melting away into the darkness of the corridor beyond. A moment more and the quiet patter of her feet were gone also.

"That was a quick exit," Azir grunted.

"Can ya' blame her?" Beathan asked. "She's got a young one t' protect."

Before Alayna could suggest they do the same, a groan from the floor behind her jerked all their heads toward the sound at once. A thin body, lying underneath a pile of a few other gaunt frames, was twitching, and trying to escape, emitting keening, whimpering sounds in its efforts. It sounded less than human.

Philip put a hand out to stop them and stepped forward carefully, cautiously making sure that the person couldn't get free. It was a woman, Alayna saw, and she was bleeding out from a particularly deep wound to the side. Even if she could free herself from the pile of bodies on top of her, she likely wouldn't last long.

"Who are you?" Philip squatted down next to the woman. She bared her teeth angrily, snapping at him like a feral dog. Philip repeated his question and with a stony-face he placed a thumb in her wound eliciting a writing shriek. Alayna clenched her teeth at the pain the woman might feel, feeling a little sick that Philip was questioning her so. But they did need answers.

Finally the woman gave in. Death seemed a certainty for her, but extra pain didn't have to be. "We are the Thinners. We follow the One."

"That *One*?" Philip jerked his bloody thumb unsympathetically toward the dead Chicheface on the floor behind him.

The woman's face crumpled, and Alayna pitied her. The loss of a god couldn't be easy.

"Tell me more. How did you come to worship him?" Philip prodded.

The woman snarled a bit more, until Philip threatened to stick his thumb in her side again. She gave in and spoke between clenched teeth, whether from pain or anger, Alayna wasn't certain. "A generation ago, the One came," she began in a half-crazed fanatic voice. "Many came. Many were changed, absorbed, transformed. Many died. It was only right to worship them. But some left. Only one stayed. The One is he who stayed. We have served him ever since." She giggled hysterically despite the blood leaking from her side.

"What the hell is she talking about, Philip?" Alayna asked sickly. The jumble of words didn't make sense. Her words all seemed to fold in on themselves.

But Philip had a dawning look in his eyes. "I think she's talking about the Great Transformation. It sounds like she's speaking of a home— perhaps her village. Some of the rural villages were hit hard by the Great Transformation. Away from cities and safety. Out of range of many of the Guild outposts many villages were overrun, wiped out in hardly more than a heartbeat if they were unlucky enough to face an onslaught of dangerous creatures."

"But that's not exactly what she's describing," Alayna responded, scratching her head absently. The Thinner—as she called herself—was drifting in and out of consciousness now, seeming close to the end.

"No, it's not," Philip pondered slowly. "But what she's saying still sounds to me like the Great Transformation. There might still be a few old people from her village alive who were present when it happened, making it still a generation ago to her people. Imagine, you live in a superstitious village and a whole raft of non-human entities threaten to overrun you, kill many of you. It might make sense to some to serve them."

"Sounds like this One—th' Chicheface—is th' only one that stuck aroun' though," Beathan mused.

Philip nodded. "It could have been enough upheaval, terror, and superstition to create a delusion—a new deity, a religion, if you will." He shrugged. "At least it seems to have been enough for them. They certainly seemed to have come here on the bidding of that creature." He paused to glance back at the Chicheface that he'd killed. "It's strange, but I've seen wilder things than humans worshipping a beast and adopting some of its attributes and characteristics."

"Well, if it is true, I certainly hope they don't hold a grudge," Alayna said worriedly. Philip nodded pensively, just as the Thinner woman gasped her last breath.

"Can we leave? I just want to get out of here," Stephen asked a bit plaintively, as he looked at the dead Thinners with a shudder of horror. For the first time tonight he actually sounded more his age.

Philip wrapped an arm around the lad's shoulder. "Lead the way."

CHAPTER NINETEEN

Beathan was relieved to see that Philip's acquaintance, Captain Keldrick, had treated Ashei well upon their arrival at the ship. Although the ship was hardly more than a barge really. It was old, sat low in the water, and leaked at the seams much more than Beathan was comfortable. But Philip and the Captain assured them all that it would get them across the channel. Sailing was one thing in which Beathan couldn't claim any sort of expertise, so he had to take their word for it.

The ship had one cabin, where Ashei had been waiting for them, but that belonged to the Captain. As sailors loosed the ropes binding the ship to the dock, Philip led them down below, into a damp cargo hold. They were forced to drape themselves across crates and boxes of goods as best they could. Beathan found the sturdiest box he could and climbed up, resolving that if he had to ride out the short voyage in this dank hold, the least he could do was try and make sure that he stayed as dry as possible —a few inches of water collected at the very bottom of the hold, enough to be uncomfortable but not enough to damage the goods, which were placed on wooden crate platforms of their own, keeping a foot above the wet hold's floor.

"Well, here we are," Philip said with an overly cheery voice. "Safe and sound and on our way to London."

Azir shook his head in disgust and Beathan was inclined to agree with the vampire, who was gingerly picking his way toward a box a little further along in the hold, darker and further from the solitary lamp that lit their little hold. Beathan noticed the lad, Stephen, was eyeing the vampire nervously. He'd clearly picked up on what he was and was unsure of him. At first glance a vampire was a lot more threatening than a half-fairy or an elfas.

"Do we have to stay down here?" Alayna shifted in discomfort as she spoke, wiggling and moving around on her crate like a cat kneading its paws.

Ashei looked hopeful at Alayna's comment, but Beathan knew that hope would die shortly. As soon as Philip answered.

"Unfortunately, love, yes. Keldrick is a good man and owes me a favor. But he knows our crew is strange and wants no part of what we do or where we go. He wants his crew kept separate from us, as well."

"Well he is doing us a favor, so I guess we should acquiesce to his requests," Alayna sighed.

Philip nodded. "Everything sorted with where we're staying when we land?" Philip turned his attention to Beathan who was in charge of their accommodations—if that was even an apt description—when they arrived. He'd spent a time or two in London, growing as wealthy as he'd ever been from such a raft of pockets to pick. So many he'd grown bored, imagine that! He'd even tried his hand at cat burglary at one point during a stay in London but stealing from a house while people were asleep just felt too easy. It lacked all the fun of picking a pocket or lifting a bracelet or ring straight from a person's flesh. It lacked the personal touch.

"Sorted?" Beathan snorted. "It's not like I sent a letter in advance o' our arrival. I just know a spot or two where we can lay low. Squattin' territory. Salynksa an' her ilk know th' few locations I've got in mind. She'll meet us there when she an' th' Shade King arrive with our reinforcements. We discussed it before we left Transylvania."

Philip grunted a sort of approval and with that he deemed the discussion closed and shut his eyes. Alayna curled up next to him. Beathan decided he might as well try to sleep also, seeing as how it had been a long night and not a wink of sleep to show for it. He yawned and stretched loudly. Come to think of it, he could hardly remember being this tired. Not since the time he'd stayed up nearly three days straight staking out a gnome nest. Beathan grinned at the memory.

Gnomes were homebodies and particularly territorial about where they resided. And when they left it was only very irregularly and for a short span of time. He'd been hoping to crawl inside and snatch a cache of mushrooms known to cause mild delusions and hallucinations—difficult for any but gnomes to locate. He'd watched that hole in the ground for days on end waiting for the inhabitants to leave for a new round of foraging. He'd been so tired once he'd crawled inside that he had almost fallen asleep. Well he might have, come to think of it, because those nosy gnomes had been there when he'd begun his escape, mushrooms in hand, and had caused him a multitude of problems.

Gnomes had a nasty sense of revenge. Beathan still had a few pricks and scars on his body from that encounter.

As Beathan slid off to sleep, as uncomfortable as he could ever remember being, the memory of those mushrooms made him smile. The gentle swaying of the ship, wallowing through the channel, rocked him into unconsciousness.

When he awoke some time later, he noticed cracks of light were seeping in through a few seams in the hold near the roof. Day had come. Surprisingly, most people were still asleep, but Ashei had clambered upon a box next to Stephen and the two were talking low and fast as if they'd been holding each other in their confidence their entire lives. Beathan's heart warmed at the sight. The lad was a good lad, fighting for those who needed it, like that fairy and her child in Calais. Likely more than a little of Philip had rubbed off on him during their few years together. And Ashei had been through enough in her short life that she deserved a friend close to her in age. Come to think of it, she might not be all that much older than the lad herself.

Beathan glanced over at Alayna curled up beside Philip and realized as he saw a warm glow in one cracked eye as she looked at the same sight as him, that she wasn't as deep in slumber as she seemed to be. A small smile formed on her face watching the two youths before she closed the eye again.

Beathan figured there was nothing else to do but sleep, so he willed himself back into the embrace of unconsciousness. It might not be long before they wouldn't get any sleep at all.

———

WHEN THEY ARRIVED, Captain Keldrick insisted they help unload his cargo—as part of their payment he said with a sour grunt—and Philip instructed them to follow orders. It didn't take long, and it also allowed them to blend in. A few extra hands—even smaller bodies like the two youths—could go unnoticed by crowds if they were mixed in with a bunch of other bodies doing the same thing. They kept their heads down and hoods up. It was late afternoon when they docked and the sun behind their heads would make them little more than dark outlines to anybody paying attention.

They finished helping and Philip said his farewells to the captain, shaking the man's hand as they left.

"After you," Philip indicated with one hand for Beathan to take the lead.

Beathan stepped up his pace to walk in front, a few of his jangles, as he liked to think of them, clinked and tinkled as he walked. He breathed in the stink of London and a smile came to his face. Ahh London, a city with more marks than good sense, where people were so practical and steadfast in disbelieving of magic that a being like Beathan with a few advantages at his fingertips could quite literally make a killing. The grin stayed as he led the group through a warren of narrow streets and alleys, ignoring the suspicious looks of passersby.

When they reached a crumbling brick building, with moss growing on the sides and a broken-down sign swinging at an angle from a solitary hinge, he stopped.

"Well, here we are, one o' me dear ol' home sweet homes whenever I happen t' chance through dreary London!"

"A run-down building?" Azir asked incredulously. "You people do enjoy living rough." The vampire shook his head in disgust.

First the cargo hold and now this. Beathan smirked as they followed him into the empty building. Or at least he hoped it would be empty. He was tired and didn't fancy the walk to his second hidey-hole in the city— as he thought of them.

Luck was with them and the abandoned building was vacant of anyone or anything. Beathan led them deep within, away from the sounds of the street. A few caved in rooms had open air to the sky, but most of the building was intact. There were even a couple of rickety chairs for sitting. They'd have to share those.

"Fortune shines on us." Beathan grinned and added, "As luck would have it, our first stop is th' right stop. An' that wily vixen Salynska will come here first, I made sure o' it."

"When exactly are they meeting us?" Alayna asked, somewhere between Beathan and Philip.

Philip was the one to answer. "We were shooting for a few days window of time, which we made. They'll likely be here within a day or two—if they kept to their own schedule. Their coordinated assaults on the outposts I gave them across the continent will have taken them much further afield than our route to get here to London." Heads nodded all around as they all listened to his answer.

And then there was really nothing to do but have one person set about preparing a cold meal from the little bit of bread and cheese that they had on them. The task fell to Philip, who commandeered Stephen for help. The rest of them, with the exception of Ashei, set about tending to their weapons. Polishing out nicks in blades, oiling, sharpening. Alayna restrung one of her mini crossbows.

Beathan kept an ear trained on Philip and Stephen as he worked. "What will you do now?" He heard Philip ask the lad.

Beathan chanced a glance over at the two of them. Eavesdropping was never polite, but as his ma had always said: 'you can be polite, or you can be alive'. She'd had a dark streak his ma did, Beathan thought with a fond grin. And anyway, he was part fairy, and old habits died hard.

"I don't really know, Sir—Philip," Stephen corrected himself. "I can't —I don't want to go back to the Guild. It feels wrong."

Philip nodded to the boy. "It'll be dangerous what we're doing. I'm not sure I want you to come along."

"I can help! I can fight. You know they start training apprentices in combat at fifteen," the desperation in the lad's voice was palpable.

Philip ruffled Stephen's hair. "I know, I know. Calm down. I'll think on it." And then in a joking voice he elbowed the lad good-naturedly. "What, has no one ever shown you how to cut cheese before? Give me that" Philip rolled his eyes and Stephen chuckled, as Philip took the knife from his hands.

Beathan stole a glance across the room and saw a warm look on Alayna's face as she watched Philip with Stephen. Dare he call it almost a motherly look? One glance at Azir's face said the vampire had noticed the same look on Alayna and sourly stood and walked away.

The vampire was still missing when Beathan, Alayna, and Ashei joined Philip and Stephen around the meager meal. Beathan had a sinking feeling that even if they managed to survive this cockamamie scheme to take down the Collectors Guild, their companionship would likely not survive, as well.

CHAPTER TWENTY

Philip watched as Stephen tossed a knife at the wall. The boy—young man, he corrected himself—was working more on form than power. His training as a solider in the Guild would have only just begun so he was still in the rudimentary phase of learning. It had taken many years of training and practice before Philip had felt accomplished enough to protect himself in a real fight. But they had some time to kill until Dracula and his henchmen—their allies—arrived. It should be soon. Hopefully. Philip didn't want to wait much longer. They wanted the Guild leaders aware of the danger, clustered together in their main headquarters, but they didn't want the Collectors Guild to find them here in London before their reinforcements arrived. If that happened, it could be over before the Shade King even arrived.

"Good, Stephen. Don't forget to flick your wrist when you release." Philip slapped the lad on the shoulder, a cue for him to go retrieve the knives laying on the ground before the rotten wall. None of them had found their mark and stuck. Philip grinned despite himself, although he was quick to hide the smile when Stephen turned around. Young men could be touchy when it came to their pride.

A tentative tug on the back of his tunic caused him to turn around. It was Ashei, and she was curled in on herself even as she stood there. She rarely spoke much to Philip. He supposed their first encounter in the mountains when she'd seen him in such a terrifying clash with that bogeyman had made him a fearsome figure in her eyes. Someone to be cautious of. He couldn't blame her. She'd suffered enough at the hands of those stronger than her. She was probably smart to be careful.

"Yes, Ashei?"

"Mr. Philip—" she began.

"You don't need to call me that," he corrected her as gently as he could.

She swallowed at his interruption but didn't cower back any further so he supposed that meant he'd managed to keep his face and tone as calm and neutral as possible.

"Mr—err Philip," she continued. "Could you show me too? Alayna said you might if I asked."

"Show you what?" he asked with eyes narrowing.

She didn't answer, she just pointed a finger toward Stephen walking back with the blades.

Philip opened his mouth slightly in understanding. "Ahh. And why do you want to learn?" It never hurt to ascertain someone's motives.

A strange steel crept into Ashei's voice, something Philip wasn't accustomed to hearing. "So I can defend myself. Protect myself from Collectors or anybody who would want to—to hurt me again." Tears began welling up in her eyes, and Philip winced as Alayna shot him an annoyed look. If Ashei burst into tears on his watch, Alayna would not be pleased.

"Easy, lass, of course I'll teach you." Philip put a comforting hand on her shoulder and was glad to see that she didn't pull away from his friendly touch. She was still skittish but growing less so by the day. In leaps and bounds really, since Stephen had arrived. The lad and she had become fast friends, despite their opposite races and upbringings.

Philip spent the next half hour or so instructing the youths as he had once been instructed himself. He showed them footwork, techniques, how to sight your target without focusing your eyes in on one spot too much—many a warrior had died for tunnel vision and forgetting to keep an eye on the periphery—and as much as he felt they could handle. Alayna and Beathan stepped in to help after a time, and Azir watched from his seat a few yards away, making cynical comments about how they'd end up dead, or worse a meal, if they didn't learn quickly.

Philip ignored the vampire's acerbic comments. He knew the vampire was on edge because the Shade King was returning. Dracula seemed to frighten him more than anyone else for some reason.

Finally when the others had sat back down, and it was just Philip and Stephen again, Philip broached the subject he'd been speaking with the lad about earlier.

"I'm not sure you and Ashei shouldn't clear out of here before the vampires arrive."

Stephen lifted his head up indignantly. "I don't need to run."

Philip sighed. Youthful pride. "It's not running lad it's simply leaving a fight that isn't yours. Especially if your allies are as dangerous as your foes."

"But it is my fight, I'm a member of the Guild more recently than you! Or had you forgotten?" Stephen muttered hotly. "I want to see changes made too. As much as you all do."

Philip pursed his lips. "Still, it's an iffy fight at best. We're taking on the might of the Guild, in their territory. I'm not even sure we'll accomplish our aims, let alone make it out alive."

Stephen shook his head stubbornly. "I'm not leaving. Not again. You got rid of me in New York, and I didn't come with you to St. Thomas prison to free Beathan. This time I'm sticking around for the fight." He slapped his chest with bravado and this time Philip sighed even more loudly.

"Those were different, you were literally still a child then—" Philip began.

"Well, I'm not anymore, am I?" Stephen tossed the knife in the air rather recklessly and then caught it by the hilt.

Philip shook his head and fought to keep from rolling his eyes. "Have you been taking secret lessons from Beathan?" He grumbled. "Such a flair for the dramatics."

"Does that mean I can stay?" Stephen asked with a breathless smile.

"Against my better judgment, yes."

"Me too?" Ashei's voice from behind him asked.

Philip turned around, looking for Alayna's confirmation, and when he got it, he nodded to the girl. "I suppose. But no fighting, either of you! Strictly lookout work, and scouting. Stephen if you get caught you might still be able to claim Guild membership and slip away unscathed. And you, Ashei, well don't get caught," Philip finished lamely, and couldn't help but feel like keeping them around was going to end badly. But if this was what Alayna wanted, and what the two of them wished, then they could use the extra sets of eyes and ears. When you were outmanned you didn't turn help away.

As the conversation ended, a slither of soft feet disturbed the dust and pebbles of the rooms beyond. Instantly tense, Philip and all the others grasped weapons and waited nervously to see who made the noise.

When dark haired Salynksa poked her head through the door with a haughty stare, Philip lowered his weapons, although he still kept a hand near to one of his wooden stakes. More and more vampires piled in through the doorway. They must have been a silent black wave, sneaking through the night streets of the city.

Their army had arrived.

———

"TOOK YOU LONG ENOUGH. We've been waiting forever," Philip grunted. Although it really hadn't. The vampires had arrived within the allotted timeframe that had been agreed upon before leaving their eastern stronghold.

Salynksa sneered. "Wrap yourself up in those lies and complaints, perhaps they'll protect you when the battle comes. We both know I'm here when I said I would be."

"And where is the Shade King?" Philip followed up flexing his hands as he looked at the vampire. He had to continually remind himself that these were his allies not his enemies. Instincts were screaming otherwise.

Azir's head shot up as Philip asked the question. Perhaps he was still concerned about being held accountable for the death of The Alchemist.

Salynksa looked scornfully at Philip before deigning to answer. "I do not keep tabs on The One Who Rules." Philip narrowed his eyebrows and stepped just an inch closer, silently daring her to speak in that haughty tone again. Apparently, Salynksa had noticed the danger and swallowed before continuing on with a slightly rushed voice. "But, we split our forces, as was planned. My Master led one prong and I the other. Just as you led the third portion of our trident attack. I am certain he will not be far behind."

The vampire was right. As the two groups occupied the space together uneasily, spreading out and covering the many empty rooms in this dilapidated old building, Dracula arrived, shaking a bit of water from his hair. London was rainy. Philip was not surprised.

Stillness followed the Shade King's arrival, even though he didn't say a word. Fear and quiet seemed to ripple through the room and even into the chambers beyond, vampires bowing their heads and shuffling back against the walls. Even Philip's group hushed and tensed as he strutted casually through the room.

Philip stepped forward to meet him. The ancient eyes bored into him, and Philip forced himself to stand tall, show no fear, even though his senses were practically shrieking that an apex predator had just entered the room, a predator that most certainly looked upon him as prey. The shadow that had seemed to accompany Dracula during their time in the castle was not present and Philip could see the mottled midnight streaks on his skin, lending a darkness to the vampire king's paleness.

They faced off for a long moment before the Shade King bared his teeth in less of a smile than a snarl and said placidly, "I've always hated how positively wet London is—was, as far back as I can remember."

A reminder to Philip. *I am old, strong, and I can crush you when I please without the slightest hesitation or remorse.*

"It's always been like this. That's why I try and make sure to stay away." Philip bared his own teeth.

"Indeed," was all Dracula said as he held the eye contact for a little bit longer than was necessary.

"Well Mr. Kingliness, where's the rest o' your army?" Beathan had crept up beside Philip. Philip wasn't sure if he was glad or not for the interjection. It was likely a support for Philip, but Philip couldn't help but feel that if, or when, the time came to handle Dracula, it would somehow be squarely on his shoulders. It might even make the vampire look at him with less respect if he allowed Beathan to squirm his way into their one-on-one discussions.

But it was done now, and there was no taking it back. Philip waited for Dracula to respond, and he might have been imagining it, but the king certainly looked hungrier to him than he had a moment earlier.

"They are camped in another underground *castle* like this one," the Shade King responded with a sarcastic twist of his mouth as he took in their grubby surroundings. "They would not have fit inside here with Salynksa's party already arrived."

Philip bristled at the king's comment. "We wanted to stay out of notice once we arrived in London, hence these ramshackle quarters. I hope you did the same."

Dracula smirked at Philip, seeing he'd struck a nerve. "We're children of the night, Collector, even en masse we can move unnoticed by the light of the moon. Now shall we get to more pressing business?"

"Like?" Philip asked, nostrils flaring. He prided himself on his demeanor; calm and collected, like any good soldier. And yet, somehow this ages old vampire had figured out just how to get under his skin. Philip was always on edge around the king, whether from annoyance or attention to danger, or both. And Philip suspected that Dracula preferred it just so. Keeping one's enemy off guard and out of sorts was an old tactic.

And aren't we allies? Philip asked himself, bitterly. Only for the near future. Beyond that Philip had no doubt he and the vampires would go back to being exactly what they had been prior to this arrangement.

"Like, final stage tactics and planning," Dracula responded smoothly.

"I'm a wee bit surprised ya' made the trip over here yourself," Beathan interjected once again, perhaps realizing just how close to an angry precipice Philip was. "I always supposed kings made a point o' not doin' anythin' they couldn't order someone else t' do."

Dracula smiled at Beathan before flicking his eyes to Philip, and there was nothing friendly in his face. "I wanted to keep my eye on certain... matters. Matters only I can attend to."

The threat was hidden but it was there. The king would come after him when this was over. Perhaps the moment the Guild leaders were done. Philip swallowed back the fear. He could practically taste it. What was it about Dracula that made him react so? He'd faced down plenty of deranged creatures and beings before.

"Well let's get on with it then," Philip said gruffly to mask his emotions. The vampires of lesser importance inhabited the other rooms of the building, clearing the one they currently occupied. A few of them prowled out into the night, no doubt looking for a snack. Philip's stomach clenched angrily at the thought.

He turned his attention back to the circle of people before him. Lacking a table, they had turned to drawing a rudimentary map in the dust of the floor. A squiggly line representing the river Thames and a few hastily sketched out shapes for various burrows and buildings of note.

"Shouldn't we send the children out to play?" Salynksa snorted, as she glanced at Ashei and Stephen, flicking her fangs out.

Philip looked over at them also and felt a little sick to see the revulsion and disgust on both of the youth's faces. Clearly, they weren't prepared for the allies they'd signed on to assist in this venture. Stephen shot Philip a look that bordered on betrayal.

Philip turned away and addressed Salynksa. "As long as your kind is around, I'll keep them close. But thanks for the concern." The vampire smirked. Alayna hovered a step closer to the two younger ones.

"Enough," the Shade King said quietly, but with force. Apparently, all joking matters were off now. Salynksa and the few lieutenants trusted to lead the vampire cohorts immediately went silent and smoothed their faces into masks. Philip had never seen such immediate and forceful obedience. Not even to high up Guild leaders. Dracula inspired fear like nobody he'd ever known. To be able to terrify his vampire brethren meant he must be fearsome indeed. Philip found himself wondering what that would look like to come up against. He also found himself positing that he might find out the answer, sooner rather than later.

"Do you care to finally share the location of Guild headquarters with us? You told us the targets to hit across the continent but held on to our final destination." The Shade King's mouth twisted and for once Philip could see that he'd gotten under the king's skin and not the other way around. It was a welcome sensation.

Philip smiled his most friendly and mocking smile. "I had to make sure I was still needed, come the end."

"Well, you are needed. Out with it," Dracula grated.

The main Guild complex is somewhat of a bunker. It has a couple floors above ground and attached to a small building, but the majority of it is subterranean, with portions of it stretching even under the Thames."

"Where?" Salynksa asked, her eyes glued to the rough map in the dust —a military commander planning her assault.

Philip drew a rather large circle in the grime of the floor.

"That's large enough to house a small city!" she exclaimed fanged jaws flexing in anticipation.

"Why do you think we made this arrangement?" Alayna purred sweetly. "It certainly wasn't for your pretty faces. We need the bodies. We need the army to sack this underground fortress."

"Yes, but where is the entrance?" Dracula swore as he asked, "You've marked out an area too large to assault all at once. We'll need the right entry point."

"I'll be holding on to that piece of information until we get there. You can just play follow the leader," Philip said nonchalantly, and couldn't help but love the wink that Beathan threw the vampire's way as Philip said it. "I'll hold that crucial piece of information until the end. Nothing's changed."

Dracula stared at him for what seemed an age, and his lieutenants grew restless and turned beady black eyes on Philip and his crew. Finally Dracula acquiesced with a slight nod of his head. Philip breathed a sigh of relief. He'd just guaranteed his company's survival until at least the moment of battle, the moment of assault, but beyond that, he had no doubt the Shade King would throw everything he had at Philip as soon as the Guild's threat was nullified. He wouldn't appreciate being made to acquiesce to anything in front of his subjects. Rulers never liked being forced into humility.

"So multiple assault forces? Or shall we simply charge their gate and storm their fortress all at once?" Dracula sounded almost exasperated. Without this crucial final detail it left the tactics and planning squarely on Philip's shoulders, the one who had that information necessary to make such decisions.

Philip paused. He grimaced slightly. "It isn't a gate in the classic sense of the word, but yes, I think a full-frontal assault will work best. Hit them hard, hit them fast, and don't let them recover."

"And how do we even know the Guild leaders—our primary targets— are even there? How do we know our plan worked?" This time it was Azir asking the question.

Philip winced again. "It's too late to hit them tonight, which means we'll need to wait until tomorrow night. I was going to sneak in myself during the day tomorrow, and verify, but now I think another might be better suited. I'm persona non grata within the Guild right now. I might be recognized."

"An' who'd be better, mate?" Beathan asked curiously. "I've been known to wiggle me way in an' out o' a hole a time o' two, but I think Collectors would realize I'm not one o' them." He indicated his shabby clothes, looking like a traveling show person from a decade prior, bracelets and necklaces jumbled and clinking at his wrists and neck.

"Not you, friend," Philip said. He slowly turned to look at Stephen.

"You cannot be serious," Dracula scoffed. Even Alayna looked alarmed at what Philip was implying. But the lad simply stiffened his back, put on a proud smile, and nodded his head.

Philip nodded back.

"That's it then. Tomorrow night, assuming all's to plan, we hit them with everything we've got—where I say. But first, to verify, Stephen goes in."

CHAPTER TWENTY-ONE

S tephen was gone for only a couple hours before he returned, a jaunty smile on the lad's face as if he'd just pulled a prank rather than completed a dangerous mission. The invincibility of youth. Only someone his age or younger could forget that mere days ago they'd been imprisoned by the Guild alongside a fairy with a real chance of death awaiting them.

The lad approached Philip, but Alayna stepped up beside her love to hear the report. Dracula, obviously annoyed at not being the sole focus of the reconnaissance information, did the same. Alayna stifled a grin. As terrified as she was of the Shade King—and most assuredly, she was—it was still fun to see him navigate the waters around co-leading this venture with Philip. In the vampire's eyes, Philip was likely nothing more than a one-time foot soldier for an organization he hated. He hadn't even been a leader in the Guild before he fled. It must rankle the king that her mate was somehow on even footing with him.

Stephen appraised the situation as people of varying importance clustered around him to hear. However the clumps of gathered people left room around Philip and Dracula. The Shade King quite obviously owned the place of deepest fear in his subjects' hearts, but surprisingly— or perhaps not, considering all she'd seen and done with her mate—Philip was eyed with considerable respect. Amongst the unknown vampires especially, there was a clear trepidation to cross him. Dracula's minions was how Alayna thought of them. Sure, Salynksa and her ilk weren't quite so cautious around Philip, but the majority of the vampires were. And with good reason. Alayna had seen the aftermath of Philip's attack on the menagerie. He'd almost singlehandedly torn through an entire compound by himself before finally being subdued.

"Ready, lad?" Philip prompted with an intent but calm nod to the boy.

Stephen returned the nod and flashed that grin of his that said he clearly did not fully comprehend the situation at hand. Did the lad wink also? If he had, it had been hardly more than a flicker. He'd been spending too much time around Beathan these last few days.

"All went according to plan, Sir," Stephen began, and this time Alayna noticed that Philip didn't correct the appellation. "Didn't even have to sneak in. So many Collectors and other Guild members being recalled from all over the continent that credentials are hardly ever checked." The lad shrugged, "Even if they had though, mine likely would have checked out. I wasn't in that cage too many days before you rescued me. It's unlikely the outpost in Calais sent word back to headquarters about my arrest yet."

"The details?" the Shade King asked with a crisp sort of irritation.

Stephen glanced at the king of the vampires, swallowed, but then clearly addressed Philip again. Alayna could have chortled at the look on Dracula's face.

"Sir, I couldn't infiltrate all levels, but I saw and heard enough to confirm what we suspected."

Philip raised his eyebrows in question, his shoulder length brown hair swaying slightly as he leaned toward the lad in subconscious tension and anticipation.

Stephen continued seamlessly. "The Guild has been pulling members back in numbers unseen since the Great Transformation. More than you might have suspected, possibly," the youth's features flickered with worry, the only sign of nerves he'd shown. "There's a whole lot of them in the complex. Nearly all the fighting men who are worth a damn have been called back. I'd say your ploy worked. You sheep-dogged them well and good sir."

"And the leaders? Helmsted?" Alayna interjected, trying to keep the desperation from her voice. She wanted that bitch more than all the rest of the Guild combined—perhaps a little too much, since this was supposed to be about more than revenge. But after what Helmsted had put her through at the menagerie, it was all Alayna could do not to gnash her teeth at the thought of the woman.

Stephen ran a hand through his hair as if thinking through his next words. "No sightings of her. I did see a few Guild leaders I'd seen before, back when I was stationed in the north of England, though, so I have visual confirmation of some of them."

"If some are here, likely they all are, especially if numbers are so large within the compound. They'd not leave their personal armies behind if they felt threatened," Philip murmured thoughtfully.

Stephen nodded his agreement. "My assessment exactly, Sir. Besides, while I don't have a visual, I did overhear Helmsted's name in conversation quite a few times. It sounds like she's grabbed the reins well and truly now. It appears that many within the Council defer to her judgment. At least that's what rumor says among the lower ranks."

"Foot soldiers often have a better sense o' th' truth than one might expect," Beathan said. "Find th' lowest soldier t' get a true pulse o' th' army, I always say."

"Indeed," the Shade King leaned in toward Stephen. "It seems our strategy has paid off."

Philip nodded slowly. "It's the best we're going to get, I think. We can't wait for confirmation. There are too many of us, eventually our presence in the city will be noticed—especially with your lot having to feed now and then."

Salynksa gave Philip a toothy grin that was not at all friendly. Dracula eyed Stephen. "It appears the lad has accomplished his task then and done it quite well." The vampire narrowed his eyes for a second and then shot a slight smile at Philip before continuing. "It seems your future with the Guild is uncertain at best at the moment, Stephen. Should you ever need work, I'm sure I can find some use for a boy of your talents."

Alayna involuntarily took a step forward. She'd only spent brief periods of time around Stephen, now and a couple years ago on their way to rescue Beathan, but both times he'd shown astounding courage for one his age. And a brain to match. Plus, he'd somehow gotten Ashei to giggle regularly these past few days, not an easy feat. Stephen had endeared himself to Alayna.

Philip quietly slid a hand into hers as she stepped parallel to him, effectively halting her in her tracks. He was composed as ever. "I think we can provide for him ourselves, thanks."

"At least let the boy answer," Dracula spread his hands apart welcomingly.

All eyes shot to Stephen again, the center of attention, perhaps even more so than when he'd been reporting. The lad swallowed again, his face pale and nervous. Facing the hungry eyes of so many vampires before even reaching adulthood would have sent Alayna quaking to the floor in a puddle of emotions when she'd been a youth. But that had been a different time, a completely different Alayna.

Stephen gathered himself, glanced at Beathan of all people, then visibly smoothed the concern from his face. "I thank you for the offer... your Majesty?"—Alayna realized none of them really knew what appellation to give to the king of the vampires. His subjects called him master, but Alayna would be damned if she'd ever do that—"but I think I can fend for myself. Besides, I have a feeling that a snack like me wouldn't live long in your court, regardless of how useful I was. Accidents probably have a way of happening." Stephen finished with a cocky grin—Alayna wasn't sure where he'd pulled it from—and managed to look the Shade King in the eyes.

She held her breath, insulting the king of the vampires, their main ally, on the eve of battle was the last thing they needed. On the other hand, she'd never let the boy go with them, so she was glad he'd said what he said. The silence hung in the air after Stephen's words, before shockingly the king laughed.

It was a dark laugh, filled with genuine mirth, but a mirth that was not one she'd want to hear without the support of allies nearby to defend her.

"A quick wit too," Dracula proclaimed. "It's a shame. You'd have done well with me. Although, I won't dispute the logic of your thinking." The king paused, and eyed the boy darkly, leaning in to loom somewhat menacingly. "But just remember, those 'accidents' you mentioned can have a way of happening regardless of where people are working."

All self-assuredness left the lad's face as he blanched, perhaps realizing just how careless an attitude had led him to say such things to the king of the vampires himself. Stephen mumbled something and then nodded to them all before slipping behind Philip.

Dracula chuckled once more. "Again he shows brains, and an instinct for danger. A shame, a real shame..."

"Can we continue?" Philip said a bit too forcefully, causing the Shade

King's eyes to snap back to him with the weight of hundreds of years of bloodletting and pain.

"By all means," the king motioned with a sinister look in his eyes. Alayna was absolutely certain in that moment that regardless of the mirth he'd just shown, and the offer of work for Stephen, that Dracula had absolutely no intention of letting Philip live past the end of this war. Past the end of tomorrow really when hopefully they'd have completed their successful assault on the Guild and brought it to its knees. No, the Shade King saw the continent as ripe for the taking, if the Guild could be decapitated as they planned. He wouldn't, couldn't, allow any to remain to stand against him once that day came.

From the way Philip was staring at the king, sizing him up, Alayna could also tell with a flash of dread and a cold sweat, that her mate was thinking the exact same thing only from the opposite perspective. She looked at it from a military perspective, a soldier—no a general's line of thought—who wouldn't want to take the opportunity to nullify not one but two great foes with the same stroke?

Yes, Philip was planning something—or at least preparing something —similar to the Shade King.

After their assault tonight alliances would change. Come tomorrow morning a power swing would be in place. Alayna swallowed back her fear.

Neither Dracula nor Philip expected—or intended—for the other to live beyond tonight's battle.

———

THEY PASSED the rest of the day planning the night's assault. It was fairly straightforward. Philip was still keeping the main entry a secret, and keeping Stephen close also, since the boy knew too. Alayna listened as Philip and Dracula haggled over the plan. Back and forth, Philip never budging as the king continuously prodded for the information he wanted.

Alayna understood Philip's hesitance. After her instincts had gone wild earlier, she had no doubt that as soon as Dracula had what he wanted from them—or at least from Philip—he'd see no point in keeping him alive. Philip was holding his cards close. Grudgingly the Shade King had to agree to let Philip lead the force alongside him.

As twilight fell, Alayna was shaken from her thoughts by the approach of Azir. The hybrid had been strangely reticent to talk with her of late. She found she missed him. As she grew back together with Philip, it appeared her friendship with the vampire was doomed to suffer.

"I feel like I haven't spoken with you in quite some time," Alayna said, slicing through the awkwardness as best she could, with a blunt statement.

Azir seemed to appreciate her efforts, because he answered with a grin, even if it was strained. "Things are coming to a head. Tonight is what we have been working toward for months now. You will finally have the revenge you want on Helmsted."

"*We* will, Azir. We'll have the revenge we want. You were in the menagerie with me."

He looked at her with the oddest expression on his face, almost wistful. "I have not forgotten, Alayna. It was a horror show, for sure, but strangely I do not look upon my time there with nearly so much hatred as you."

Alayna contorted her face in confusion. "What kind of nonsense? We were tortured!"

Azir smiled again, this time almost sadly. "Ah yes. But oddly enough, I find myself remembering it more for the fact that it was the only time I've ever spent alone with you."

Alayna felt the words hit her chest like an anvil. Not now. This was not the time—on the eve of battle—to have this conversation.

Azir seemed to read her mind. "It is the only time we have left to speak of this. We may soon be dead."

"The plan will work, we have strong numbers, and the element of surprise," Alayna debated, desperately hoping to avoid what she knew was coming.

"Surprise?" Azir quirked his eyebrows up in scorn. "Come now, Alayna, you are not a simpleton to trick your mind into believing something simply because you wish it true. Our gambit across the continent was effective. Their numbers are here, en masse. We may have the initial moment of surprise when we attack, but do not fool yourself. They know we are coming."

"Your point?"

"My point," Azir paused dramatically, "is that if there are things that must be said, then now is the time to say them."

"Please, Azir," she whispered, "let's not do this. There's nothing to be said."

Even though she could tell that he'd expected and prepared himself for such a response, she could tell that Azir—the normally cold, and aloof hybrid who had an unspoken connection with her and had saved her life —was crestfallen.

"I see. Well, I suppose that is that then," the hybrid sighed bitterly.

"Maybe in another lifetime, under different circumstances these feelings would be enough, Azir. But not now, not this time."

The vampire took a deep breath as if her words had freed him somehow. "At least you admit that there are feelings." He turned to walk away.

Alayna found herself almost reaching out. "Azir?"

He turned back and waited expectantly for her to continue.

"Are you sure you want to stay—now that you know definitively where I stand?" She mumbled. "It's not too late for you too leave."

He sighed again. "I have come this far, my dear, I might as well stick around for the whole show," he said with a sardonic twist to his mouth. Then he melted off into the shadows of the room, amongst a clump of his own kind.

Alayna watched him go, feeling dirty and guilty for some reason. But there was no time to wallow in emotions, however, because Salynksa's voice echoed through the room.

"Alright, it's our time now, the dark of night. Twilight is settling across the unsuspecting city. Glory and payback is waiting for us, and a tiny little thing called the Collectors Guild headquarters is all that stands in our way," her mocking voice was caustic to Alayna's ears, and for what might be the last time Alayna felt sick to her stomach that these creatures were her allies. They were horrible.

No, not all of them, she corrected herself, as unwillingly her eyes searched for Azir, her friend, amongst the crowd.

Vampires stood at attention and prepared themselves to move. Alayna wound her way through the people back to the small clump of her friends near the room's exit. Philip, and all the rest, even Azir were waiting.

"You're leaving," Philip was saying firmly to Stephen. "And you also, Ashei. My allowing you to come and help, never included the idea that you'd stick around for the actual assault."

"You can't make me, Sir," Stephen was arguing almost shrilly. The harder he argued to stay, the more his voice warbled and the younger he seemed. Alayna swallowed back the pain that his face and Ashei's face gave her. Philip was right, this was no place for two youths, not yet into adulthood.

"You'll die if you stay," Philip said, his voice brooking no nonsense, no questions. "You've done your part. It's time for you to leave." Alayna saw a tear forming in the corner of Stephen's eye. He'd been left on his own by Philip on multiple occasions. She'd seen the way he looked at her love, like a father or a worshipped older brother at the very least. But Philip was right.

"Ashei will need help getting back home to her people," Alayna said quietly. "Perhaps you can escort her there. Help keep her safe—keep each other safe," Alayna amended.

Stephen eyed her sullenly, but her words seemed to have quelled the objections. Whatever he might be feeling now, she knew the youth cared about the elfas girl, Ashei. The ploy might get them both out of the way, and on a safer course.

Alayna turned to the elfas girl who'd fallen into her care somehow. "It's time to leave, Ashei." She hugged the girl tightly, feeling tears on her neck as the girl buried her face in Alayna.

"We'll see each other again soon. I'm sure," Alayna murmured the platitude, grasping the girl tightly for one last moment.

"If you survive that long," Ashei said sadly, almost bitterly, and Alayna couldn't bring herself to correct the girl, because it wasn't wrong.

And then it was goodbyes all around. Stephen received a wink from Beathan, a clap on the shoulder from Azir and a rough embrace from Philip, who tussled Stephen's hair and spoke quietly to him.

Alayna heard a snatch of what he said, and it was mostly a reminder about the ancient Guild rendezvous locations they'd both been trained in, points that they could use to find each other again. Perhaps not immediately, but eventually, one day. Ashei said her goodbyes to the males with smiles and a light kiss on each cheek, but the girl was still skittish, reserving the only hug she had for Alayna. When it was time, Philip leaned in close to Stephen and whispered in his ear again, and again Alayna could hear the words.

"Take care of each other, lad. This venture might work out for us, but it might go sideways." Philip gave the youth a bag of coins. "Take the quickest ship across the channel that you can and get her home. I don't want you around if things don't work out. Don't forget, that whatever you think they do or do not know, it wasn't too many days ago that you were in a Guild cell awaiting who knew what fate. Don't trust anyone but each other."

Stephen, to his credit, wiped his eyes, steeled his back at the words, looking at Ashei with a smile that she returned. He gave Philip one last hug and an admonishment to survive, and then led Ashei out the door and away into the night.

Alayna cried for a moment. The two youths had wormed their way into her heart. It felt like part of her family was leaving. And perhaps it was.

But they had a battle to fight, a war to win, and a Guild to overthrow.

CHAPTER TWENTY-TWO

Alayna moved with the running rush of bodies toward the river Thames. There were too many of them to go unnoticed, even in the dark of night. She'd heard shouts of alarm, hastily closed shutters, and locked doors as they'd swept through London's narrow, nighttime streets. But as Philip had explained to her, it didn't really matter whether or not they were seen at this point. Moving this quickly, any lookouts trying to send word of their advance on the main Guild complex wouldn't be able to reach their destination ahead of them. The final phase of their plan was in motion—all out assault on the Guild headquarters.

Philip had stationed them very close to where they needed to be. Little more than a quarter mile of running and they were approaching the river. A squat, blocky set of buildings looking like unused factories rose up in the darkness, and as Philip gave the hand signal, Alayna realized this must be it.

It didn't look like much, but Alayna had come to see that the Guild often preferred obscure premises, at least when operating in the middle of a city. Fewer eyes on an old warehouse than a fancy manor, like the menagerie Helmsted had operated from far out in the countryside.

A downward sloping street led them up to a set of double doors in a solid brick wall. Alayna could smell the water nearby, and the muck and mud of the shoreline.

Dracula and his vampires raced along beside them, shooting furtive looks at Philip whenever he got a chance, but Philip, having waited until the last moment to reveal his final card, the details of the main entrance to the Guild compound, had ensured that he'd at least survive long enough to begin the battle. Dracula couldn't exactly pause to take care of him right now—not when they were a mass of hundreds upon hundreds of bodies racing toward a blitz attack on the doors in front of them. When it was clear where they were going, Alayna saw the Shade King give a covert signal, and Salynksa broke off from the rest, circling backward and sprinting to recover the rest of the vampires in the secondary location and lead them here. They'd be welcome reinforcements in a matter of minutes, Alayna was sure. It would have been helpful to have them now, but they were quartered just slightly farther away, far enough that alarm could have gone before them to alert the Guild.

Alayna didn't have time to spare another glance for Salynksa however, because they were closing the last few meters toward the gate. Nobody was stationed outside of it, but there were peep holes stationed at eye level in both doors, which clearly would have had people watching. So, the Guild was feeling cautious, not a single guard stationed outside. They were bunkered in and shut up tight. Luckily, the attackers had the equivalent of a living cannonball at their disposal.

Philip spurred himself forward and curled in on himself as he ran and dipped his shoulder as he struck the door ahead of the rest of the crowd. He struck it with such force that it sounded like an earthquake had hit London, reverberating back out into the night. There would be no chance of hiding this battle from the public tonight. But then again, that had always been Guild protocol, wasn't that yet another example of what they were striving against?

Shouts of dismay could be heard within the building. The surge of bodies pushed up against those in the front, Alayna alongside Philip, and their companions, as well as Dracula and his lieutenants. The mass of bodies made her feel like she couldn't breathe, couldn't move. Somehow Philip freed himself enough to surge back and then forward again bursting the doors inward with the added weight of the bodies behind them.

They crashed into the main Guild complex in London and saw a rash of defenders ahead of them. Lines upon lines of hard-eyed Collectors— exactly what Philip had once been—ready and waiting for them. Alayna saw what Stephen had meant. Maybe their tactics had worked too well. It looked like every Collector on the continent and perhaps beyond had been called back from active duty to play guard dog for the Council.

However, there was no slowing down. Alayna freed her miniature crossbows from where they hung beneath her cloak and fired two bolts through the intervening and ever shrinking distance. She didn't even pause to see if they struck their mark. Because the clash of bodies was upon them. Alayna slipped her bows back in their place and pulled her knives. It was time to fight.

Philip and the vampires threw themselves at the wall of Collectors before them and Alayna followed suit. She'd been in skirmishes enough over the past years running, hiding, and fighting with Philip, but nothing quite like this. Come to think of it, she doubted whether Philip had ever been in a pitched battle quite like this before either. He'd been Guild his entire life, not serving in the army of a country, so this must be a first for him, and likely many of the vampires too.

Perhaps Dracula, and his centuries old animosity had experienced battles before—who knew where or what that being's past entailed? But for the Collectors too, this was probably a new experience, being more used to hunting and capturing creatures.

Due to many being unaccustomed to such a clash, the battle was a frantic melee, not a tactical endeavor. Bodies slammed into bodies. Vampires tore out throats and in turn, died in agony as stakes pierced their hearts. Men and creatures fell in droves. And still more vampires poured in the front gates, cracked wide open, while more Collector reinforcements appeared from the darkness beyond.

"Helmsted!" She could hear Philip bellowing in a primal rage of battle fury, over and over again. A call to face him, or at the very least to show her face. Stephen's reconnaissance indicated she had assumed control of the Guild during this time of crisis and Philip was calling her out. But as of yet she hadn't shown.

Alayna ducked a sword thrust and swept in close like a deathly wind to eviscerate her opponent, her body's momentum harnessed into the next move of death as she hamstrung a Collector with his back to her. It might not be the blow that took his life, but she had surely killed him all the same.

She saw Philip fighting with his fists as always, calloused knuckles as hard as stone, the ancient blood in his veins lending him rage and strength. At one point her mate, in the most terrifying fashion, simply grabbed a smaller Collector by the ankles and began swinging him impractically as a make-shift club. He battered skulls and slammed bodies with the body of one of their own and something about that fact made it more frightening to behold than if he'd simply killed them with the brute strength of his hands.

Arrows began streaming from the dark corners of the room attempting to bring him down. It wasn't a rain of them for fear of hitting their own, but marksmen would do their best to pick him out when they could. Arrows missed and arrows struck. Some few did exactly what they hoped to avoid and struck their own Collector brethren when they missed Philip, but a few hit home. Philip just snapped them off or yanked them out, counting on his fast healing body to carry him through. As the battle continued, a few arrowheads with snapped off ends could be seen buried in his arms and shoulders. Alayna would have felt concern for him if she hadn't had her own duels to fight.

She tried to fight as close to Philip as possible; they never liked to be far from one another during danger, but a full-scale battle was more difficult to manage than a skirmish. They were swept slowly but surely further and further apart.

Attacks swarmed her and it was everything she could do to defend herself. Her blades and her body became slick with blood, some from her opponents, some her own. At one point, a vampire skewered a Collector with a sword it had picked up just as the Collector had been about to bash Alayna's brains in from behind with a club. Frozen for a moment at having a vampire save her, Alayna opened her mouth to thank the female vampire when the shock wore off, only to see a stake protrude through the front of the vampire's heart, having taken a deathly wound to the back.

A Collector grinned wickedly as the corpse before it dropped to the ground and advanced on Alayna.

And so the battle continued.

On and on.

On.

And.

On.

Alayna sucked for air as she felt like she'd never been so tired in her life. There were too many of them, too many Collectors. Their plan had worked too well, the Guild had bunkered in with too many of its foot soldiers. They were going to lose.

Alayna saw Philip hard pressed by no fewer than five Collectors at once. Beathan, having activated his enhancement charm, flitted about with an almost exaggerated speed and agility, laying waste to those around him, but even so, he took wounds. Azir, mouth bloodied from tearing throats, warily faced down two Collectors advancing on him with a stake.

Alayna was suddenly overwhelmingly glad that they'd ensured that Ashei and Stephen were away from this mess. What had they been thinking trying to take on the Guild in open warfare. There were too many of them. Too many men stacked up at the back of this entrance room, this empty warehouse, kept empty to provide the cover, the excuse, if necessary that it was just an abandoned factory.

Still Philip bellowed for Helmsted. Still she didn't show her face. She had no need, the tide of battle was in her favor.

And then abruptly it changed. A wave of moans issued through the Collectors and Alayna heard a hiss of approval wash through their own dark forces. She chanced a moment to turn her head and saw Salynksa at the head of their second contingent of vampires, essentially a second army. How had Alayna forgotten about it? Had it really been that short of a time since they had begun fighting? It felt like all night. Salynksa hit the back of the battlefield room and many vampires pulled back to breathe allowing the fresh fighters to the fore.

They hit the Collectors like a black wave, swarming them, biting them, wreaking pain, and havoc. Alayna heard cries and prayers. She heard the sickening crunch of throats tearing, heard bones breaking.

And finally, as the Collector resistance, its defense, began weakening, a voice cried out from the shadows at the back. "Hold! Hold you bastards! Hold or we're all dead." It was a voice Alayna could never forget, a voice she heard in her nightmares, whispering promises of pain and retribution. It was Helmsted, finally forced into the open to bolster her forces.

Alayna saw other hard faces, a coterie of what had to be important men and women, Guild Council members at her back. Desperation and a turning battle had, by necessity, lured the head of the snake into the fray.

―――

HANDS PAWED AT HER, clubs swung at her, blades of all shapes and sizes swung in her direction, but Alayna only had eyes for Helmsted. Alayna fought almost mechanically, as efficiently as she had ever fought. Philip and Beathan had been swept toward the other side of the warehouse room, near to the heart of the vampire thrust, near to the Shade King, but Azir was not far from Alayna.

He fought his way to her side, clawing his way through Collectors to get there. Grinning viciously as he reached Alayna's side, he swept a fist at the jaw of an onrushing Collector and connected with a solid thud. Alayna poured her focus into the battle. Every fighting form, every training session, every single time she'd been beaten and tortured in that cursed menagerie came flooding back in a rush of emotions as she fought, eyes fixed on her targets, but always, always aware of where Helmsted was in the distance. Some of those memories helped her keep that focus, others threatened to shatter it, but they all helped coalesce that focus into a hardened rage, nearly a frenzy to reach Helmsted.

"Let's teach that bitch a lesson this time?" Azir proposed with a sneer, that was half question.

Alayna jerked her head in agreement and led the way. She sliced her way through tendons and muscles and took no fewer than three wounds —shallow though they might be—in order to cleave her way toward the object of her fury.

Azir cut a swath through the men in front of him. Like the vampire who had saved Alayna's life earlier, Azir had picked up weapons from the dead, opting for two rapiers with which he laid waste to the people before him. With his formal speech, and his elegant sword forms, he reminded Alayna of the most deadly courtier she'd ever seen. A noble without a king—unless you counted Dracula, which Alayna wasn't sure she did. Not in the way she was thinking.

They fought side by side, inching their way closer to their target, wading through blood to get there. And all the while Helmsted's commanding voice rang out. When it did, backs firmed, lines hardened, and the Collectors before her stiffened their resolve. There was no debating that Helmsted was born to command, born to lead. Alayna just hoped to send her to the grave as she did.

Alayna gritted her teeth as she saw Helmsted skewer a vampire on her blade, then watched as it clawed its way frantically down the sword, cutting itself further in the process, in the hopes of reaching her with its teeth. But Helmsted calmly pulled a stake and exploded the archaic but effective weapon through its heart.

Cool under pressure. Well Alayna would show her what pressure really was. Then it happened. Helmsted glanced across the fray in Alayna's direction. She must have been surveying the scene as a battle leader, but when her eyes caught Alayna's she smiled just a little. That smirk even in the face of impending defeat, frustrated Alayna more than anything. She would take everything from Helmsted, just as the woman had nearly taken everything from Alayna.

Helmsted beckoned her closer with a lazy motion of the hand, still smiling despite the circumstances. Alayna snarled wordlessly and rushed on, hacking her way through. Men fell before her like grain before a scythe in a manner she'd only seen happen when Philip was fighting. She was on another plane now completely as a fighter.

Somehow Azir managed to keep up, cleaning up the mess and finishing off any who didn't die in her wake. Through Helmsted's marshaled forces they advanced, the two of them in tandem, the two of them there with the most grudges to bring to bear against the woman who led the Guild now.

A patch of vampires led by Salynksa saw the swath of bodies that Alayna and Azir were leaving and took advantage of it, punching through behind them into the gap they created. Alayna, not Philip, was the cannon ball this time and it felt good. All the anger she'd bottled up after the menagerie was being let off like steam boiling over the edge of a pot. Salynksa flashed her a hard grin as they drew level and the Collectors' resolve finally broke. Men scattered, and a battle turned into a rout. A running man couldn't defend, not how a fighting man could, and vampires were not ones to take prisoners. It was a blood bath. Oh, the fighting didn't stop completely, pockets held out, but the battle was over, and everyone knew it.

And yet, Helmsted didn't run. She stood her ground, killing vampires that attacked her left and right. In the face of defeat she just sneered, fought, and waited for Alayna to arrive.

"We will do it together," Azir promised as their final approach began. Alayna slashed the artery on the arm of a Collector and the man went down in a heap clutching it, hoping to stem the red flow. Hungry vampire eyes followed him to the ground.

"No," Alayna snarled. "You took the last kill that belonged to me, you killed The Alchemist. I want this one. Helmsted is mine!"

Azir took one look at her face and seemed to decide that disagreement was not his best option. "I'll be near, beside you, if you need it," he agreed in an understanding voice, loud enough to be heard over the din of battle.

But Alayna didn't need understanding, she needed revenge. Justice. She wanted retribution from the nights spent crying in pain, from seeing Azir dragged back into his cell next to hers after a bout of torture, wondering if he'd live. She wanted retribution for the schism the menagerie had caused in her relationship with Philip—a relationship that was only just now becoming repaired, becoming whole.

She needed Helmsted.

Alayna stepped through a spray of blood from a vampire and a Collector fighting next to her, and the red mist painted a side of her face. What she must look like now. A vengeful elfas spirit, she hoped.

And there she was, Helmsted was waiting for her. As if the entire battle had been staged just so that this moment could come to pass.

"Coming to try your hand against the devil, darling?" Helmsted smiled, sickly sweet.

"You're not the devil, you're just some bastard I'll barely remember when I'm done killing you," Alayna spat.

Helmsted chuckled. "By the look on your face right now, we both know that isn't true. I'll be in your dreams, your nightmares, for eternity. Regardless of how this plays out."

And with that Helmsted acted in a blur of motion. The pistol she kept at her hip, loaded and ready with one shot, was in her hand and blurring upward toward Alayna's face. The firearm discharged, but Alayna was ready, remembering the woman's affinity for that weapon. Alayna somersaulted into a roll, and the lead ball careened past her, whizzing through the air viciously until it struck some poor soul amongst the mass of fighters behind her.

Alayna came up from the roll into a three-point crouch and heard Azir's worried shout from the side. But she was ready, and her hand grasped a mini crossbow, fed it a bolt and quickly was up and released.

The bolt flew true and struck Helmsted in the thigh. And the woman cursed and fell to one knee. Alayna grabbed the other crossbow under her cloak and the next bolt was raised and ready in seconds. It struck true as well, this one finding the hateful woman's fleshy side, below her ribs.

Helmsted swore again and in a fit of strength stood and ripped the bolt free from her leg, striding vengefully toward Alayna. This wasn't a fair fight. This was war. This was revenge. Alayna felt no remorse at the bolts she'd fired into her opponent before their hand-to-hand duel even began. Helmsted had shot at her first, after all.

But the rage of the woman before her, her face contorted in hatred, disdain, and pain, carried Helmsted forward into the fight. And fight she did. Helmsted swung a dangerous swipe of her dueling sword just as Alayna stood and leaned barely out of the way. Alayna swung forward with a knife and Helmsted avoided it just as easily as Alayna had evaded Helmsted's sword. It was almost as if she didn't even feel the wounds. But no, that couldn't be. Helmsted was just a hint slower, just a bit more tired than she should be after a few parries and thrusts, a few circular passes against one another.

Alayna would make use of that fatigue.

Alayna pressed Helmsted hard, the harder she worked the woman, the quicker that bastard would tire out for good. Azir urged her on from the sidelines, keeping any and all Collectors who sought to get involved out of the way.

They fought for an endless time, minutes probably, but the bubble of fury and focus that encompassed Alayna as she fought was enough to blur the edges of reality, of her normal comprehension of time. Cut, thrust, dodge swipe. Strike with the hilt, kick at the knee. Before long she was breathing hard, but Helmsted was breathing harder, and wobbling a little as she stood. Now was the time.

Alayna feinted, drawing a sweeping arc of the sword from Helmsted, but Alayna ducked it, dodging in to close the distance and get within the sword's range.

In a flurry of anger, Alayna exploded her forehead through Helmsted's nose in a vicious head butt and grabbed the remaining bolt in Helmsted's side with her hand. Alayna twisted the weapon into the wound and delighted to hear Helmsted shriek in pain, whether from the blow to the face or the twisting of the bolt, she wasn't sure.

Alayna pulled her head back to grin in satisfaction at the agony on her enemy's face, at the woman's will, so usually iron hard, crumpling as she felt her strength go.

"This is the end for you," Alayna whispered victoriously.

Helmsted had the self-respect not to argue. She just spat in Alayna's face with the last of her strength. Alayna responded by using the hilt of her belt knife to hammer the bolt all the way into Helmsted's body, disappearing within, forcing a spout of blood to fountain from the woman's mouth.

It was over.

Alayna took a step back. Helmsted was still standing. Barely. She was swaying on her feet, eyes glazed in pain. But she was done. Finished. Alayna picked up the miniature crossbow discarded from earlier, loaded another bolt into her favored weapon and aimed it at the woman's face.

"Do it!" Azir hissed in excited anticipation. This death meant almost as much to him as it did to her.

Helmsted opened her mouth groggily, but whatever her last word would have been, whether to beg for her life, or curse them for bastards, Alayna would never know. She released the bolt and it flew straight and true. It entered Helmsted's open mouth at top speed and speared out the back of her throat and beyond without slowing.

Helmsted slumped to the floor, a spatter of blood and death, and Alayna felt vindicated for the first time in a long time. However, this venture might end, at least there was some closure. At least that bitch Helmsted was dead.

CHAPTER TWENTY-THREE

As the battle raged, Philip saw Alayna drift away from him, the ebb and flow of bodies smashing together gradually putting some distance between them. Azir happened to stay close to her, however, and for perhaps the first time that Philip could remember, the idea of Azir being beside her to watch her back when he couldn't was relief rather than a thorn in his side.

Philip wished he could have fought beside her, but skirmishes had a mind of their own sometimes, let alone full-scale battles. Hundreds of forms darted in and amongst each other in the empty factory room that was a front chamber and decoy for the main complex of the Guild. The main complex stretched back into the darkness and eventually dove deep underground, reaching underneath the river so near to where they'd entered.

Thoughts were a distraction however, as a man threw himself at Philip, vicious snarl on his face and a hatchet ready to split brains. Philip swung a forehand at him, almost like a bearswipe and sent the man tumbling to the ground never to rise. Philip felt his strength coursing through his veins, the pure power and cold fury of the north within him. His troll blood sang at the sound and feel of battle, each Collector he faced another contest of might and wills. Philip had to shove the extra, extremely raw side of his northern heritage aside at the sight of all that gore and flesh. He would not eat humans. Chasing Beathan after he'd believed Alayna dead and lost his mind was a one-time occurrence.

The battle swept back and forth until the reinforcements led by Salynksa arrived. Once the second wave of vampires struck into the building out of the cold, damp night, everyone who had eyes could see it was over. Philip heard Helmsted and a few other Council members shout rallying cries that staved off the inevitable for a short while, but nothing could change the outcome. Yet, even with a foregone conclusion the battle stretched interminably, the Collectors refusing to break and run, to give up.

It was around that time that Philip began to notice a few wounds being dealt his and Beathan's way—the half-fairy had managed to stay right beside him—from none other than their supposed allies. Vampires occasionally clawed at them or snapped their teeth. Always under the guise of accident, always with an apology or explanation. They were always turning toward him and reactionary attacks, or shaken off as a bout of battle berserk, quickly recanted with hands raised and the vampire turning toward another human attacker.

But Philip knew better. He and Beathan shared a concerned glance as Beathan caught a tossed stake Philip had kept at his hip just in case—it never hurt to be prepared with vampires around—and fended off a brutal assault of a young female vampire, who then quickly shook her head and acted as if it was an accident just like the rest.

"It's turnin', mate," Beathan shouted above the fray, and Philip knew his friend didn't just mean the tide of the battle shifting in their favor. No it was more.

Philip turned to look around and saw enemies everywhere. Guild members were fighting vampires, but it was clear by the looks in the eyes of all, that sooner or later every single person in that room save the people he'd started this venture with would likely attack him.

"They're under orders," Philip grunted to the fairy, as he blocked a Collector's cudgel with his troll-hardened forearm and smashed his calloused fist into the man's face. Brawlers tactics. They'd always been his strength.

"Evil, bastard. Couldn' even wait 'til after th' fight was over t' turn on us," Beathan swore as he cast a knife end over end, its point striking home and felling a Collector. The fairy bent in the moment's break and picked up a few more wooden stakes from the ground, lost by fallen

Guild members, and shoved them through his belt. With a shrug he looked at Philip, "Doesn't hurt to be prepared."

"No, it does not."

Philip saw with a clench of fear Alayna followed by Azir spearing their way through the other wing of the battle, driving directly at the Council members led by Helmsted. Alayna was shouting something incoherent; it could have been nothing beyond guttural rage, or it could have been an instinctual battle cry in some elfas tongue from her heritage that burst forth from her lips.

Philip steeled himself to fight his way to her. No way would he let her face her deadliest enemy without him there. But as he cast a glance at Beathan and saw the fairy read his gaze with a nod of agreement, the accidental swipes and jabs, the apologies for nips disappeared and their vampire allies as one finally turned upon them to attack. He'd not reach Alayna's side now. Philip sent up a prayer that Azir would do what was necessary in his place.

Collectors were fighting in small pockets and falling by the dozens. Enough so that Philip's devilish allies finally felt the battle had swung enough in their favor to let the truth out. Black eyes turned upon him and he felt the weight of their hungry angry stares as vampires circled and prowled closer, a trap already springing. Smirks and sneers marked their faces and Philip couldn't help but wonder how he'd get out of this one. There were too many. He'd gambled, and achieved his goal, but ultimately led his friends to the death. Led Alayna to her death. Even if she survived her duel with Helmsted, there were too many enemies all around.

Philip grimaced and thrust Beathan behind him. "Run! Get to Alayna and get her out of here." He didn't wait to see if the fairy complied.

Philip lunged to engage the first vampire, the final stake in his immediate possession wrenched from his hands when the creature twisted as it fell. But before Philip could lament the loss of his weapon, shrieks of pain and surprise sounded from the entryway. Vampires snarled in anger and shock. Philip chanced a glance and with a mixture of hope and trepidation saw that a new host of people were barging into the building. Thinners, hundreds of them, flooding into the room. How they'd crossed the channel in such numbers, whose ship they'd had to commandeer to get here, Philip didn't know, but here they were all the same. It couldn't be a coincidence. They were after him. Philip had killed their god—of sorts. And they were here for vengeance. But they were also crazed fanatics who could barely tell one being from another, and an entire small army of them had just plowed their way into the rearguard of the vampires who were still finishing off Collectors and were causing mayhem. They tackled anything near to them, biting scratching, picking up stakes and stabbing wildly. They didn't usually find the heart, but they caused pain and some vampires still managed to fall and not rise.

Salvation and danger for Philip and his company all wrapped up in one.

Barehanded, Philip faced off again with the vampires circling him and readied himself for the fight, when a darkness swept up from the side. The Shade King stepped forward and his followers melted out of his way without hesitation.

"Finally. This is what you want to happen?" Philip asked a bit breathlessly, trying to steady his heart rate for the duel he knew was to come. The question was more to stall for a moment. Dracula had hardly had to fight, leaving his minions to do that on his behalf.

"This is what has to happen. What has always had to happen since the day you arrived at my castle. Too valuable to turn away, too full of knowledge of my ancient enemy. Yet, too dangerous to be allowed to live. To shake the very core of power on this continent in such a way, with so little time and planning." The vampire tsked and finished, "No, no, no. You can't be allowed to live. There's a void of power now, and I—we—" he magnanimously swept his hand around to the followers around him, playing to his crowd, showing his people love, even as he ruled them with iron and fear, "—plan to fill it. You can't be around for the new era."

"Not sure your bastard henchmen can finish me off without your help?" Philip spat, unsure why he was so angry. He'd known this was bound to happen. But betrayal was still betrayal he supposed. The sounds of Thinners screaming and wailing and moaning as they fought with desperate vengeance for their dead pagan deity still filled the air.

Dracula smiled. "No, Collector. They could do it," and the vampire paused to hear their hisses of approval. "But they'd lose more warriors than I care to spare in doing it. You've some small amount of strength, I'll grant you that. No, I'll take care of you and then we can dispatch this rabble behind us and be done," he finished with a look of disgust at the dirty, unkempt followers of the dead Chicheface still filing through the broken double-doored entry.

"Well then, what are you waiting for? And by the way, I'm not a Collector!" Philip roared and burst forward with all the power and strength he had, in hopes of catching the Shade King off guard. Chivalry and code of conduct meant nothing here. If he could kill Dracula and have seen the end of the Council leading the Guild in one night then it would be a productive venture, even if he lost his life.

However, Dracula was much too fast and wily to be caught unaware. "Ah, ah, ah," he taunted as he darted out of the way, sending Philip crashing into the vampires nearby, nicking and scratching him with their nails. "You must be better. I haven't lived this long to be brought low by tricks." Dracula bared his teeth and Philip saw a set of fangs and teeth that were ready for war, like an old armory finally getting a chance to fulfill its purpose.

Silently Philip disentangled himself from the onlookers and doubled back ready for anything. He didn't dare take his eyes away from the deadly fast Shade King for even a moment, as much as he might wish to search the ground around them for a loose wooden stake.

Dracula was a vampire and vampires had a predatory way of innately, instinctually targeting the weaknesses of their opponents, their prey, as they fought. Philip tried to catalogue all the old injuries he had, ready himself for where the thrusts might be, but Dracula with all his ancient and uncanny insight and evil wisdom struck elsewhere.

"Your only friend, the fairy, will die. You can't stop it. And that traitor to his own kind, the hybrid fool who chose your ilk over us, will die also. He'll finally pay for disobeying my protection of The Alchemist," Dracula said with vicious delight. "I don't need you anymore so I don't have to spare your companions." Philip fought the effects of his voice. Lies. Nothing was foregone yet. His companions might still get out of here alive. Especially if Philip could distract the Shade King for long enough.

The vampire struck again mentally. "You'll never keep her safe," Dracula crooned, his voice caressing Philip's mind. "Her life has been nonstop terror and danger since you arrived. She's not even the same species." Dracula's words hit Philip like a stone, striking every fear he possessed deep down. The injuries Dracula was targeting were internal, emotional. Philip rocked back whether from the words or from the vampire's powerful crooning persuasion, was unclear.

The Shade King lunged in on the back of his words and struck a staccato of quick blows to Philip's face and body and for moment Philip was too stunned to react, just barely managing to get his arms up and deflect the worst of them from his face at the last second.

A scornful laugh sounded as Philip turned his bloodied face toward the direction in which the Shade King's momentum had carried him. "She'll die because of you. All because of you. Without you she would have lived a happy, peaceful life."

Again, Philip fought the words as much as he fought physically. Something about the vampire's crooning voice—especially that of a centuries old bloodsucker—added an extra weight to them, made them strangely difficult to disregard. Philip shook his head to clear it, hoping that Alayna had dispatched of Helmsted and that Beathan had indeed fled and reached her side via his enhancement charms—if anyone could move fast when needed it was the half-fairy.

Philip focused on Dracula and advanced again. He might as well take the fight to him as defend. Defending never won a fight. Cackles from the vampires sounded roughly in his ears as Dracula strutted out of reach, enjoying the adulation of his subjects.

"Lay down and die, perhaps I'll make it quick," Dracula sneered loudly.

Philip lunged in with a jabbed feint then quickly followed with a roundhouse swing that connected with the vampire's jaw soundly. Dracula reeled backward from surprise and from the speed and power of the blow. He'd clearly thought his mental battle had worn Philip down further than it had. Philip hardened his resolve; he'd show the evil bastard what a part-troll hybrid could do.

Dracula spat the equivalent of blood from his mouth and turned a livid, black eye on Philip. The vampire's midnight-mottled skin, seemed to shift and move like a summer storm beneath a hidden moon. But Philip was winter and ice, and he was stronger than he looked.

Philip hardened his resolve and advanced again, and this time the Shade King didn't spout taunts, but rather focused and moved with Philip, finally seeing him as a threat. The onlookers cheered their master on, shouting curses and promises of what they'd do to Philip and his people once he was defeated. Philip ignored them.

Sweat and blood dripped down his face from exertion and from the initial blows Dracula had dealt him, but they caused his vision to blur and he risked a wipe of his shoulder across his face. It was a mistake, as Dracula darted in—faster than anyone had any right to be—and delivered a kick to the knee Philip had injured so many years ago as a Collector. Philip felt it buckle, but instead of working to steady it, he leaned with it and rolled under the next swipe of the vampire's claw-nailed hand and thrust upwards, tackling his body through the chest of Dracula, sending them both flying upward and then crashing back down to the ground with Philip upon his enemy.

Brawling tactics again, and Philip was pummeling the vampire with his hardened knuckles as fast as he could, driving blows into Dracula's face that would have ended a lesser being immediately. Philip put all the force he could into those blows, but they didn't have the desired effect. Instead of finishing his foe, they enraged the Shade King who subsequently tossed Philip off like a rag doll. Philip flew through the air and landed, skidding into the feet and shins of the watching vampires. They bit and clawed and kicked at him until he shook himself free and drifted back inward to the battle before him.

Dracula was picking himself up and looking angrier than Philip had ever seen him. The vampire had wanted to humiliate Philip, finish him quickly. Instead, he found himself facing off with someone much stronger than he'd expected. If there was one thing Philip knew about leaders who ruled by fear, it was that they couldn't afford to be seen as anything less than they claimed to be—infallible, unbeatable, and genuinely impenetrable in all ways imaginable.

Right now Dracula was looking very vulnerable, to Philip and to his followers. Vampires ruled by night, and Dracula needed to prove he still deserved it. Wobbling a little, but steadying himself as he advanced, Dracula closed the distance, bruises marking his face from the pummeling. Philip grinned to himself, belief suddenly coursing through him. He was the renegade. He'd defeated Astori, broken into and out of St. Thomas, sacked Helmsted's Menagerie, and managed to orchestrate the decapitating of the Guild leadership—and he'd accomplished that last feat in just a few months. He could handle a vampire, regardless of how old or powerful he might be. Was Dracula as old as winter in the north, as ancient as the cold that seeps in and freezes a person's bones in the arctic? Could Dracula send gales and blizzards to destroy civilizations like the great north beyond could, and had done for thousands of years? No! The north within him was stronger and Philip knew it. He just had to channel it.

Dracula seemed to sense the shift in Philip's mood, and it made him nervous. He bared his teeth and screamed at Philip. "You're nothing! I've eaten kings and murdered emperors. I'll feast on you, as well."

"Well, as I said before, what are you waiting for?" Philip beckoned him in with a casual flick of the wrist.

The insulting mannerism enraged the vampire further, and Dracula lost the mental battle. He sprinted toward Philip, all speed and fury, spearing his body forward, latching teeth into the base of Philip's neck as his body clashed into Philip's. They tumbled to the ground, landing blows, striking in short brutal bursts. Philip felt the vampire's teeth tear out of his neck and was relieved to feel the wound at the base, almost the shoulder, not a mortal wound. Not to Philip, who healed faster than most.

The Shade King wound up on top of Philip as they tussled, as the sounds of a still-ongoing battle roared around them. Dracula struggled to gain purchase again with his teeth, Philip's hands on the vampire's face, all that was desperately keeping his jaws from clamping down on a part of Philip he couldn't afford to sacrifice. Philip felt the vampire's breath upon him, somehow hot and cold at the same time. Philip's fingers slipped into the mouth and sliced open on a fang. Still he barely managed to keep the vampire at bay.

Shouts and cries from the vampires watching were a mix of pleasure and worry. Philip couldn't wait any longer, worried that eventually one or more of them would see how long this fight was taking and rush to their master's aid, consequences be damned.

No, he couldn't risk that. Philip had to end this.

Philip felt the sharp, hard edges of the vampire's teeth as Dracula slavered and savaged his fingers. He was already partway there, he might as well just give in and go with it. Philip felt the Shade King's shock as Philip stopped fighting the jaw and instead slid his fingers further into the vampire's mouth, capturing the tongue with his fingers in a viciously quick maneuver.

"You should have said more while you had the chance, oh *One Who Rules*," Philip snarled mockingly. He just heard a panicked moan from Dracula before his clenched fingers yanked backward as hard as he could pulling the tongue out at the root in an avalanche of blood and mindless screams.

Philip flipped the stunned Dracula over on his back and knelt over him, driving a few fisted blows to his sides just to subdue him from the panicked thrashing, before gripping the jaws once again, this time with both hands.

The Shade King's fear plastered across his face and practically flooding out of his eyes was a sight to see. The vampires and the Collectors Guild would lose all their leadership in one night. The continent would have a new look come first light, and Philip was glad of it.

Philip's hands were slippery from blood as he grasped the jaws and stared down into Dracula's face for the last time. "I'd ask for your last words, but I think we both know you won't have much to say at this point. No? That's what I figured."

Philip wrenched the jaws open and apart, tearing the bottom one from the sockets and ripping it clear off of the face. Stunned moans erupted from the crowd as Philip then finally took a moment to look for a loose stake on the ground. He found one quickly within arm's reach and plunged the sharp wooden stake into the already dead vampire's heart. It never hurt to be certain.

Dracula was dead.

———

STUNNED SILENCE OCCUPIED the little space around Philip, but the rest of the room was still awash with noise. The fighting still raged, humans against vampires against Thinners, against Philip and his company. He saw a look of awe on Alayna's face from across the room as she had seen the ending of his fight. He didn't care what she'd seen, or what she thought. She was alive. She'd survived this long. That was all he cared about. And sure enough, Beathan had made it to her side and was tugging her deeper into the complex beyond, with Azir beside them as Philip had instructed. Philip caught the fairy's eye and without waiting to see how quickly the spectating vampires recovered, he plowed into the crowd, shrugging off his injuries and wounds as best he could, fighting to get near to the only people he cared about left alive in this building.

He saw the three companions heading out the back end of this entrance warehouse room due to the fact that the front entrance was still much too clogged with fighting. Philip heard the shriek of anguish from Salynksa as she saw the remains of her master and knew it would only be moments before someone was after the four of them—whether vampires or Thinners.

Philip sprinted into the gloom ahead and quickly caught the others, even with the limp from the blow to his knee. A pack of Thinners surged after him and the four of them stood side by side and managed to fight off five of the gaunt humans, creepier than just about anything Philip had ever seen.

"We have to keep going," Philip gasped as the last Thinner fell. "More will come, and vampires too. They won't rest."

"I know, I saw what you did," Azir said with the closest thing to admiration Philip had ever heard in the hybrid vampire's voice.

"Angry?" Philip asked quickly but carefully.

"Hardly," Azir responded with a flashed grin. "He would have punished me eventually for that bit about me killing The Alchemist."

Vampires were now rushing after the Thinners who'd already been killed. And more Thinners were rushing their way also, fighting each other still as they went, but moving toward the four of them like an inexorable wave of anger and retribution.

"Pleasantries later, eh? I'd rather not die t'night," Beathan suggested.

"Agreed," Alayna said breathlessly.

Philip nodded. "Follow me. I know this building better than most. I was in and out of here all the time during my days as a Collector. James used to hate how often we'd have to report back. James his old partner. It had been a while since he'd thought about him.

They raced after Philip into the darkness, blood, and limps, just like him. A maze of passages, doors opened and closed, but they couldn't manage to lose their pursuers. The complex was a ghost town, as if every able body had been fighting in the front room. They managed to stay ahead of their pursuers, but only barely. Philip heard the snarling and slashing as vampires or Thinners or both—he wasn't sure—pounded on a door Philip had locked behind them. It wouldn't hold long, as Philip could already hear the hinges creaking.

"One more door and then it's the back passage out, and under the river to the other side." Philip spoke quietly out of habit, even though their pursuers new their direction by scent and sight in the darkness.

"Tunnel under the river?" Azir asked intently.

Philip nodded as he heard the crash of a door breaking open behind them.

"Long stretch without a door?" the vampire asked again.

Philip narrowed his eyes before nodding again.

"You'll never make it. I've never seen them whipped into a frenzy like this before, and that's not to mention those lunatic humans on our tail." Azir wiped sweat from his brow as they approached the door to the tunnel passage out.

"That's because ya've never seen a Dracula executed," Beathan chimed in cheerfully, only a hint of nerves in his voice.

Azir grunted something unintelligible and opened the door to the back passage. It was a narrow door, small enough for only one person at a time. At one point it had even been a secret passage in and out, before the complex had expanded and needed to utilize all its assets more fully. Azir ushered Alayna and Beathan through. He motioned for Philip to go as well, and Philip obliged.

Alayna and Beathan turned back to wait for them but Azir motioned them forward. "Go!" he urged.

"What?" Alayna cried in confusion. "There's no time, come on!"

Alayna took a step back and Beathan caught hold of her. Azir smiled a sad smile at Alayna, yet somehow managed to keep a dark glint of something in his eye as he appraised her. "I would say we should stick together but we need to buy more time. I would prefer it was Philip, but you would never leave *him*." Azir jerked his head unceremoniously at Philip.

He turned to Philip. Philip opened his mouth to object, but Azir cut him off. "We are hopelessly outnumbered and have run out of doors to lock and bar. They would catch us before the end of this passage. I want her safe. I want her out of this mess. Besides you have always wanted me out of the picture," he finished with a bitter smirk.

Philip swallowed. "No, Azir, not like this."

"I appreciate the sentiment, but we are out of time. I will hold them off. Go!" Azir imbued that last word with all the croon and persuasion he had as a vampire, using his mental acuity to the fullest, and with that Azir shoved him toward Beathan and Alayna.

Almost against his will Philip felt the wave of persuasion hit him. He could have fought it, but a part of him knew the vampire's words were true. They'd never make it without someone holding the door. At least for a while. It was narrow enough that one body could stand for a time before eventually succumbing.

Alayna was crying as Beathan was already tugging her away when Philip caught up to them.

"Run," Philip said grimly. "Don't make his sacrifice for nothing." All he heard were Alayna's whimpered words of *no* as they went. One last look over his shoulder saw Azir lock the door and brace himself against it as the first impact hit the frame. It held. For now.

Feeling shame that he should leave a comrade and pain that Alayna should lose a friend, Philip ran.

———

HE BRACED himself against the door as the pattering footsteps of his friends disappeared into the distance. His friends. There had once been a time that would have seemed to be impossible. At least for Beathan and Philip. Alayna was a different story. Azir felt the added strength in his limbs, his will, from the fact that she would escape.

As long as he could hold. As long as he bought her enough time.

Azir had never been one for emotional farewells or sentimentality. As the door shuddered beneath his shoulder a tear trickled down his face at the thought of never seeing her again. But he smiled as he thought of all the many days she'd have because of him. He chuckled as he realized that both she and Philip would never forget him. He'd be with them forever in a way. Just the thought of Philip living out the rest of his life in the shadow of Azir's sacrifice was enough to make this worthwhile.

Amusement somehow managed to strengthen him. He leapt back as the door cracked and burst open. It was narrow, barely more than a few inches from his shoulders on either side. They would have to meet him one at a time.

And so Azir set himself, bared his teeth, and prepared to die.

So that she could live.

CHAPTER TWENTY-FOUR

They burst through the door to the passageway into the faintly lightening sky of early morning. Sunrise was close. If Azir could just hold for a little while, then the vampires at least might not be able to pursue. Sunrise couldn't be more than minutes away.

Beathan grimaced slightly at the thought of leaving a comrade behind. It hurt something fierce to continue on. At least they were far enough away to not have to actually hear it happen.

Alayna was weeping. "We have to go back." She half turned to do so, before Philip and Beathan grabbed her shoulders and turned them back forward, keeping her at a run.

"We cannot, lass. Not unless, ya' want it t' be for nothin'. He did it for ya' personally, certainly, out o' care for ya', but he did it for th' rest o' us, as well. I'll not let a man—well, vampire really—die for me an' then spit on that sacrifice."

"He's right, love," Philip said as they ran. "We can't go back. Azir wouldn't want it. He was clear in his wishes."

"Best way t' die is with your mind full o' mischief. But barrin' that, dyin' for friends is about as good a death as a body can get, Alayna." Beathan put a comforting hand on her shoulder, which was difficult as they were moving too fast to really do so.

Alayna sniffled some sort of agreement but didn't really answer. They ran on for a few more minutes until the sun began to rise. "Sunrise should keep the bloodsuckers off our tracks," Philip said, "although who knows about those Thinners."

Beathan shrugged. "Hopefully they tore each other t' pieces."

"I wouldn't count on it," Alayna muttered bitterly and Beathan was forced to agree. Things tonight—last night, he supposed—hadn't exactly broken their way. Azir was gone, and regardless of Dracula and Helmsted being dead, there were still plenty of foes left alive behind them.

They neared the docks, ships being the best, most logical option now. He wished they could catch up with the youths, but with a little luck Ashei and Stephen had caught a ship out on the evening tide last night. Safer to find their own ship and trust fate to wind their paths together again if it wished.

"At least we accomplished what we wanted," Alayna said dully. "Helmsted and the council are dead, and so is the Shade King."

They slowed to a walk, as morning greyness infiltrated all areas of the quay. Captains of ships, small and large, roused crew with shouts and kicks. Early goers threw the ropes off small vessels and cast away from the dock into the river.

Philip led the way, as usual. He probably had a contact in mind, some captain that could get them away. He was resourceful. Almost as resourceful as a fairy with leprechaun blood in him, Beathan thought.

"Where to now?" Philip asked.

"The two powers of the continent are shaken to the core. I just want to curl up and sleep somewhere, and not fight again ever—well at least for a while," Alayna amended with a sad yawn. Philip hugged an arm around her shoulders, keeping an eye behind them for Thinners. Although as of yet, they hadn't seen any pursuit. Maybe they'd gotten lucky, maybe the vampire horde had finished off those maniacs and then Azir and daylight had stalled the vampires. Perhaps they were in the clear.

"I guess I wouldn't mind heading north again," Philip said a bit dubiously, as if after all these long months of focusing so hard on the objective they'd now accomplished, he had no clear line of vision for the future.

Beathan squinted his eyes at the sun, thinking thoughts he would have never once thought. But well, the time to play lone wolf seemed to have gone.

"I might have an idea."

CHAPTER TWENTY-FIVE

The two of them turned their heads toward Beathan and waited expectantly. Alayna shielded her eyes with her hand to block the brilliant morning sun from behind the fairy, feeling a pang that Azir would never see the sun again.

"Well?" Alayna asked.

"Well, Ireland's mostly north—by way o' west I guess. I have family, friends there, places we could hide if need be. Them Thinners might still be on our tail, and th' vamps will certainly be a wee bit miffed at us—at Philip in particular," Beathan raised his eyebrows suggestively.

"I didn't think you have friends," Philip joked, even though the joke rang hollow with only three instead of four of them to hear it.

"More acquaintances really." Beathan shrugged.

Alayna couldn't help but smile. Beathan was one of those people who could do that, elicit a smile or a laugh where it seemed it wasn't possible. Alayna thought about it for a moment. Part of her wished to find Stephen and Ashei, but another part of her knew that staying clear of them, at least for now, was safest for their two young friends. Get free of London, lay low for a while, make sure they'd lost whoever might have their scent. And only then would it be a good idea to go looking for the youths. She had to trust they could take care of each other.

Alayna looked at Philip. "I've never been to Ireland," she said with a questioning tilt of her head.

Philip nodded slowly as he thought, before turning to the fairy again. "You're sure you have places for us to lay low?"

Beathan looked at her mate with the most affronted look Alayna had ever seen him give and this time she couldn't help but let out a low quiet laugh.

"Mate, I have hideaways hidden within hidey-holes like you'd not believe," Beathan bragged. "Safe as we're likely t' be."

"Alright, then," Philip said.

And that was that.

Philip hired a captain, the first that was leaving for Ireland—anywhere in the entire island would do at this point—and within the hour they were sailing out on the morning tide.

Alayna sat with Philip and Beathan in the prow of the ship, hoods up even against the sun, so as not to alert the crew to their natures.

"What will happen now—with the Guild and the vampires, I mean?" she asked, turning toward Philip.

Philip was silent for a long moment. "Both lost their leaders last night, and both lost massive numbers, the Thinners at the end ensured that consequence. Whatever happens, it'll take years, maybe decades for them to recover."

"But without the Guild, people might suffer, right? Humans..." Alayna trailed off.

Beathan spoke up for Philip, answering her question. "Worth th' risk. Th' Guild was growin' unchecked, we knew that. Too much so. Ya' cannot hope t' make a better future without layin' a foundation. And ya' have t' break some stones to lay that foundation, now, don't ya'?"

"Beathan's right," Philip agreed. "The Collectors Guild was drunk on power. We stopped that last night. Hopefully, they realize they can't operate the way they were. If they do come back with any kind of strength, we can only hope they'll learn from their mistakes. Anything else is out of our control."

Alayna and the other two fell silent then, gazing at the river slipping past them. Soon they'd be out at sea and curling toward the Emerald Isle, one of the many places in this great wide world that Alayna had yet to see.

She loved Philip. With all her heart. She had no regrets about choosing him. She'd choose him over and over again. He was hers and she his.

But she couldn't help but wish that Azir was with them now, to see the sunrise on a new day, a new era that he had helped them purchase.

Philip grabbed her hand as if he could sense what she was thinking. Alayna leaned into his side and breathed in the tangy air. Salt of the sea was not far away. She closed her eyes and smiled at the feel of him along her back. A new adventure waited.

CHAPTER TWENTY-SIX

They weren't long at open sea before they were making port in Cork. The Irish coast greeted Philip like an old friend. He'd spent many a journey, many a mission here during the decades of service to the Collectors Guild alongside his then partner James.

Philip smiled fondly. James had been a Guild man, through and through. He'd believed in the goodness of people—of humans—the love of family, and above all the idea that he—that anyone who tried, really—could help protect people from the dangers that were out there in this world. Philip had often agonized over what James would have thought of his course of action over the last few years since his friend's death. In fact, for a long time, Philip had been quite certain that James would have been bitterly disappointed in him.

But things felt different today. A little time to grieve—not much, but enough to clear his head—had shed a new light on circumstances. Azir's death was still fresh, but his sacrifice had meant something. If James had been able to see a snarky, vampire do what was right and good and sacrifice his life for the safety of his friends, among them a former Collector, he might have changed his mind about what beings other than humans were capable of. Philip certainly hoped he would have. He might have seen the virtue of opposing the Guild, of protecting more people than just humans.

Azir was proof that people could change. He was proof that what they were doing was right. At least Philip hoped that he was. It was entirely possible he was rationalizing to himself everything he'd done these past months, to overthrow the Guild.

They paid the captain and disembarked. Philip was glad to be out from under unfamiliar eyes. The battle last night would not have gone unnoticed. The sooner they were away from strangers, the less chance of people tracking their progress.

Stop, Alayna smiled and spoke gently into his mind in a way she hadn't managed to do since their separation before the menagerie.

"Stop what?"

She shook her head fondly. *Just stop thinking. Sometimes you think too much. You get all caught up in your head.*

He laughed quietly. "Alright, love."

"Well, are we ready?" Beathan asked with a jig of his feet.

"You seem cheerful," Philip said.

"Comin' home always puts a scamper in me feet, mate." There was a twinkle in the fairy's eyes.

"Which way?" Alayna directed her question to Beathan since he was leading the way for now.

"Yes, now that we're on your island, where do we go from here?" Philip gazed at the cobblestones of the streets around him and couldn't wait to get out of the city and into the wild.

"North, I know how much you like that direction." The fairy threw a wink in Philip's direction and almost subconsciously Philip drew in a relieved breath at the thought of heading back toward his homeland, his icy heritage, even if it was just within the confines of this island.

"And then what?" Philip asked as he grasped Alayna's hand, the open-ended question feeling right for some reason.

Beathan shrugged in the most cavalier, fairy way possible, and quirked a smile as a wild, icy wind of the not-yet-ended-winter whipped through the street. Despite where they were, it somehow managed to carry with it the scent of uninhabited places.

"Well, then I guess, we see what kind o' trouble we can find."

THE END

Don't miss out on your next favorite book!
Join the Melange Books mailing list at
www.melange-books.com/mail.html

THANK YOU FOR READING

Did you enjoy this book?

We invite you to leave a review at the website of your choice, such as Goodreads, Amazon, Barnes & Noble, etc.

DID YOU KNOW THAT LEAVING A REVIEW...

- Helps other readers find books they may enjoy.
- Gives you a chance to let your voice be heard.
- Gives authors recognition for their hard work.
- Doesn't have to be long. A sentence or two about why you liked the book will do.

ABOUT THE AUTHOR

Mathias Colwell grew up in far Northern California exploring redwood forests and cloudy beaches. He loves God, his family, and friends. Mathias has been a writer for most of his life, drafting his first stories as young as eight years of age. His desire to write fantasy was inspired by such authors as J.R.R. Tolkien, David Eddings and the late Robert Jordan. He is an avid traveler and all-around adventurer, having visited or lived in 27 countries. His travels have led him around the world to five continents including stays in Siberia, Spain, and Chile, and he attributes many of his passions and goals in life to these experiences. In his free time, he enjoys reading, outdoor activities such as soccer, snowboarding and water sports. Mathias has a passion for issues pertaining to social justice and human rights and hopes to influence these areas in the future.

mathiasgbcolwell.wixsite.com/author

facebook.com/Mathias-GB-Colwell-225647397579547

twitter.com/MathiasColwell

ALSO BY MATHIAS G. B. COLWELL

with Melange Books

The Collector Series

The Collector

Blood Loss

Menagerie of Shadow

Reckoning and Retribution

Dark Arrow Trilogy

Dusk Runner

Entrance to Dark Harbor

Black Water Well

Novellas

An Age of Mist

A Burning Hope